Advance Praise for David Wood's *Cibola*

"Ancient cave paintings? Cities of gold? Secret scrolls? Sign me up! *Cibola* is a twisty tale of adventure and intrigue that never lets up and never lets go!"
Robert Masello, author *of Blood and Ice*, *Vigil*, and *Bestiary*

"With the thoroughly enjoyable way Mr. Wood has mixed speculative history with our modern day pursuit of truth, he has created a story that thrills and makes one think beyond the boundaries of mere fiction and enter the world of 'why not'? *Cibola* is a worthy tale!"
David Lynn Golemon, Author of *Event, Legend, Ancients*, and *Leviathan*

"*Cibola* by David Wood is a page-turning yarn blending high action, Biblical speculation, ancient secrets, and nasty creatures. Indiana Jones better watch his back!"
Jeremy Robinson, author of *Kronos* and *Antarktos Rising*

"History is turned on its head in this gripping tale of sects, secrets, and double-crosses. With mesmerizing treasures in beautiful locations, beautiful women and rugged heroes, mysticism and mystery, Wood spins a yarn that keeps the pages turning."
Alan Baxter, author of *RealmShift* and *MageSign*

"David Wood is an exciting new author to watch!"
Bill Craig, author of *the Hardluck Hannigan* adventures.

Works by David Wood
Dourado
Cibola

CIBOLA

DAVID WOOD

Gryphonwood

Gryphonwood Press

CIBOLA. Copyright 2009 by David Wood

Published by Gryphonwood Press
www.gryphonwoodpress.com

ISBN: 0-9795738-7-4
ISBN 13 : 978-0-9795738-7-3
Printed in the United States of America
First printing: March, 2009

For my father David, who always
believed I was a writer.

Prologue

April 11, 1539

Fray Marcos de Niza muffled a curse as he dragged his shirtsleeve across the still-wet ink. He pushed the offending piece of fabric up to his elbow and surveyed the damage. Only a smear in the upper left corner. Nothing too grave. That ought to teach him to blot with better care.

Sighing, he turned away from the log book and refilled his cup. He held the bottle up to the light and swirled it around, looking mournfully at the very last of his wine. Three fingers, no more. Hopefully, something of a decent vintage would soon arrive at this remote outpost civilization had forgotten. He reflected on his fall from grace, and hoped that word of it had not reached his family back home. He wondered if his father still lived. If so, he hoped his father had not heard tell of what he had done. If only he could tell him the truth. If only he could tell *the world* the truth. If so, he would not have been sent to this place to do nothing of value. Oh, they promised him he would return to Mexico some day, when he was no longer "needed" here. It was probably true. Whenever Coronado forgave him, he would be permitted to come slinking back, tail between his legs.

Had it all been worth it? Of course it had. There were too many reasons that what he had discovered could not come to light. The truth of it alone might do the church irreparable harm. It had even shaken his faith, strong as it was. There was a greater reason, though. Who could be trusted with such power? Certainly not Coronado. Not the king, not even the Pope. Perhaps no one.

But was it right and proper for him to hide this secret for eternity? He was confident that he and Estevanico alone knew the true story. He had removed the sole written record of it from the library in which he had found it, and the final key was in Estevanico's hands… at least for now.

No. He could not let it die with him. It was not his secret to keep. This was God's secret, to be revealed in His time to the man of His choosing. Marcos would continue with the plan that had been laid upon his heart. He would leave a single clue for the world. If God wanted it to be found, it would be found. If not… well, it was in His hands. Marcos returned to his journal.

…I know that what I do is wrong in the eyes of the king, but I believe that it is good and proper in the eyes of God. Some secrets are meant to remain just that. I have seen the horrors wrought by my countrymen upon this innocent land. I shudder to think of the consequences if such power should fall into their hands. I do not fear for myself. They accepted wholeheartedly the tale I have spun, and only two of us remain alive who know the truth, though the second is believed by them to be dead. At least, I hope he is still alive, and he lives to complete his task. I know that it is foolish of me to record these thoughts, but I feel that I must write them down, reflect upon them. I know the secret is safe.

Yet I find that I cannot bear to hide this secret from humankind. It is too terrible to reveal, but too precious to bury. I have prayed and searched the scripture for guidance, and I have received an answer. God Almighty willing, the day shall come when this secret comes to light. Only the chosen servant shall decipher the clues I and my faithful companion leave behind. He must begin by searching the depths of the well of the soul…

~*~

Sun-on-Lizard ducked down behind the stone outcropping and peered out upon the moonlit landscape. Silver light illumined the rocky plain, casting all in a ghostly glow beneath the blanket of darkness. It was a night for spirits.

The sound came again, much closer now. One less

experienced might have missed the faint brush of foot on rock. Someone was moving almost silently through the night. It was possible that whoever it was meant no harm, but he would not take any unnecessary risks. Finding a comfortable position, his weight balanced on the balls of his feet, he settled in to wait. Patience, his grandfather had said, was a good thing, and Sun-on-Lizard had plenty.

With great care he lay the two small rabbits on the ground; a poor fare for an overlong hunting trip. He had been foolish to stay out so late. He did not fear the coyotes, but they could be more than an annoyance in this land where even the meanest game was hard won. And if the stories could be believed, there was more to be feared in this particular place. Slipping his short bow from his belt, he strung it with a practiced ease. Three arrows remained in his quiver, but he let them stay there. Should the need arise, he could put an arrow in the air faster than anyone he had ever met.

He stared up at the velvet blanket of the night sky, sprinkled with stars and washed in pale moon glow. He had grown up with stories of the star pictures, and the stories of the ancient ones in the sky. His brother, Sits-at-Fire, had always been fascinated with the lore, but he had no interest in such things. He believed in the earth beneath his feet, the bow in his hand, and the challenge of the hunt. He respected his adversaries, even the small rabbit, and appreciated a resourceful quarry. He always thanked the game that fell to his bow for providing him with food and clothing. Yes, there were enough things of this earth to contemplate that he need not concern himself with things of the sky.

Once again the shuffling sound whispered across the rocky landscape, and a glint of silver caught his eye. A dark figure appeared from behind a distant rock formation, moonlight outlining his dark form. Another figure emerged, and then a third. Sun-on-Lizard sucked his breath in between his front teeth, and he narrowed his eyes. It could not be! As the figures drew closer, he saw that he had been right. They had the heads, arms and legs of men, but their bodies were covered in snake scales! His left hand tightened around his bow, and he grasped an arrow in his right. Could such creatures be killed? Suddenly wishing he had listened to more of the elder's fireside tales, he hunched as low as he could without obscuring his vision. He willed himself to be a shadow, a dark patch on the night landscape.

A vagrant breeze, cool and dry, wafted toward him. He inhaled deeply, but caught no odd scent. Of course, the snake had no scent of which he was aware. At least he was downwind of the strange creatures. They moved closer, and with each approaching step his heart pounded faster. Blood coursed through him, the vein in his temple pulsating with every beat of his heart. They were coming right at him. He would fight them if he must. There were three of them, and he had three arrows. He made up his mind that he would aim for their heads. That part of them, at least, appeared human, and as vulnerable as his own. It was only the serpentine scales that made them look unassailable.

He nocked his first arrow and drew it halfway. He was about to spring up and fire when the three suddenly veered from their path, the one in the lead gesturing toward a particularly bright star. They headed off to his right, to the north. As they made their way, Sun-on-Lizard had a good view of the snake men, and what he saw made him grin.

They were not beasts, but men. Men wearing the hard, silver vests of which he had heard tell. The same clothing worn by the fabled outlanders with their cloud-white faces and thunder sticks. Another story he had never believed. Sun-on-Lizard had traveled farther than anyone in his village, down to the red rocks and up to the great salt water, and he had never seen a man with a white face and a stick that made fire. Of course, he had not seen their silver vests before today, either. It struck him as more than passing strange that the men he saw were not white-faced, but dark. It was difficult to tell in the darkness, but the first two looked to be of the Dineh, as they called themselves, or perhaps some other southern tribe. The third man, though, was a head taller than the others, and as dark as night. So dark, in fact that his head seemed to vanish when he passed through the darkest shadows. Sun-on-Lizard had never seen such a man. When they were almost out of sight, he made up his mind to follow them. He had to know more.

Sun-on-Lizard rolled the pebble around in his mouth, trying to stave off thirst with the cool, round stone. Two nights and two days had told him precious little about his quarry. He was quite proud of himself that he had avoided detection during that time. He kept his distance in the daytime, remaining just out of sight, and relying on his tracking skills to keep him on the proper path. Twice he feared he had lost them, but in each instance a small sign reassured him. He had sharp eyes, and could find a scuff on a dusty stone, or a pebble pressed into the sand by the soft tread of one trying not to leave a trail. He had to admit, the Dineh moved well, as did the dark fellow. From one that size, he would have counted on more than the occasional marking to indicate his passage.

It was full dark now, and he lay secreted within a rock fall surmounted by scrub brush. The rabbits were long gone, roasted over a banked and shielded fire the night before. He had eaten a bit of dried meat before creeping up on the others' camp. A discontented stomach could make all his stealth for naught. Reclining on his left elbow, he peered out from his hiding place at the strange trio of men. Or at the strange duo, rather. The dark fellow was gone. Careful not to move too hastily, he scanned the area around his hiding place, but saw nothing.

He focused all his senses on the two men seated at the tiny fire. They had stripped off their serpentine vests, and now looked much less sinister in their native garb. The one on the left, a squat, muscular fellow with a scarred face and shaggy black hair was roasting lizard tail skewered on a long, sharpened stick. The other, equally short, but with a leaner build and a raptor-like face, sat with his knees against his chest, and his hands clasped together. They were speaking softly, but he could not make out the words. Of course, he spoke very little of their tongue.

A sound behind him caught his ear, and he whipped his head around, his hand going to his knife. The dark man stood behind him, a long knife at the ready. His smile shone in the darkness, and his eyes caught the starlight like dark pools. Sun-on-Lizard saw no threat in the man's countenance, but he did not doubt that the fellow could and would kill him if he so chose. He had the high ground and the better weapon. If Sun-on-Lizard were in the clear, he might be able to throw his knife at the man and get away, but not lying here within a tangle of brush. He spat the pebble from his mouth.

"You track well," he said to the big man, not that the fellow would speak his tongue. "You leave little sign with your passing, and I did not hear you coming up behind me."

"I thank you for the compliment," the man said in a rich voice, deep like the bottom of a canyon. "You are not without skill yourself. My name is Estevanico. Put away the knife and come sit by my fire." He leaned down and proffered an ebony hand.

It took Sun-on-Lizard a moment to recover from the shock of the strange fellow speaking his language. "I suppose you would have already killed me if that was your intention," he said, sheathing his knife and grasping the man's hand in his.

Estevanico hoisted him to his feet as if he was a child. The big man regarded Sun-on-Lizard with big, brown eyes for a long, silent moment before answering. "That remains to be seen."

Chapter 1

Jade tapped on the dive light strapped to her forehead. The beam flickered again, and then shone at full strength. *Shoddy university equipment.* Drifting back to the wall, careful not to disturb the fine layer of silt that coated the floor of the subterranean cavern, she again ran her fingers across the striations in the rock. They were definitely man-made. Much too regular to be natural, and this part of the wall appeared smooth and level underneath the coating of plant life and debris that had accumulated over a half-millennia. She scrubbed her gloved fingertips harder against the rock, instinctively turning her head away from the cloud of matter that engulfed her.

Turning again to inspect the spot she had cleared, she waited with heart-pounding anticipation for the sluggish, almost non-existent current to clear her line of sight. With painstaking slowness, the haze cleared away, and her eyes widened. It was a joint, where precisely-hewn stones fitted neatly together. She could see the vertical lines where the blocks met end-to end. She scrubbed away another patch, revealing more worked stone.

Raising her head, she let her eyes follow the beam of light as it climbed the wall. About six feet above her head, the regular pattern of the ancient stones gave way to a rough jumble of broken rock and tangled roots. It was a collapsed well, just as she had believed she would find. Remarkably, the web of thick roots created a ceiling of sorts, preserving this bottom section almost intact. She made a circuit around the base, inspecting the rocks. They appeared to be solid, with no apparent danger of further collapse. Nonetheless, she grew increasingly aware of the mass of stone directly above her. It had obviously been in place for hundreds of years, but the thought of loose stone filling the shaft of a well made her feel distinctly vulnerable.

She checked her dive watch and was disappointed to see that she had exhausted her allotted time. She had carefully planned her exploration so that she would have time to return, plus two minutes, giving her as much time as possible to seek out the well.

Reorienting herself toward the upstream channel, she kicked out and felt resistance, like something tugging at her from behind. Cautiously she again tried to swim forward, and again she felt something pull her back. She was an experienced diver, and knew that she needed to move slowly and remain calm. A sudden movement could tangle her further, or worse, tear a hose loose. She turned her head back and forth, seeking out the obstruction, but to no avail. Whatever she had snagged was directly behind her. Reaching back, she felt for the obstruction but found nothing. A moment's irrational fear rose up inside of her, but she quelled it almost immediately. She had to approach this rationally.

Reaching behind her head she ran her hands along the surface of her breathing apparatus, and soon found the obstruction. A root was wedged between her twin tanks. What were the odds? She tried moving backward, then from side-to-side, but to no avail. She freed her dive knife and tried to saw at the obtrusion, but it proved ineffective against the gnarled root. Besides, it was nigh impossible to accomplish anything while working blindly behind her back. She would have to unstrap her tanks and free them from the obstruction. The thought frightened her a little, but she had practiced the maneuver as part of her training. She again looked at her watch, and realized she was now well past time to be done.

Her heart thundered and her pulse surged. *Stay calm, Jade,* she reminded herself. Panic led to unnecessarily heavy breathing, which led to faster oxygen consumption which led to… *Stop it!* None of it mattered right now. She would work the tank free, and then she would make up the lost time on the return swim. Yes, that would work.

Taking two calming breaths, she methodically unbuckled the straps holding her tanks, and slipped free. With a last breath of sweet air, she took her mouth from the mouthpiece. Holding her breath and keeping a firm grip on the tanks, she turned about in the tight space. A few deft tugs and it was free. Putting the gear back on was awkward in the dark, confined space, but she managed nicely, and was soon breathing the blessed air again. No time to pat herself on the back, though.

She set out at a rapid clip up the dark, narrow channel, swimming against the current, and what had seemed like a lethargic flow of water now seemed to be putting up serious resistance. Particles of silt and bits of vegetation flew past her face as she shot recklessly up the channel. She passed through a twisting section a little too carelessly and scraped her shoulder against the edge. She felt her neoprene suit tear, but under the present circumstances that was no great concern.

She wondered if Saul knew something was amiss. Did he even know how long she had been gone, or when she should have returned? Probably not. He was not a diver. *Great. No one to send in the posse. When I get out of here, I'm finding a dive partner.*

The ceiling was low at this point, and her tank banged against a low-hanging rock. She kept going, certain that the distance had not been so great on the way in. *What if I've missed the way out? What if I've gone too far?* Panic again threatened to seize control, but she forced it down. She remembered this low spot: it was about the halfway mark. Halfway! Down to the dregs of her tank, and she was only halfway.

Her legs pumped like pistons, her cupped hands pulled at the water as if she were dragging herself through sand. She tried holding her breath for longer periods, but soon gave up on the idea. Her body needed oxygen that was no longer there. Her muscles burned, and the rushing of blood in her veins was now an audible roar. She tasted copper in her mouth, and her lungs strained against invisible bonds. Shadows appeared around the perimeter of her vision, and slowly crept inward. She was going to die.

Still biting down on her mouthpiece, she screamed in mute frustration. She tried to fight, but her desperate flailing and kicking quickly subsided as darkness consumed her. She released her bite on her useless air supply, and surrendered. As consciousness faded, she saw a light coming toward her.

What do you know? All the stories are true. She watched with detached awareness as the light grew brighter. She was drifting up to heaven… or wherever. The glare grew intensely bright, and then she could have sworn she felt arms around her. *An angel has come to take me to heaven…* A sudden tightness encircled her middle, pinning her arms to her sides, and before she knew what was happening, something was forced into her mouth. She tried to protest, and cool, sweet air poured into her lungs. A coughing fit immediately ensued. She had taken more than a bit of water into her mouth, and now it felt like all of it was in her lungs. She tried to twist free, but whatever it was held her tight.

Instinct took over, and she gradually regained control of her lungs, and spat the water free. With the fresh flow of oxygen came a renewed sense of calm and awareness. Someone had come to her rescue after all. He was holding her tight so that she would not, in her panic, drown both of them. She took few long, calming breaths from the pony tank her rescuer was holding in his right hand. At least, she hoped those thickly muscled forearms belonged to a *he*. Making a point to keep her body as relaxed as possible, she slipped her right arm down, and tapped him twice on the thigh. His grip relaxed a touch, and she raised her hand and she circled her thumb and forefinger to make the "OK" sign. He slid the mini-tank into her hand, and let go of her.

Turning to face her rescuer, she saw that it was indeed a *he*, but other than his blond hair, she could not tell anything about him. Giving him a nod and a quick wave of thanks, she led the way back up the channel. She could not believe how close she had come to dying. What's more, she could not believe someone had rescued her.

Relief gave way to embarrassment and anger as she neared safety. She couldn't believe how her own bad judgment had almost killed her. *Stupid!* She was a professional, not some weekend scuba diver. This guy, whoever he was, probably thought she was one of the dozen grad school bimbos working the dig aboveground. She was going to beat herself up over this for a long time.

The glow of sunlight flickered in the distance, and soon she was up the shaft, and breaking the surface. Strong hands grabbed her under the arms and lifted her free of the water. Her feet touched ground, and then she dropped down hard on her backside.

"Why were you down for so long?" Saul rounded on her, his square face marred by concern. "What happened in there? Are you trying to kill yourself? Because you nearly killed me from worry. Do I need to take up diving so I can keep an eye on you?"

"I'm fine, Saul. Really I am." She shrugged off her tanks and grinned, reaching up to pat his short, neatly coiffed brown hair like she would a faithful pet. "Thank you for sending someone for me. I was wondering if you had even noticed." She didn't catch his reply because her attention was focused on her rescuer, who was clambering out of the water.

He wasn't the tallest fellow, not quite six feet, even with the spiky blond hair, which was already sticking up as it dried in the hot Argentinean sun. He pulled off his dive mask to reveal a lightly tanned face, a friendly smile, and intense blue-gray eyes. Jade smiled back, taking a moment to admire the thickly muscled legs. The guy wasn't the type she usually went for, but he was definitely cute. He took a step toward her, and she hauled herself to her feet to greet him, but Saul was quicker.

"Thank you again for helping us." Saul stepped

between them, clasping the man's hand in both of his. "She had been down for so long, and I always tell her she takes too many unnecessary risks. Thinks she's immortal, she does." He suddenly seemed to realize that he was still shaking hands with the fellow, and let go.

"It's quite all right."

She liked his voice. It was cheerful yet firm, and had a rich timbre, like one of those guys who reads audio books. What was she thinking about? She hadn't even spoken to the guy and already she was mentally babbling.

"I'm just glad I was nearby. It was a close thing getting her out of there."

Saul was about to say more, but Jade pushed him to the side and offered her hand.

"Thank you so much for your help, Mister…"

"Maddock," he replied, looking her directly in the eye. "Dane Maddock. And you're welcome."

"I'm just so embarrassed that I let myself run out of air like that. I'm really an experienced diver. I just pushed it a little too far." She stopped, realizing she was on the verge of babbling for real. He was still looking her in the eye, though, which scored him a few points in her book. Most guys would have let their gaze drift a little lower by now.

"You know what they say," he replied, waggling his finger like a grade school teacher. "One third of your air going in, one third going back out…" He was grinning ear-to-ear.

"…and one third in reserve in case of an emergency, one of which I did arise. I'm well aware of the rule of thirds, Mr. Maddock. I just…" she felt her face grow warm. "I just didn't follow them this time." She wanted to be annoyed at his condescension, but his grin told her he was only joking.

"Understood. I would tell you to call me Dane, but I still don't even know your name."

"Oh, I'm sorry. I'm Jade Ihara."

"A beautiful name. "You don't have a Japanese accent."

"My father was Japanese," she said. "My mother is Hawaiian. I was raised on Oahu."

"Well, that explains it." He cupped his chin and looked thoughtfully into her eyes. "I was trying to figure it out, but I couldn't place it."

"Explains what, may I ask?" She resisted the urge to squirm like a schoolgirl under his cool gaze.

"You have the traditional Japanese beauty, with just a touch of the robust splendor of Polynesia."

"I don't know whether to be flattered or totally creeped out." He had her laughing—another point in his favor. "Where did you get that line about 'robust splendor of Polynesia' anyway?"

"From a coffee commercial," he said, grinning.

"So, what are you anyway? Some kind of professional 'damsel in distress' rescuer or something?"

"I'm a marine archaeologist," he said. "We were working nearby. The discovery of this outpost has been a great opportunity for us."

Saul cleared his throat loudly, reminding them of his presence. He stood with hands on hips, tapping his foot. His mouth was twisted in a sour frown.

"Saul, if you will please pack up my equipment, I'll be with you in a moment." She cut off his protest with a raised hand. "Thank you, Saul. I'll join you shortly." She met his stare with a level gaze until he turned away, muttering something under his breath. He snatched up her dive gear and stamped off through the tangled growth. "I'm sorry," she said, turning back to Dane. "Saul is very protective of me. He means well."

"Not your boyfriend, I hope."

"No, he's definitely not my boyfriend. He's my assistant." That was technically true, she supposed.

"Well, I need to get going," Dane said. "By the way, did your mother ever teach you about the old Hawaiian tradition? When someone saves your life, you have to have dinner on his boat that evening." He made a show of checking the time on his dive watch. "At exactly 18:00 hours. Give or take a few minutes, of course."

"Is that so?" She really didn't have time to socialize with this, or any guy. But he *had* saved her life. Besides, an idea was forming in the back of her mind. "Who am I to flout tradition? Six o'clock it is. I'll need directions to this boat of yours." What was she getting herself into? "And Dane? Dinner had better be spectacular."

Chapter 2

Man, I cannot believe you're kicking us out," Matt Barnaby, Dane's engineer and first mate for this expedition while his partner Bones was on vacation, complained as he swung his leg over the side of their boat, the *Sea Foam*. "And for a girl of all things." He shook his head, turned, and hopped into the waiting motorboat. "Unbelievable."

"Hey, it's not that unbelievable," Dane protested. Actually, it was. Since the death of his wife and unborn son nearly five years ago he had sworn off women. Recent experiences had changed his outlook, and he was beginning to come to grips with some of his inner demons. "I like girls."

"I thought you liked Kaylin." Corey Dean, the ship's tech-head and sonar guru stumbled out of the cabin, trying to slather on sunscreen and spray himself with insect repellant at the same time. His fair skin was no match for the intense sun, but he loved the sea. "I didn't know you were playing the field all of a sudden."

"Kaylin's my friend." Kaylin Maxwell was the daughter of Dane's former commander. The two of them had been through a harrowing adventure together, and come out of it barely alive. The experience had forged a strong bond between them, but sometimes it felt more like brother and sister than anything romantic. Perhaps it was because she was the first woman since Melissa to get close to him. "And she isn't your problem in any case."

"So you won't mind if I ask her out," Matt said, "seeing how you're just friends and all." He smiled a gap-toothed smile, and ran his fingers through his close-cropped receding brown hair, pretending to primp in front of a mirror.

"She's from a Navy family. She'd sooner date a pig

than an army grunt," Dane jibed.

"See there, Corey? You've got a shot after all!" Matt helped Corey over the side and into the small craft.

"You know what really blows?" Corey replied, ignoring Matt's dig. "Bones goes on vacation, and now Dane turns into the player. I thought we were going to get a temporary break from the college dorm room shenanigans."

Uriah Bonebrake, nicknamed "Bones", was Dane's partner and a longtime companion. They had been best friends since their days in the Navy SEALs. The big Cherokee had a way with the ladies, and was known to kick his crewmates off the boat for an occasional evening of entertaining.

"That's right," Dane called back, warming to the banter. "I'm picking up the slack for Bones. Bet you I…"

"You what?" Jade sat astride a jet ski just off the starboard bow. Dane had been so busy bantering with his friends that he had not heard her approach. Her brown eyes sparkled, and her straight white teeth shone against her almond complexion. She was wearing a loose fitting white tank top over a turquoise bikini top. Her black shorts were rolled at the waistband, showing off her flat stomach and a few extra inches of her firm thighs. "Come on now, I'm dying to hear."

"Epic fail!" Corey laughed and fired up the motorboat. "Good luck climbing out of that hole, Maddock." He and Matt made mock salutes as they cruised away.

"Bet you," Dane said, turning back to Jade, "that you absolutely love the dinner I've prepared for us." Leaning over the rail, he offered her a hand, which she clasped firmly. He hauled her over with one tug, and she landed nimbly on the deck, her bare feet making barely a sound when they hit. Martial arts training, he supposed, or perhaps dancing. "By the way, totally unfair shutting down the engine and drifting up on me like that."

"I'm full of surprises." She gave him a coy grin. "If

dinner's good enough, I might let you take it for a spin around the harbor." She surveyed the *Sea Foam* with an appraising eye. "Nice," she said. "She's obviously been worked hard, but I can tell you take good care of her."

"Done much sailing?" he asked, intrigued by this beautiful young woman who seemed to have a great deal of depth. "I suppose if you've done enough diving, you have to have climbed your share of rigging."

"Is that some sort of innuendo?" she teased. He shook his head and she laughed. "I grew up around the water in Hawaii. My uncle had a fishing boat, and I spent a lot of time out with him. My mother hated it, said it wasn't ladylike, but I didn't care. Even then I loved the sun, the salt spray, the dips and the swells." Her eyes had a faraway glint as she remembered. "I don't get out on the water as much as I used to. Mostly when I go back to visit my mother and uncle."

"What about your father?" Dane asked. He could tell by the way she flinched that he had touched on a sore subject. "Sorry. I don't mean to pry."

"That's all right," she said. "He left before I was born. Went back to Japan. He wasn't really part of my life." She stared down into the blue-green water, her face now downcast. "I did all right, I suppose. What about you? What's your story?"

"Navy brat," Dane said. "Did my time in the service, met my friend Bones, and we went into business together when we left the SEALs." He shrugged. "It's a good life. Lots of sun. The occasional interesting diversion," he gave her a meaningful look and grinned.

"I think you skipped over quite a bit in that lovely ten-second autobiography." She narrowed her eyes and stepped close to him. "But that's okay. I have all night to pump information from you." Raising her head, she closed her eyes and inhaled deeply. "What's on the grill?"

Dinner was one of Dane's specialties: broiled sea bass

with lime and herbs, steamed vegetables and fresh fruit. Jade was duly impressed, and dinner conversation was relaxed and enjoyable. An archaeologist by trade, she had graduated from the University of Utah with a specialty in Native American tribes of the southwest, and now served on the faculty of Central Utah University.

"So," Dane said, squeezing a lime into his second Dos Equis, "what is someone with your background doing working an early Spanish dig in Argentina? Seems pretty far out of your area." He took a long drink, savoring the strong flavor, the cool drink perfect on such a muggy evening.

"It's not as far afield as you might think," she said. "The Spaniards who founded this settlement were some of the same men who explored the American southwest, even up into Utah." She put her bottle down and folded her hands in her lap, suddenly serious. "I have a business proposition for you."

"Bummer," Dane said. "And here I hoped it would be a proposition of a more personal nature." He smiled, put his beer down, and leaned forward, mirroring her posture. It was a technique by which Bones swore. He said it created empathy and identification. Then again, when had Bones ever cared about either of those things? Dane suppressed a laugh and leaned back, letting his arms hang over the sides of the chair.

"Very funny," she said, misunderstanding the reason behind the grin on his face. "Personal comes after I've known someone a great deal longer than one evening. Or did you think I was, shall we say, promiscuous?"

"Didn't think, only hoped." That was a comeback worthy of Bones, but it didn't gain him any points. Jade just smirked. Bones had a natural way with women, while Dane had to work hard at it. It wasn't fair. "Seriously, what's your proposition?"

"I need to have another go at that underground stream." She raised her voice and hurried on when she saw

Dane grimace. "I think it will take only one more time. I need to go back to the place where you rescued me." She paused, her brown eyes boring into him. "And I need a dive partner."

"I hate fresh water dives," Dane protested. "They're dangerous, as you found out today, and they're not something I'm comfortable doing." Jade kept staring at him in silence. He knew what she was up to, waiting for him to fill the gap in the conversation. She would try to keep him talking until he talked his way through all his objections and right smack into doing what she wanted. Not biting, he retrieved his beer and took another swig.

"I don't blame you. I know it's dangerous work, which is why I need an experienced diver with me." Her voice softened. "This is very important to me. I've been working on it for ten years. It's not..." She broke off, uttered a distinctly unladylike curse, then mumbled something that sounded a lot like "Why do I get so flustered around you?" before turning her attention to her beer.

He made *her* feel flustered? He swore he would never understand women. The look of disappointment on her face was heartbreaking. "Why don't you tell me what you're working on?" he said.

"If I tell you, will you dive with me?" She cocked an eye at him.

"No," he lied, knowing full well that he was going to let her have her way because... well, just because that's what was going to happen. "But I'll think about it. Tell me what you're doing here."

Jade leaned across the small table, close enough that he could smell her perfume. Jasmine or something like it. "Are you familiar with the story of the Seven Cities of Cibola?"

"I've heard the name," he replied cautiously. "That's about it." A creepy déjà vu feeling blanketed his mind, enveloping him in a muzzy semi-conscious state. He couldn't possibly be getting into another weird mystery.

"Part of the impetus behind Spanish exploration of New Spain, what we could term Colonial Mexico, was the myriad of myths about treasure and magical places." As she spoke, she sat up straighter and her voice gained strength and confidence. She would make a great lecturer. "One of the greatest was the legend of Las Siete Ciudades Doradas De Cíbola, the Seven Golden Cities of Cibola. The myth was an outgrowth of the Moorish conquest of Portugal in the early eighth century. Allegedly, in the year 714, seven Catholic bishops and their followers fled across the Atlantic to a land called Antilia."

"The Antilles," he chimed in, to show that he was paying attention.

"Correct. The story goes that they fled to the New World and established the seven cities, where they hid gold, gems and religious articles to keep them safe from the Moors."

At the mention of religious articles, Dane bolted upright. "Oh no. No friggin' way!" He struck the table with his fist so hard that both their beers tipped over. Jade managed to catch hers, but his hit the table, spewing its foamy contents everywhere.

"Nice," Jade deadpanned. "Are you always this erratic? What did I say, anyway?" Her smooth features were tense with concern.

"Nothing," he muttered. "I just had a bad experience recently and..." What could he tell her that she would actually believe? "It's not important." Before she could reply he hurried to the galley to retrieve some paper towels. Returning, he sopped up the mess as Jade looked on with an expression somewhere between amused and offended.

When the spill was cleaned up, she nodded like an officer at inspection time, and inclined her head toward the bow. "How about we move back there and watch the sun set?" Dane liked that idea just fine, but was disappointed when, once they were seated, she resumed her story.

"The Antillean islands failed to produce the great quantities of gold and silver the Spaniards were expecting, so they set their sights on the continent and its purported riches. As soon as Cortes and his men finished conquering the Aztec Empire in the early 1520s, they set out to find these legendary Seven Cities of Gold. The expedition took them as far as the Texas panhandle, but needless to say, they found no sign of Cibola.

"And then, in 1528 a Spaniard named Cabeza de Vaca was shipwrecked on the Texas Gulf Coast. He wandered through Texas and into northern Mexico before his rescue in 1536. He told of fantastic treasures he had seen in villages to the north, "with many people and very big houses." And thus, what is now New Mexico became targeted as the mythical Cibola.

"Viceroy Antonio de Mendoza soon became intrigued by the fantastic riches rumored to exist in the Seven Golden Cities of Cibola beyond New Spain's northern frontier. In 1539 he sent an expedition led by Estevanico, a black slave who had been shipwrecked with Cabeza de Vaca, and Fray Marcos de Niza to verify de Vaca's reports. Estevanico did not return. It is reported that he died in western New Mexico at Háwikuh, one of the Zuñi pueblos."

"I notice you emphasize 'reported' that he died," Dane observed. "You don't think so?"

"Be patient, I'm getting to that," she reproved, smiling. She was warming to her tale, and obviously thought he was as well. And he was, despite his better judgment. "Get yourself another Dos Equis and shut up. Get me one too."

He produced the drinks in short order, and settled back in to hear the rest of the story.

"Fray Marcos returned to New Spain, declaring he had seen golden cities, the smallest of which was bigger than Mexico City. These strange people were said to possess in great quantities domestic utensils and ornaments made of gold and silver, and to be proficient in many of the arts of the Europeans."

"I think I know how this story ends," Dane said, recalling a bit of history. "Coronado took a stab at it, and failed miserably. Seems like these seven golden cities were just mud villages and such. Nothing but a pipe dream."

"Right. He spent almost two years searching for the seven cities, but finally concluded that they were a myth. His expedition was branded a failure." She bit her lip and stared out at the water.

"This Fray Marcos guy, why do you think he lied? Didn't want to admit to having failed? Maybe he didn't want his friend to have died in vain?"

Jade turned and met his gaze with wide-eyed seriousness. "The kindest historians think that, from a distance, he saw sunset on adobe walls containing bits of silica, and believed he was looking at glimmers of a city of gold."

"That doesn't make sense," Dane protested. "Why would he see a city of gold from a distance, and never go close enough to get a good look? And what about all the details he provided? How would he know those things if he observed from afar?"

"You're right," she said. She took a sip of her beer, then rubbed the bottle across her forehead. Dane watched the cool beads of condensation trickle down her tanned skin. Illumined in the setting sun, they put him in the mind of gold. "Marcos did find Cibola, and he concocted his story to protect the truth." She took another drink, waiting for his reply.

"Come on, now. Don't leave me hanging," he said. "You've got to fill in the blanks."

She reached into her small black bag and withdrew a plastic folder, opened the catch, and produced a small stack of paper-clipped sheets. "I'll hit the high points, so I don't bore you," she said, smiling mischievously. "Fray Marcos's journal turned up in a collection in Spain. I've scanned the pertinent pages. Translations are on the back." She held them out to him.

Dane felt strangely detached as he took them. His fingers were numb and his mind was muddled, and not because of the beer. "Another journal," he muttered. Jade cocked her head and frowned, but said nothing. "Unbelievable." He didn't feel like elaborating.

"Uh huh," Jade said. "He provides precious few details, but he makes it plain that he found something fantastic. He is also very clear that the story he told Mendoza was not only a fabrication, but a tale carefully crafted to lead them astray." She took a deep breath and held it, regarding him as if taking his measure. "I don't know why, but I feel I can trust you." Dane nodded and waited for her to continue.

"The journal indicates that Marcos wanted to hide Cibola from Mendoza, Coronado and the rest, but he didn't want to hide it from the world forever. I believe he left a clue in the bottom of a well." She paused, either for effect or to see if he had any response. "I found that well just before you rescued me. The top caved in long ago. No one even knew it was there. The bottom portion is intact." She leaned back, picked up her drink, and peered at him with an intense stare as she sipped her beer.

Dane made a show of examining the papers, all the while turning things over in his mind. He could tell himself that he didn't want to get involved in another caper like he had before, but truth was his heart was racing from sheer excitement. He had chosen his particular field not only because he loved the sea, but because he loved the mystery, the search and discovery. This was right up his alley. And then, of course, there was Jade. He glanced up, his eyes meeting with hers long enough to register the crinkled brow and tiny smile. She knew she had him.

"So, what exactly do you want me to do?"

Chapter 3

The water was colder than he remembered, and the tunnel darker. He supposed adrenaline had drawn his thoughts away from such things when he was coming after Jade. Now he had time to examine his surroundings, all of which reminded him how much he hated cave diving. Too many skilled divers had met their ends in caves just like this one. Dark, twisting, precarious arteries of peril, all of them. He couldn't wait to get out of here and make up for the sleep he missed the night before.

The two of them had stayed up late, planning the dive. By the time they were finished, Matt and Corey had long returned to the ship and called it a night. He had suggested that Jade stay the night, but she laughed and gave him a chaste hug before heading back to shore. Thoughts of her blended with images of gold and treasure until he couldn't say which was the most responsible for keeping him awake.

He snapped out of his reverie when the narrow channel opened into a wide chamber. They were in the well. He looked up, allowing the beam of his headlamp to play across the ceiling. A thick snarl of ancient roots held up massive chunks of stone, bound together by mud and clay that had seeped down into the collapsed well shaft. The whole thing had a precarious feel to it. He couldn't wait to finish up and get out of there. Jade drifted up alongside him, and motioned toward the floor as if to say "get on with it." He needed no convincing.

Reaching into the small dive bag strapped to his waist, he fished out his metal detector. About three times the size of a cell phone, the rectangular instrument with its fat red buttons and large digital display reminded him of the hand-held football game he had gotten for his fourteenth birthday. The 'players' were little red dashes, and it emitted an annoying tweet whenever you scored. His parents had regretted buying it for him by the end of the first day. He grinned at the memory as he punched the buttons and waited for the instrument to boot up. It was still hard to think about Mom and Dad, but it didn't hurt the way it once had.

The screen was black, with green indicator bars up each side. He drifted to the downstream side of the well, chose what passed for a corner, and began his search. The little detector could penetrate about three feet in ideal conditions, and he was banking on the bottom of the well being silt and mud. He hoped that whatever they were looking for was made of metal. If it wasn't.... well, it wouldn't be the end of the world if they had to excavate the entire floor, but it was worth giving the unit a shot. Besides, it was an expensive toy, and he wanted to play with it. Better than a power tool any day.

Jade shone a high-powered dive light on the floor in front of him, leading the way as he crisscrossed the well bottom. Thankfully there were few obstructions, the gentle current having kept the floor swept clean over the centuries. He held the detector a half-meter off the bottom, sweeping it slowly back-and-forth, feeling like a hotel maid cleaning the floor.

The first hit came almost immediately, small and faint. He stopped and swept the area again. He felt certain that it wouldn't amount to anything, but he indicated the location to Jade, who swam over to meet him. She produced a long, thin digging tool and probed the area, careful not to stir up more dirt than necessary. The steady flow of the underground stream should keep the silt down, but it did not hurt to take care. In short order, she dug free a small, dark object about the breadth of his thumbnail. Perhaps a button or a coin, but they wouldn't know until they took it up top and cleaned it. Jade shrugged and deposited the item in her own dive bag.

The search continued with few results. They turned up

a couple more unremarkable chunks of some metal or other, but nothing more. Dane found himself growing impatient when suddenly his screen went supernova. The indicators on either side shot up, the bars hovering near the top. The display was a solid green square. He moved it back and forth over the spot, which was almost in the very center, trying to get a feel for the size of the object. He quickly determined that it was no larger than a meter square, and no smaller than half that size. He switched the detector off and put it away. He would finish his sweep after they had exhumed whatever this was, but he had a good feeling that this was what they were looking for.

He withdrew his digging tool, a ten-inch titanium rod with a blunted, triangular tip and a six inch rubber grip on the other end, and drew an imaginary circle around the target area. Jade nodded and began working on one side while he took the other. Firmly, but with great care, he probed the perimeter of the target area. Given the intensity of the signal, he hoped it was not buried too deep. The well bottom, mostly silt and clay, gave way easily as he pushed the rod in up to the handle again and again until finally he met with resistance. A glance told him that it was about seven inches down. He withdrew the tool and tried a spot six inches closer to the area where Jade was working. Again he struck something solid at a depth of seven inches. He tapped Jade on the shoulder, and indicated the area, giving her a thumbs-up, which she returned with enthusiasm. Together, they began removing a half-millennium of dirt, clay and rock. A cloud of fine particles enveloped them, but the lazy current carried it away, though not quite fast enough to keep pace with their digging.

When they had cleared a hand's-width channel about two feet in length, he was finally able to see what they were excavating. It was smooth and dark with a gently-angled edge. The exposed surface was slightly convex. Encouraged, Dane produced a larger digging tool, a small shovel with a wide blade that Bones liked to call his "beach toy", and began scooping away the soil in large chunks. Jade tapped her wrist, and he consulted his dive watch. They had been down longer than he had thought. They had five minutes to get this thing out of the ground and start their return with a reasonable amount of time to spare. After Jade's near-disaster, he wasn't willing to take chances. They each carried a pony tank, but he would prefer to avoid using them altogether.

They worked fast, and soon had all but a thin layer of dirt and clay cleared from what he no longer thought of as an object, but an artifact. He swept the dirt away until his gloved fingertips touched the surface. It was hard and smooth with regular raised bumps and lines. His fingers searched for the edge, and found it, squared off and a half-inch thick. Increasingly confident in the solidity and durability of the artifact, he worked the edge of his shovel around the sides, clearing away the debris, while Jade brushed the surface clean.

When the object was fully exposed, they paused, letting the silt drift away. As the water cleared, the object seemed to rise up toward them. It was a breastplate, though its thickness and apparent weight made it obvious to Dane that no man had ever worn it. Time and the elements had turned it almost black, but in the glow of the dive lamps he could discern raised markings. His heart pounded with eager anticipation as the two of them grasped it by opposite edges and pulled.

Nothing.

They tried again, but it would not budge. He checked his dive watch and found that they had less than two minutes. Retrieving his small digging tool, he worked it under one edge, and tried to pry it up, but to no effect. Jade did the same on her side. He reminded himself that, if need be, they could come back with better tools and fresh tanks. After five hundred years, the thing wasn't going anywhere soon, but he was stubborn enough to not want to leave it for even a short while. He managed to get the titanium blade underneath the breastplate, and levered it back and forth, working it along the edge. Soon he had enough leverage to try and pry it up from the bottom. Hoping that it was as sturdy as he reckoned, he braced his feet on the floor and lifted. The breastplate budged a millimeter, then two, and then it broke free with a massive upsurge of dirt and clay.

Knowing they were on borrowed time, Dane motioned for Jade to help him with the breastplate, which was sitting on its edge on the well floor. She took hold of it, while he opened his mesh bag, pulled out two sturdy straps, and secured them around the breastplate. Where they crossed in the middle, he hooked a quick-connect, then snapped that onto a thick, folded object. Jade tilted her head questioningly. He unsnapped his pony tank from his belt, and secured it to a valve. Jade nodded and gave him a "thumbs-up" as the object grew into a torpedo-shaped bladder with two handles on the top. He took hold of the bladder, and lifted, the added buoyancy making it an easy burden. He was about to lead the way out when Jade pointed at his feet.

He looked down to where they had pulled up the breastplate. The silt had drifted away to reveal a dark circle embedded in the floor. A sigil, a cross inside a clover, was engraved in it. Jade dove down and began trying to work it free.

It looks like a seal, Dane thought. A cold certainty swept over him, and he shook his head. He wanted to shout, for all the good it would do. He watched as if in slow motion as Jade gave a twist, and the edge of the seal crumbled. Cracks appeared in the surface, and then it imploded. Knowing she had screwed up big-time, Jade turned and headed for tunnel leading out, with Dane right behind her. Giant bubbles burst forth and then a muffled sucking sound filled the watery cavern. The gentle current was now a daunting foe, and he struggled to make headway, the breastplate dragging him down.

A chunk of rock bounced of his mask, knocking it

askew and letting a in a small trickle of water. The ceiling was coming down! Invisible hands pulled at him, seeking to draw him back into the well. He was in the shaft, but he was making little progress. His legs burned, and his aching lungs reminded him that air would soon be in short supply. Letting go of the breastplate with his right hand, he grabbed for the side of the tunnel, searching for a handhold. His legs still doing double-time, his fingertips found a crack in the rock and he pulled himself forward. He hoped Jade had made it out.

He suddenly felt himself being hauled forward, and he was dimly aware of a gloved hand clutching his shoulder. He kicked and paddled as Jade pulled him into a recessed area on the side of the tunnel. Thick vertical cracks ran down the wall. Still fighting the current, he shoved his free hand into one the cracks, made a fist and twisted until it was wedged tightly. Jade had done the same, and she wrapped her free arm around both him and the breastplate, helping him hold on.

The current raged, and Dane's legs were slowly pulled out from under him. He kicked furiously as he felt himself drawn inexorably toward the well and certain death. Jade still clutched him tightly, and he was glad to know she was still holding on as well. His shoulder screamed in agony, and he feared it would pop out of its socket, but he tensed his muscles and held on. Dirt and debris battered them as it was sucked down the tunnel and into the well.

And then his hand slipped.

It happened suddenly. One moment his fist was painfully wedged in the rock, the next instant he was pulled free, taking Jade with him.

A tremendous crash sounded in the darkness behind them, loud in the watery tunnel, and then they were hurled back up the channel, away from the well. He careened into one wall, then another. He tumbled forward, the breastplate banging painfully against his shin. He was flipped upside down, and he crashed into a wall of stone, his breath leaving him along with his mouthpiece, and he slid to the bottom amidst a shower of dirt and rock.

Woozy, he tried to get a handle on his wits. He found his mouthpiece, forced it between his teeth, and tried to breathe, but his lungs were constricted from the blow. Schooling himself to calmness, he relaxed. It was no easy task to will himself to be at ease underwater in the dark, but soon he was able to take a sip of air. A few more tentative gasps and he was breathing again. He did not need to look at his dive watch to know he would soon need his reserve tank. He felt for it at his hip, and was not completely surprised to find it gone.

Righting himself, he tried to get his bearings. The well must have finally collapsed, re-sealing the hole Jade had opened, and sending the wave of water that had sent them shooting back up the tunnel. That was good. It meant that he was closer to the way out. But how to find their way in the dark?

He ran his hand along the wall, and discovered that he had struck a sharp curve in the channel. Trailing a hand along the edge, he swam forward, hoping he was headed in the right direction. Several times he collided with obstacles, or banged into the opposite wall in particularly narrow stretches of the tunnel, but he kept moving forward. The darkness was absolute. *If I hit the collapsed well, I'm dead. I'll never make it back from there.* The thought did not strike him with fear so much as it disappointed him. He wasn't ready to go. *Where is Bones when I need him?*

A faint glimmer appeared far ahead of him, and then a bar of yellow light sliced through the dirty water. Jade was somewhere up ahead with a flashlight. He swam furiously, the light shining brighter as he the intervening space grew smaller. Before he knew it, Jade was with him. She took hold of the breastplate and together they swam out of the murky tunnel.

Dane spat out his mouthpiece as he broke the surface, and sucked in a lungful of hot, humid air. Matt and Corey were waiting for them, along with Saul. The three of them lifted the breastplate from the water, and then hauled the two divers out.

Dropping to one knee, he removed his mask and turned to look at Jade, who lay on her side, breathing hard.

"I don't know about you," she panted, "but I'm thinking we shouldn't go back down there anymore."

"Do you think?" Dane said, grinning despite the dozen or so pains he felt throughout his body. "Do me a favor. If we ever dive together again, check with me before you pry anything out of the floor." Still panting, he took a few deep, calming breaths. "I just hope that whatever we found was worth it."

"It will be," she said. "Did you see the symbol on the seal?" Dane nodded, remembering the clover around the cross. "That was the mark of Fray Marcos de Niza.

Chapter 4

"Dude, this place is seriously dry. Somebody turn on the humidifier." Bones unscrewed the top of his bottled water, chugged half of it, and dumped the rest on top of his head. He let loose with a massive belch, and tossed the empty bottle into the back of Isaiah's pickup. "You didn't tell me it would be like this, Cuz."

Isaiah frowned. "You realize this is a desert. What did you expect?" He hitched the backpack over his shoulder and leaned in through the driver's side window to grab his clipboard and notebook. Straightening, he fixed Bones with a level gaze. "Bones, this is a serious dig, and the first one I've ever directed. Promise me you won't be…" He paused, searching for the words.

"Be myself?" Bones asked. He had to laugh when his cousin nodded in affirmation. "All right Cuz, I'll behave. Honest injun!" He raised his hand like a plains warrior.

Isaiah rolled his eyes. "Bones, you know I hate it when you talk like that. It degrades our people." He shook his head. He knew Bones well enough to know his sense of humor would never change. "Forget it. Grab that other bag." He nodded to a black duffel bag in the bed near the wheel well on Bones' side of the truck.

"Are you sure we're related?" Bones kidded, hefting the bag. "Sometimes it's hard to believe we're swimming in the same gene pool, know what I mean?"

"Our mothers were related. I don't claim you at all, *Cuz.*" Isaiah grinned and winked. "Let's get going. I don't want to be late on my first day." He led the way down a dusty gravel drive past a line of dirty trucks and SUVs that Bones assumed belonged to the workers on the dig. Falling a few steps behind his cousin, Bones licked his finger and wrote "YOUR MOM IS THIS DIRTY" on the back of a

Range Rover before picking up the pace to catch up.

"You know you love having me around," he said, clapping a hand on the smaller man's shoulder. "By the way. Think you could explain to me how my Tonto act disgraces our ancestors, but it's all right for you to dig up their bones?"

"We're not exhuming any graves," Isaiah said. His long, thin face visibly pained. "We're examining pictographs, and excavating artifacts from the site

"Oh," Bones said, shrugging. "I thought it was because these guys are Fremont and we're Cherokee."

Isaiah snapped his head around and raised a finger, looking every bit the junior college professor that he was. His lecture was thankfully cut off by an attractive young woman in a business suit.

"Excuse me. Are you Dr. Horsely?" she asked, though her tone indicated that the question was a mere formality. She knew exactly who Isaiah was.

Bones chuckled, drawing annoyed glances from her and Isaiah. His cousin's family name was Horse Fly, but Isaiah had legally changed it when he went to college.

"Yes, I'm Isaiah Horsely. How may I help you?" Isaiah took the woman's proffered hand, looking distinctly uncomfortable. He had always been shy around women.

"I'm Amanda Shores of the Deseret Bugle. I'd like to ask you a few questions about the dig." Not waiting for Isaiah's reply, she thrust a digital recorder in his face and pushed the record button. "What do you expect to find in this site?"

"I can't say yet," Isaiah said, taking a step back. "This site's very existence is a new revelation, and we've made only a preliminary survey. There are quite a few fascinating pictographs…"

Amanda cut him off. "Why do you think Mr. Orley has kept this site a secret for so long?" She took a step toward him, keeping the recorder in his face. "What do you think he has to hide?"

"He kept the site a secret in order to protect it." Isaiah looked decidedly uncomfortable. "I have no reason to believe he is hiding anything."

"We really have to go Miss Shores," Bones said, taking Isaiah by the arm and guiding him around the reporter.

Amanda was not deterred. She stepped in front of Bones, blocking his path. "And who might you be?" Challenge shone in her hazel eyes as she faced him.

"Uriah Bonebrake, but you can call me Bones. I'm just a grunt on this expedition, helping Dr. Horsely with his project. But if you're going to do a write-up on me, would you mention my band? We're called 'Custer's Next-to-Last Stand'. I've got a demo tape…"

"I'm sorry, that's not my department," Amanda said, cutting off the recorder and tucking it into her purse. She pointedly turned her back on Bones as she turned back to Isaiah, proffering a business card. "Here's my card, Dr. Horsely. If you find anything of interest, I would appreciate a call." She said it as if it was an order rather than a request.

Isaiah nodded and tucked the card into his pocket. Together he and Bones made their way toward the dig site.

"What is Deseret, anyway?" Bones asked.

"That was the proposed name of a state that Mormon settlers tried to establish back in the 1800's."

"So, you gonna' call her? The reporter chick, I mean." Bones stole a glance over his shoulder as Amanda climbed into her car. "She's cute in a brunette gymnast sort of way."

"You're crazy, Bones. I don't know how you lived this long." Isaiah chuckled and clapped a hand on his shoulder. "And yes, I just might call her."

They walked in silence for a short while. Bones took in the high skies and rugged terrain. It was beautiful, but a bit confined for someone accustomed to the sea. He tried to imagine being a native tribesman a thousand years ago, fighting to survive in this desolate land. Isaiah had assured him that despite appearances, Utah was far from barren. In fact, the land was teeming with life if you only knew where to look for it. Bones supposed that made it like the ocean in a way: bleak on the surface, but abundant life concealed within its depths.

They had not walked far when a short, square man in a weathered John Deere hat hailed them. He wore a flannel shirt in spite of the heat, and sweat rolled down his florid face. He drew a pack of Beech Nut from the back pocket of his jeans and packed a wad into his cheek before speaking.

"You gonna' keep them diggers over at the site where they belong?" He looked at Isaiah as if daring him to say 'no'. "I don't want 'em nowhere else. This is a working ranch, and I ain't got time to be chasin' college kids all over the place."

"We're fully aware of the parameters of the dig site," Isaiah said. "Mr. Orley, I'd like you to meet my cousin, Uriah Bonebrake. People call him Bones."

Bones reached out to shake the rancher's hand, but the fellow just stared up at him for a long moment. He spat a small stream of tobacco juice onto the dusty gravel. "You're one big damned Indian. I think you're the biggest 'un I've ever seen."

"I used to model for the cigar store Indians," Bones said, "but chewing tobacco put us out of business. Now I just go around making white people hurt their necks."

Orley frowned and pursed his lips, glaring at Bones. He looked like he might spew out a stream of curses, but suddenly he laughed and clasped Bones' hand. "By God, you're a funny fellow too. This 'un here," he nodded at Isaiah, "you'd sooner get a tater out of a goat's behind than get a smile out of him."

Bones shuddered at the bizarre mental image. "He's a college fellow," he said in a conspiratorial tone, eyeing Isaiah out of the corner of his eye. "You know the type. Serious all the time."

"I do know it," Orley said. "You mean you ain't a college fellow yourself?"

"Me? Not a chance. Retired from the Navy." He left

out the fact that he had earned a two-year degree while in the service. "You ever in the service, Mr. Orley?"

"Hell yes! Did my tour in 'Nam and got the hell out of there." He nodded at Bones, as if satisfied, and turned back to Isaiah. "Anyways, keep them diggers over there," he pointed to the dig site just visible in the distance. "And stay out of the small barn," he indicated a large shed built against a sheer rock wall about a hundred yards to the east of where they stood. "I got a sick bull in there. I don't know that you'd catch anything, but I don't need you upsettin' him. We clear?"

"Absolutely," Isaiah said, smiling. "And let me thank you again for opening up your ranch for this dig. I admire the way you've preserved the site for so many years, and I appreciate the opportunity to be the first to excavate it."

"Ah, forget it!" Orley waved a calloused hand at him, and spat another brown puddle on the ground. "Ever since that feller at Range Creek opened up his place, I knew it was just going to be a matter of time before you college 'uns started poking around. Might as well get it done." He turned away and strode off toward his small house just visible to the southeast.

Bones looked at Isaiah, who grinned and shrugged. "He's not a bad fellow," Isaiah said. "I can imagine that after the undisturbed Fremont sites were opened up on Range Creek, he probably did feel like he needed to share his site on his own terms."

"Whatever," Bones said. "Let's head on to the site. I'm anxious to do some digging. Should be fun."

"This is the most boring thing I have ever done." Bones scuffed the ground with the toe of his boot. "I had this crazy idea that a 'dig' might involve some actual digging." He snapped another picture of the pictographs adorning the rock face, and let out a dramatic sigh. They had spent what felt like hours photographing and cataloguing the various pictures etched into the rock. The others members of the dig were mapping the lay of the land and making records of the artifacts that lay strewn across the ground. He had been surprised to see how plentiful they were, and that Orley had apparently left them untouched where they lay.

"Are you sure you've been on a dig before, Bones?" Isaiah did not turn to look at him, but instead kept his eyes on the pictographs. "You told me you loved archaeology."

"Yeah, but the last dig I was on, there was climbing and people shooting at me and stuff." He knew he sounded like a sullen schoolboy, but he didn't care, because at least it annoyed his cousin. "It was fun!"

"You're a piece of work, you know that?" Isaiah shook his head. "I swear, sometimes you even have *me* believing your wild tales." He paused to lean in close and scrutinize a picture that looked to Bones like a lumpy cow. "Anyway," Isaiah continued, "if you don't want to help me with this, grab a notebook and start counting the potsherds."

"Counting the potsherds. Thrilling. Forget it dude, I'll just stay here." He moved along the wall, looking with disinterest at the pictographs. Isaiah had called them "fascinating", said they were the best he'd ever seen. To Bones, all of them looked the same. The same people, the same four-legged beasts, the same weird shapes. Except for one that drew his attention. On the far right end of the rock face, where the overhanging ledge arched down, the wall receded back into the hill. The recessed area looked like it had been bricked over with inch-thick flat rocks and mud. To the left of the bricked in area was a rendering of a person. Unlike the pictographs, this one was a painting, and the fellow in the picture looked like he was bowing down to something or someone.

"Hey, check this out," he called out to Isaiah. "This one is different." He ran his fingers along the stone around the edge of the image, wanting to touch it, but fearing he might damage it in some way. His eyes drifted to the stacked rocks closing off the alcove. Perhaps it was his imagination, but they looked like they had been put there intentionally. He touched it with a tentative finger, and found it solid. He pushed a bit harder to no effect. Stealing a glance at Isaiah, who was still scrutinizing the pictographs, Bones balled up his fist and rapped on the rocks. The sound rang hollow in his ears. There was a space behind there, he was sure of it! He knocked again, harder this time. With a loud clatter the rock wall collapsed, falling back into the empty space behind in a puff of dust. Bones gasped when he saw what lay behind.

"Bones!" Isaiah shouted. "What did you do?" He rushed over to Bones' side. "I can't believe you…" Words failed him when he saw what Bones was staring at. His dark face blanched. "It can't be," he finally whispered.

A detailed cave painting, so unlike the simple pictographs that covered the rest of the rocky face, stared back at them. A man stood in the center of a group. Light shone all around him, creating a glowing aura about his beatific face. Although the artwork was primitive, it was clear that he was not an Indian. He had shoulder-length hair, a moustache, and a beard. He stood with his hands upraised, and all around him the primitive-looking men bowed down to him.

Bones took a step back and shook his head. It was several moments before he found his voice.

"Who in God's name is that?"

Chapter 5

Dane scrubbed the last bit of corrosion off of the breastplate, admiring its dull glow under the artificial light. It was iron with a copper coating, unless he missed his guess. The artifact was not in bad shape considering its age. The clay and silt of the well had protected it all these centuries.

"What do you make of these markings?" Jade asked, her fingers resting lightly on his shoulders. "Some of them almost look like lines on a map." She leaned down for a closer look, her cheek brushing against his. He was painfully aware of her jasmine scent and the softness of her skin. "The cross is obviously the most significant marking, but what does it tell us?"

Running diagonally across the breastplate from top left to bottom right, a cross lay in raised relief. At each of the four tips, halfway up the longest segment, and at the point where the two lines crossed were seven-pointed sunbursts. Dane looked at the etchings that surrounded it. It did look like a map. Lines that might have represented mountain ranges filled the top left and center. A low, oddly shaped range lay beneath the center sunburst, and a single jagged peak abutted the bottom left star.

There were pictures as well. There was a tall, squat tower at one point, and what might have been statues at another. And on the bottom, a semi-circle, its center filled with a variety of patterns.

"Is that the moon?" Saul spoke for the first time since Dane had started cleaning the breastplate. Dane didn't care one bit for Jade's assistant. There was something about the man's demeanor that rubbed him the wrong way. "These could be craters," he said, pointing at the circles that pockmarked the half-circle.

"I don't know," Jade said. "That wouldn't explain the

squares. It looks familiar, though." She stepped to the side and folded her arms across her chest, scrutinizing the artifact. "Let me get some pictures of it, then we'll see what we can figure out. All right," she said, raising her voice and clapping her hands twice like a schoolteacher calming an unruly class, "everybody clear the room. I like lots of peace and quiet when I work."

"Wait a minute," Dane said in mock-protest. "I could have sworn this was my boat." The look Jade gave him, disapproval mixed with mild threat, told him not to push it farther. He followed Matt and Corey, who had been hanging out quietly by the door, out onto the deck, with Saul trailing behind.

Jade emerged twenty minutes later, a satisfied look on her face.

"We're finished for today," she said. She turned to face Saul, who stared at her with an air of impatience. "You can go back," she told him, ignoring his twisted scowl. "I'll be along in a little while. You and I can look at the pictures tonight if you like."

Saul's eyes flitted to Dane and then back to Jade. He pursed his lips and worked his jaw. "Do you want me to help you with the breastplate? It's not really a one-man job."

Dane expected a sharp retort from Jade at the word "man", but none was forthcoming.

"I've decided I'm going to leave it here," she said, "at least for the night."

"The university wouldn't like that," Saul protested. "I really think you should…"

"What the university would not like is my concern." Jade spoke over him in a firm tone. "Not yours."

Saul tensed, the veins in his neck standing out and his face twisting into a scowl, then relaxed and gave a curt nod.

"Do you want me to come back for you later?" When Jade shook her head, Saul gave Dane an accusatory look. "Of course," he said, his voice sour. Without further comment, he turned and walked away. Shortly thereafter the sound of a boat motor heralded his departure.

"That guy is a real treat," Dane said, shaking his head. "Wish I had ten just like him." Saul reminded him Marc Paccone, an upperclassman he'd encountered at the Naval Academy. Like most bullies, Marc was a sadist, and used his station to abuse his underlings, but deep down he was a coward.

Years later, Dane had encountered him in a bar. A couple too many shots of Jose Cuervo, and Marc was inviting him outside. Happy to oblige, Dane had made quick work of the big fellow and been gone before anyone had even thought of calling the cops. Saul struck him the same way, though what power the man wielded over Jade was not immediately apparent.

"You seem like a no-nonsense girl," he said. "Why do you keep him around?"

"I'm afraid he's a necessary evil," Jade said, smiling. "His father is my biggest backer." Dane thought that explained a great deal. "But enough about Saul," Jade said, slipping her hand into his, "how about grabbing me a beer?"

Dane tried to sleep, but slumber eluded him. He had spent a pleasant evening with Jade, but now the mystery was foremost in his mind. He would have gone back for another look at the breastplate, but at the last minute, Jade had decided to take it back with her. He bundled it up and gave her a lift back to shore.

One particular picture on the breastplate now gnawed at his mind. He was sure he had seen the moonlike image somewhere before, but he could not place it. It was driving him crazy. He rolled out of his bed, pulled on shorts and a t-shirt, slipped out of his small cabin and made his way up to the deck.

The night air was damp, but could only be considered cool in contrast to the day's heat. The full moon danced on the water, glistening on the gently rolling sea. It seemed to taunt Dane, a tantalizing clue to the memory that abided just beyond recollection. He rested his elbows on the stern rail and stared at the silver circle.

Something caught his ear. A sound that was out of place. He cocked his head and concentrated. He heard the scrape of a shoe on the deck on the port side. Moving quickly and silently, he hurried toward the sound, painfully aware that he was unarmed. Perhaps either Matt or Corey was also having trouble sleeping, but something told him that was not the case.

His instinct was correct. A small boat drifted just off the port bow. He heard its engine fire up as a dark form vaulted the Sea Foam's rail and landed in the smaller craft.

"Hey!" he shouted as the boat tore off, leaving a frothy wake. He didn't know why he had yelled, but it had seemed like the thing to do. He could make out few details of the rapidly receding boat. A hunched shadow was at the helm, but he could see no more..

He heard a commotion below, and soon Corey and Matt joined him. He quickly explained what had happened, and they set about inspecting the *Sea Foam*. She was clean. The only sign of intrusion was the cabin door, which had been pushed to, but not quite closed. Inside, everything was in order; nothing was missing or out of place.

"Weird," Matt observed, shaking his head. "But you gotta' appreciate a burglar who cleans up after himself."

Dane gave a half-smile, but he didn't have to say what he was thinking. There was only one thing anyone would have been looking for in the cabin. But how many people even knew that the breastplate had been here? The discovery was not a secret. News of the find had spread around the town and among the various researchers. He immediately suspected Saul, but that didn't make sense. Surely he would know that Jade had brought it back with her. And why would he want to take it anyway? As Jade's assistant he had plenty of access to it. It was too much for his brain.

"I'm wide awake now," Corey said. "Anybody else want a beer? I'm dry as the desert."

The desert! Dane glanced up at the moon, a broad smile spreading across his face. He remembered where he had seen the image on the shield!

Chapter 6

Come on Cuz, your public is waiting." Bones clapped Isaiah on the back as they left the dig site. Up ahead, a throng of people stood outside the gate to Orley's ranch. He counted at least two vans from local television stations. A few others were too far away to identify. He spotted a bored-looking young man with an expensive camera slung around his neck, and two other men armed with note pads and tape recorders. At the front of the pack, looking quite pleased with herself, stood Amanda Shores. They were walking smack into a press conference.

Orley waited just inside the gate, his face even redder than usual. "You answer their questions and you get 'em out of here, or I'm shuttin' the whole thing down, you hear me?"

"Yes, I understand, Mr. Orley," Isaiah said, his voice tired. Public relations was definitely not his strong suit. "But you must understand, the discovery we've made might be of great significance. It's understandable that the public is interested."

"To hell with that." Orley cleared his throat and spat a wad of phlegm in the dust at Isaiah's feet. "Like I done told you, this is a working ranch, and I want 'em out of here." He shoved past Isaiah without giving him a chance to reply. Bones wondered at the man's comment. He hadn't noticed much work of any kind going on at the ranch, save the dig.

"Dr. Horsely," Amanda called out above the din of voices. "Amanda Shores from the Deseret Bugle. We spoke yesterday."

"Yes, I remember," Isaiah said. Warily he approached the crowd of reporters. Bones trailed behind, feeling wickedly amused. This ought to be good.

The photographer started clicking away, while two men

with television cameras appeared from the throng and started rolling. Amanda asked the first question.

"Dr. Horsely, is it true that your dig has found an image of Jesus Christ among some undisturbed pictographs?"

"Wait a second," Isaiah said, holding up his hands. "We don't know what the picture is, save that it appears to be a bearded man who is not Native American. Beyond that, we cannot say who the picture represents."

"Is it true that the image shows natives worshipping Jesus?" asked one of the news reporters, his hooked nose and piercing eyes giving his stare the intensity of a hawk on the hunt. He held his pen poised above the paper like something out of 'The Pit and the Pendulum".

"Um, the figures in the picture do appear to be bowing," Isaiah said, looking stunned. He obviously was not expecting the details to have gotten out so quickly. Someone on the dig needed to keep his or her mouth shut, Bones thought, or have it shut for them.

"Was it common for the native peoples of this region to bow down to bearded men on a regular basis?" Amanda chimed in. People in the crowd laughed. Even Isaiah cracked a smile.

"You have to understand that there are any number of things that are uncommon about this find," Isaiah protested. "Aside from the fact we're talking about a painting rather than a pictograph, the representation is done with a level of detail unheard of for the time period, and in a style that is inconsistent with the other images found at this site. We aren't ruling out anything just yet."

"But do you have any reason to believe that the painting, or whatever it is, is not legitimate?" This reporter, a willowy blonde in a navy suit, looked and sounded unhappy to be out on this hot, dry, dirty piece of earth. "Aren't forgeries easy to spot?"

"As I said," Isaiah said, "we aren't ruling anything out. The image in question was concealed behind a false wall of sorts, and was not really a part of the other images, which are simply pictographs. I wish I could tell you more, but we just don't know very much."

"You are aware that the L.D.S. church has a belief that Jesus visited the New World?" Amanda asked. "Wouldn't that be the simplest explanation? These natives encountered Jesus and worshiped him?"

"There is no simple explanation for what we've found," Isaiah said. "At any rate, I'm not interested in the simplest explanation, only the truth."

One of the newspaper men, thick around the middle and thin and gray on top, raised a manicured hand, letting the sun glint off of his fake Rolex. "What sort of proof will you need before you can conclude that this is, in fact, the image of Christ?

"I'm not gathering evidence to support any particular hypothesis. There are local legends that could tie in with this find. There are stories of men with scales that some believe represent Spanish armor. This could very well be evidence of contact with Spanish explorers."

Not liking the answer, Amanda turned to Bones. "What about you Mr. Bonebrake? What do you think about what you've uncovered? I understand it was you who discovered the painting?"

"No, it wasn't like that," Bones said, wishing she'd left him out of it entirely. "I accidentally busted up some rocks, and there it was. I stepped out of the way and let Dr. Horsely do his thing."

"We'd still like to hear your thoughts," the blonde interjected, sounding as if the only thing she'd like would be to get out of there pronto.

"I really wouldn't be of any help," Bones said, putting on his biggest dumb smile. "Like I told Miss Shores yesterday, I'm not an archaeologist, just a…"

"You're just a hard rocking Indian," Amanda said, her voice cynical. There was a triumphant look in her eyes that made Bones distinctly uncomfortable. "I did some checking on you. Fortunately, Uriah Bonebrake is not exactly an everyday household name."

"That's just my nickname," Bones said, his tension rising at what he suspected was coming. "My real name is Fred Smith. I'm a landscaper from Topeka."

The blonde actually giggled, but Amanda swooped in for the kill. "What would you like to tell us about first, Mr. Bonebrake? Your service in the SEALS? Your career as a treasure hunter and marine archaeologist?" The other reporters were now looking very interested. "I know," Amanda said as if she had just thought of it. "Why don't you tell us about the last archaeological dig you were on? I believe it was at Petra?"

"It was nothing," Bones said. "I was just a tourist on one of those volunteer digs. I didn't do much."

"That's true," Amanda said. "You only found a carving of Goliath that had been hidden since Petra's re-discovery." This statement elicited a loud murmur from the gathered crowd. The blonde reporter even appeared interested. Amanda continued to press him. "You seem to have a knack for uncovering ancient pictures of biblical figures, don't you?"

"I didn't actually find the Goliath carving," Bones said. Isaiah grinned at him, enjoying the turnabout.

"I'm sorry, was it your partner Dane Maddock who discovered it?" Amanda asked sweetly. "I have a call in to him."

"Don't hold your breath," Bones said. "He's not a people person like I am." He was filled with a growing certainty that he wasn't going to be able to talk his way out of this one.

"Tell us about the part where you and Mr. Maddock crawled out of an underground chamber behind the carving, having managed to bring down a whole mountain and effectively destroying the dig."

Bones thought fast. He had always been a risk-taker. Time to take a chance. "You're absolutely right, Miss

Shores. I do have a fascinating story to tell." He strode to the gate and vaulted it, landing nimbly on the balls of his feet. Not bad for a sea dog. "I have decided to grant an exclusive interview to this young lady right here." Two steps took him to where the blonde stood, looking surprised and pleased with the turn of events. He hooked an arm around her waist. "Where is your vehicle Miss..?"

"Dixon," she stammered, blushing furiously. "Emily Dixon, from Channel.."

"We can discuss all of that later, Miss Dixon. Right now, what I need is a tall, cold cervesa. That's Cherokee for Budweiser. Care to join me?" Emily laughed and nodded her assent.

Bones turned back toward the tangle of reporters, all protesting vehemently. "I'll be leaving you now, but Dr. Horsely will be happy to continue this discussion with you." He ignored the frustrated look in Isaiah's eyes, and turned back to his new friend. "Shall we go?" She nodded, and he led her toward his truck.

"Mr. Bonebrake!" Amanda shouted. "Will you at least tell us if you think it's possible that the image is that of Christ?"

"Who knows if Jesus came to America?" Bones shouted back. "I mean, he's the son of God. I guess he could… I don't know… fly."

He didn't know if it was the rattle of his cell phone vibrating on the nightstand, or the "Detroit Rock City" ringtone, but one of the two awakened him in a most unpleasant way. He rolled over, groaning at the pain in his head, and grabbed the phone. The number on the display was unfamiliar, but it was from the local area code. It was probably Isaiah.

He flipped it open and held it to the ear that was ringing the softest. "Bones," he croaked.

"Uh, I'm sorry," said a soft, feminine voice. "What did you say?"

"This is Bones," he growled. He really wasn't in the mood for a wrong number, especially after Emily had played him like a violin. He had been completely sucked in by her ditsy reporter act, and when he finally spilled the Petra story, she'd suddenly remembered that she needed to be home early. He'd always been a sucker for the sorority girl types, but they'd never been any good for him. In fairness, she had said goodbye with a kiss that had some potential, and a phone number that might even have been hers. He hadn't bothered to check it out. "How can I help you?"

"Did you say Bones? I'm looking for someone who knows Isaiah Horsely."

Bones sat up straight, his head clearing fast. Something was wrong. "This is Uriah Bonebrake. I'm his cousin. What's up?"

"Bonebrake, Bones, sorry about that I'm just upset." A nervous laugh. "And I'm babbling. I'm really sorry."

"It's all right ma'am. What can I do for you?" He struggled to keep the impatience out of his voice.

"My name is Allison Hartwell. I'm Doctor Horsely's neighbor. I found your name and number on a notepad on his kitchen table. I need to let someone know that there's been..." The pause seemed interminable. He was about to tell her to speed it up when she finished the sentence. "There's been an accident."

Forty minutes later he was wandering through the mostly empty corridors of the local hospital looking for the pre-op room. There weren't many people to guide him this time of night, but thankfully it was a small place. He soon found the door, and walked in without knocking.

"Excuse me, but what are you doing?" A gaunt young doctor with stringy ginger hair and a clipboard stepped in front of him. He had guts. The fellow was almost Bones' height, but couldn't weigh more than a buck and-a-half.

"You can't be back here."

"I'm here to see Isaiah Horsely. I'm his next of kin."

The doctor's eyes narrowed and a look of skepticism crossed his face. "Mister Horsely is about to go into surgery."

"I understand the concept of pre-op," Bones said. He leaned in, the two of them now nose-to-nose. "I'm asking nicely. Please."

The fellow could take a hint. "Come with me." He turned and led Bones to a curtained room where a uniformed police officer stood.

"Who is this?" the cop asked. He wasn't foolish enough to stand in Bones' way.

"He is the next of kin," the doctor said. "He'll only be a moment."

"I'll want to talk to you when you're done in there," the officer said. Bones nodded and stepped into the pre-op room.

Isaiah lay under a pristine white sheet. His face was swollen, and his head heavily bandaged. His swollen lips were an ugly purple under the too-bright lights. He had taken a hell of a beating. The neighbor girl, Allison, had warned Bones, but it was still terrible to see. Isaiah's arms were atop the sheet, and both were badly bruised. Defensive injuries, Bones supposed. His eyes followed the I.V. drip from Isaiah's hand up to the bag. He looked at the vital sign monitors, but the numbers meant little to him. He couldn't believe someone would do this to Isaiah, who had always been so bookish and gentle of spirit, and was a good man. Bones grimaced. The culprits had better pray the cops got to them before he did.

A nurse stepped into the room and cleared her throat. "We're taking him back now. You can say your goodbyes."

Bones knelt down next to Isaiah's right shoulder and laid his hand on his upper arm. "I'm here. You awake?"

Isaiah opened one eye as much as his swollen lids would allow. The corners of his mouth twitched. He was trying to smile.

"They're going to get you all fixed up, man." Bones said, hoping this was true. "And when you're all better, we'll get this mess cleaned up. All of it." He gave Isaiah's shoulder a gentle squeeze and stood to leave.

"Bones," Isaiah said in a soft voice that was almost a wheeze.

"Yeah?" Bones leaned down so that his ear was close to his cousin's face. "I'm listening."

"Orley... doesn't have a bull." Isaiah closed his eyes and said no more.

"What was that?" Bones asked, but Isaiah's steady breathing indicated that he had lapsed into sleep.

"I'm sorry sir, but we have to take him now," the nurse said. "The waiting area is down the hall to your right. The doctor will find you when the surgery is over."

Bones thanked her and headed to the waiting area. He wanted to sleep, but something told him he would be up all night trying to figure out why in the world it mattered that Orley did not have a bull.

Chapter 7

Chaco Canyon was the root of Anasazi Culture. This desert country, with its long winters, short growing seasons and minimal rainfall seemed to Dane an unlikely place for civilization to take root, yet it was once the center of Anasazi life. From the end of the first millennia to the middle of the second, people had farmed this canyon and constructed fantastic great houses and kivas. In terms of architecture, life and social organization, the Anasazi of Chaco Canyon had reached heights unsurpassed by their kindred of the Four Corners region.

The Chacoans constructed their magnificent center of trade and worship on a nine-mile stretch of canyon floor, with an eye to longitude and the cycles of the sun and moon. Working with only primitive tools and without a system of mathematics, they raised massive buildings that still inspire awe.

Dane was too focused on the sheer desolation of the land to take notice of the architecture. Most of the ruins were just far enough off the road to make it nearly impossible to see much of anything. He was road weary from the seemingly never-ending trek from the highway to the park, which lay in the midst of sparse, dry land.

Saul had insisted on driving the car even before their plane touched down in Durango, Colorado. Dane sat in the back of the rented Range Rover, poring over a park map with Jade.

"Are you sure there's anything out here?" Saul asked, not for the first time. "This is the emptiest place I've ever seen. There aren't even any tourists around."

"Yes, I'm sure," Jade said, not looking up from the map. "Just keep going." She sighed loudly, but Saul was focused on his own thoughts.

"And people really lived out here? Hard to believe, it's so dry."

"Chaco Canyon was actually the center of Puebloan culture for a long time," Jade said. Saul snorted but said no more.

"So, go over the plan with me again," Dane said. He remembered the plan well enough, but he preferred Jade's voice to Saul's any day. He was still weary from the whirlwind of the last three days. Since he had recognized the picture on the breastplate as being that of Pueblo Bonito in Chaco Canyon, they had scrambled to make arrangements. Willis Sanders, an old SEAL comrade who helped Dane out from time-to-time, flew to Argentina to help Matt and Corey finish the job on which they and Dane had been working in Argentina. Meanwhile, Jade worked furiously to research Chaco Canyon and any possible connection to Fray Marcos.

"The cross on the breastplate," Jade said, pulling a folder out from underneath the map, "is, I think, more than a cross." She laid the folder on top of the map and opened it to reveal the photos she had taken of the artifact. "A line with a sunburst at each end is a symbol commonly associated with a solstice or an equinox." Her finger traced the vertical bar of the cross, coming to rest on the top sunburst. "It can't just be a cross, or else why bother putting sunbursts there?" She closed the folder and slipped it back beneath the map.

"Here," she indicated a spot far from the park entrance they had passed not long before, "is Fajada Butte. Atop it sits the most famous astronomical marker in Chaco Canyon, perhaps the most famous in Anasazi Culture: the Sun Dagger. At midday, three large, vertical slabs cast a dagger-shaped shaft of light onto a spiral petroglyph carved into the rock face behind the slabs. The carving is used to demarcate solstices, equinoxes and phases of the moon. We'll climb to the top and check it out."

"And you're hoping we'll find what?" Dane asked.

"We'll know when we get there," Jade said. "The pictures I found on the internet didn't tell me much, but there could be something there. I think there's a clue carved into the rock, or possibly buried." She sounded determined, if not confident.

"I still think we're going to have to blast through that petroglyph to get to whatever is behind it," Saul interjected. "That spiral looks just like a bullseye to me."

"We aren't going to blow up the Sun Dagger," Jade said. "We don't even have permission to climb the butte. Besides, the petroglyph was carved long before Fray Marcos came to the New World. In fact, the Chaco Canyon settlement was nearing its end during his time."

Saul shrugged. "Suit yourself. I'm still bringing my toys." Apparently Jade's assistant fancied himself a demolitions expert. "By the way, did I tell you what I learned this morning?"

"How to tie your shoe?" Jade quipped.

"No, really," Saul said, ignoring the jibe. "I was reading an article about Chaco Canyon. The people who lived here were famous for their Cibola-style pottery. Cibola! Pretty cool, huh?"

"Uh huh," Jade said, returning her gaze to the map. "I feel like we can get in and out of there pretty quickly. The park doesn't get many visitors, so they likewise have very few rangers. I'm figuring they spend most of their time inside the air-conditioned welcome center. The butte is off the beaten path, so we should be all right."

Saul stopped the car in a small turnoff amidst sand-colored hills. "We're hoofing it from here, ladies and gentlemen. Grab your jocks and your socks."

"Lovely, Saul," Jade mumbled as she stepped out of the car.

Saul opened the trunk and they each donned a heavy backpack. They had outfitted themselves with climbing gear, analytical instruments and water. Lots of water.

A twisting, sloped trail wound its way up into the bare

hills. Dane was soon reaching for a water bottle. They called a halt upon gaining the top of one of the rocky promontories. Years on the water had helped him grow accustomed to the sun beating down on him, but in this place the air seemed to suck the last drops of moisture from his body. He took a long, cool drink and scanned the horizon. It was beautiful, if such a desolate place could be called so. The sky was high and slightly hazy from the heat. He tried to mop his brow, but the sweat evaporated almost instantaneously. How had people ever lived in this oven?

"Down the hill and to the east," Jade said, leading the way. The trail was gravelly but not particularly precarious. Saul lost his footing more than once, each time falling heavily onto Dane's back, cursing all the while. The man was a buffoon, but there was nothing Dane could do to get rid of him, so he gritted his teeth and continued bearing Saul up, hoping all the while that it wouldn't be much longer.

Twenty minutes later they stood at the base of Fajada Butte, staring up at the massive red rock. As Jade had predicted, there was no sign of a park ranger, or any other human being for that matter. Dane circled the base, looking for the most promising climb. He finally settled on the southwest side, stripped off his pack, and began pulling out climbing gear.

"I don't know," Saul said, walking up beside Dane. "This thing looks pretty tall to me."

"One hundred thirty five meters, to be exact," Dane said. "Not the easiest free climb I've ever made, but far from the most difficult." He and Bones had done their share of rock climbing together, and they had never agreed on who was the more skilled. Dane was more agile, but longer legs and arms allowed him to reach crevasses and holds that Dane could not. Until a few years ago, they had placed bets on all of their free climbs. Dane chuckled and shook his head at the thought of his friend. Bones had promised to join them as soon as Isaiah was out of the woods. Dane hoped it would be soon. It just wasn't right doing this without his partner.

"Are you all right?" Jade asked in her satin-over-sandpaper voice that reminded him of a young Demi Moore. "You look worried."

"No, I'm fine," Dane said. "Just got distracted thinking about Bones' cousin. Wondering if he's going to be okay."

"I'm sure he will," Jade said. "He has to, so I can meet this Bones character you've been telling me about. In any case, if you're serious about free climbing this thing, you'd better keep your focus."

"Yes ma'am," he replied in his best military voice. He sprang nimbly to his feet. "When I get to the top, I'll set a rope for you. Send Saul up first, so you can belay for him." *That, and if the rope breaks, we'll have one less problem to deal with.* "You bring up the rear." No one had told him he was in charge of the climb, but sometimes a given set of circumstances seemed to dictate it. Since neither Jade nor Saul objected, it must have been the right thing to do.

He set to climbing, and was pleasantly surprised at the ease with which he scaled the rock. The cracked, pitted surface provided ample handholds, and none of the angles were too treacherous. Soon, the three of them stood atop Fajada Butte, admiring the surrounding landscape. He found it truly amazing that a people had not only lived but flourished amidst this hard land.

"The Sun Dagger," Jade said, her voice filled with reverence and wonder. She indicated a spot against a high rock wall where three slabs of rock stood against the rock wall beneath an outcropping. The tallest was just over nine feet tall, and they all were tilted slightly to the left, like slices of bread.

"It's not much to look at," Saul said. And he was right. Despite having seen snapshots, Dane had created an image in his mind of something larger than life, something magical and mysterious. This was something quite ordinary.

Jade's enthusiasm was not dampened in the least. She

hurried over to the stone slabs and ducked down, vanishing behind them. Dane followed her. Slipping into the shade beneath the stone pillars, his eyes were immediately drawn to the pictograph—a large spiral, twisting into a point in the center of the sandstone slab. He had read that the spirals carried different meanings depending on whether they spun out clockwise or counterclockwise, but he could not remember anything more.

"It's beautiful," Jade whispered, her fingertips mere centimeters above the rocks surface, tracing the spiral line without touching it. She was right. There was something in its simplicity, its balance, its perfection that moved Dane's spirit. "Maddock," she said, "a thousand years ago people sat in this very place and followed the earth's journey around the sun."

"Sort of makes Mount Vernon seem trite, doesn't it?" Dane was partial to the colonial period of American history, but this was truly American history.

They sat for a while in silence, neither replying when Saul stuck his head in and asked what was the holdup.

Jade finally let out a long sigh. "I guess we'd better get to work."

After making a thorough visual inspection and taking pictures with a high-resolution digital camera, they began work with a hand-held ground penetrating radar unit. Jade looked like a cop laying for speeders, her tanned face and almond eyes solid and serious as she held the radar unit in a two-handed grip. She first took readings below the slab, then around it, and finally of the slab itself.

"Nothing," she said after taking her third reading of the slab. "It's solid rock all around. Time to re-think the plan, I suppose." Her shoulders sagged and her face was downcast.

"That means it's my turn," Saul said, picking up his backpack. "Stand back, ladies and gentlemen."

"Saul, you are not blowing up the slab." The downtrodden Jade of a moment before had vanished, and the stubborn ball of fire had returned. "If there was anything to be found underneath the rock, the radar would have picked it up. I'll not have you destroy a piece of history for your own amusement."

Saul turned around and was about to protest when something caught Dane's attention.

"That's enough," he said. Jade rounded on him but he did not give her a chance to speak, taking her by the shoulders and turning her toward the west where a black spot on the horizon was growing larger by the second. "You see that? That's a Sikorsky S-70, a military helicopter, though it doesn't have any markings to indicate it's anything other than a civilian craft now. It probably has nothing to do with us, but just the same I think we should get out of here."

Chapter 8

Dane was relieved that Jade did not argue with him. She squinted and looked at the approaching helicopter for a moment before nodding her assent. They collected their gear, and Jade and Saul made a rapid descent. Not wanting to leave any evidence behind, Dane took the ropes loose and dropped them down to Jade. He looked back at the Sikorsky and found that it still seemed headed directly toward them, and it was coming fast. There was no way he could make the free climb to the bottom before it was upon them. He knew he was being overcautious, but his instinct told him that the black bird on the horizon was bad news.

"Go on! I'll catch up!" he shouted down to Jade and Saul. She put a hand to her ear and tilted her head. "I can't get down in time!" He pointed toward the path along which they had hiked. They understood then. Jade shook her head, but Saul took her by the upper arm and trotted away. Jade had to follow or be dragged. *He's happy enough to get rid of me,* Dane thought.

He stole a last glance at the approaching helicopter before beginning his descent. It was slow going, feeling for the cracks and ledges he had climbed earlier. He wanted to look back and see if Jade and Saul had gotten away, but it was critical that he maintain his concentration.

A low hum filled his ears, quickly growing into a sound like a thousand angry hornets. The bird was almost there. Down and to his right was a crack in the stone face that looked almost wide enough to squeeze into. He made for it, his fingertips clutching at the most miniscule lumps of stone as he scooted across the rocky face. He slid his right foot out onto an egg-shaped protrusion, and shifted his weight to his right hand and right leg. Almost there.

With a soft crunch the rock broke away and he was

dangling by scraped, raw fingertips. He held on tight, not panicking. A less experienced climber might scrabble his feet against the stone searching for a foothold, and actually force his body away from the rock. Dane took a deep breath, ignoring the scorching hot pain that coursed through his wrists and forearms. Sliding his right foot upward, he found an angled crack in the rock into which he could push his toe. Soon he had found purchase for his left foot, and he was on steady footing four feet away from the fissure.

The helicopter was virtually on top of him now. Bits of sand and rock blown by the wash of the rotors rained down on his head. He searched for a way to get to the fissure, but the intervening space was worn smooth by sand and wind. He looked up to see the craft hovering over the butte. Had they seen him?

His senses sharpened by adrenaline, he spotted a crack running horizontally along the far inside wall of the fissure, level with his waist. Ignoring his better judgment, he flexed his knees, ankles and wrists as much as possible, gathered his strength, and leapt sideways across the face of the rock.

For a panicked instant he thought he was going to fall. As he had intended, he overshot the fissure, reached in and hooked the crack with his left hand. A violent yank nearly tore his shoulder from its socket, but he held on. His feet swung out, and he felt as if he were going to be upended, but then he swung back and caught hold with his right hand. Sucking in his breath he squeezed back into the shadowed opening.

He waited there, listening to the beat of the rotors. His arms burned with the effort of holding his weight, and he squeezed deeper into the crack, forcing the rock to bear some of the load. After about thirty seconds, though it seemed a half hour to his weary mind and body, the bird flew away to the east. As the sound faded away, he heard voices.

"See anything?" The voice was a man's, youthful with a

Midwestern accent.

"Nothing. I wondered if we'd find anyone out here. This place is pretty remote." The second speaker pronounced "out" so that it rhymed with "remote". Canadian, perhaps. "I'm just glad we got here first."

"How can you tell? The rotors would have washed away any footprints. Never mind. What's the radar say?"

"It says…" The man Dane now thought of as Canuck paused. "Rock. Lots and lots of rock." He paused again. "All over the damn place. Rock."

For no apparent reason, Dane thought of songs with "Rock" in the title. "Rock Rock Til You Drop", "Rock of Ages", "Written in Rock", "Rock Me"… He corralled his subconscious and focused on what was being said up above.

Midwest man uttered a vile oath, and must have kicked a fist-sized stone, because one nearly cracked Dane's skull as it tumbled down. "You're absolutely positive?"

"Yup," replied Canuck. "The big man won't like it so much, but that's how it is."

"Fine." The tone of Midwest's voice said that it was anything but. "I'll call the bird back."

"Suit yourself."

The chopper returned less than a minute later, hovering over Fajada Butte long enough to pick up the two men, before heading west, back in the direction from which it came.

Relieved, Dane scrambled down the rock faster than was safe, but he'd had all the rock climbing he could take for one day. At the bottom, he scanned the horizon but saw no sign of the helicopter. No reason it should return anyway. Not stopping to regain his breath, he set off at a jog toward the hiking trail.

Jade met him halfway back to where they had left their Range Rover. He wondered where Saul was, but did not care enough to ask. After assuring her that he was hale and healthy, he recounted what had happened on the Butte.

"Who could they be?" Jade frowned, her intense eyes

boring into him. "And what are they looking for?"

"Probably the same thing we're after," he said, taking her by the hand and setting off down the trail. He had thought about it, and nothing else made sense. Surely Jade wasn't the only person in the world who had heard of Fray Marcos de Niza and his connection to the legend of Cibola.

"But how would they know?" she protested. "Do you think it's the same person who broke into your boat?"

"I suppose there's a connection," he said. "Right now, that's our only suspect in any event." With nothing left to them but idle speculation, they lapsed into silence.

Ten minutes later they stood in the empty spot where they had parked the Range Rover. Jade exhaled noisily and punched Saul's number into her cell phone. She made a face and snapped it closed. "No signal. The jerk! We had an argument. He read somewhere that Casa Rinconda, which is the largest kiva in Chaco Canyon, and not too far from here, has a solstice window. Every year at the summer solstice the sun shines through into an alcove. He wanted to check it out, but I told him the kiva had been excavated before. Whatever sat in that alcove, if anything, is long gone."

"Let me guess," Dane said, "He wanted to blow it up." The look on Jade's face was answer enough. "If he's fool enough to try it, let's at least hope he leaves the keys in the Range Rover before they cart him off to jail." That got a grin out of her. "Are you up for a hike?" he asked cheerily.

They took their time walking back to the park's main loop. Dane went through two of his water bottles and still felt parched. They passed the time looking over park brochures Dane had stuffed into his pack. As he was flipping through a pamphlet on Pueblo Bonito, something caught his attention. "Listen to this," he said, "it might be nothing, but in Pueblo Bonito there are *seven* corner doorways."

"The doorway is on the corner of the structure?" Jade echoed. "That's unusual."

"Very rare. And one of them is an astronomical marker. It's a second floor doorway, and at the time of the winter solstice, light passes through and shines on the base of the opposite corner of the room." Jade looked skeptical. "Think about it," Dane said. "The picture on the breastplate was of Pueblo Bonito. It's a solstice marker, and it's cast by a highly unusual doorway. It's one in seven, as in…"

"Yes, I know," Jade said. "As in the 'Seven Cities'. All right, Maddock, I'll grant you it's worth a shot. But if we're wrong, don't say anything to Saul. He takes great pleasure in my mistakes."

"Few though they are," Dane added.

"Of course."

Pueblo Bonito, the largest and most complex of the Chaco Canyon ruins, was an amazing sight. Set against the backdrop of sand colored hills, it was built in a half-circle, the outer rim a complex of multi-storied stone rooms that reminded Dane of college dorm rooms, except of course for the odd, keyhole-shaped doors that led into each section. Another, narrow line of rooms ran across the straight edge, and another bisected the half-circle. There were many kivas here of varying sizes. He marveled at the scale and workmanship of the structures. Unlike the more famous Anasazi cliff dwellings that were constructed of large block, Pueblo Bonito was entirely constructed of small, flat stones that fit together with precision, giving the impression of a brick structure.

"The walls were built in the 'core and veneer' style," Jade explained. "The inner core is made of mud and sandstone. The shaped stones are the veneer. When people lived here, the veneer was plastered over and painted bright colors."

"So it wouldn't be out of the question for something to be hidden within the core of a wall?" Dane said. Jade shrugged. "It's more likely than something being hidden under the slab up on Fajada Butte."

"I suppose so," she admitted. "The place is deserted. Let's find this room and you do whatever it is you're going to do before someone shows up. By Chaco Canyon standards, this is the most popular attraction."

They quickly located the solstice room. A small, keyhole-shaped second story window was cut into the corner of one of the larger structures. It was about eight feet off the ground, no problem to reach, but it would be a tight squeeze to get inside.

"Make it quick, Maddock," Jade said, watching for any unwelcome approach.

"My, aren't we testy?" he teased. "I didn't take you for the nervous type." He took off his backpack and dropped it at her feet. He'd never fit through the window with it on his back. "Toss that to me when I'm inside." Not waiting for a response, he sprang up, catching the wider parts of the keyhole with his tender fingertips. He ignored the stinging- at least there were no helicopters around this time- and pulled himself up. It was not easy to find toeholds in the well-fitted stone wall, but he managed, and was soon squeezing through the small window. He wasn't the biggest guy, though broader of shoulder than average, but he was forced to go in on his side, which made for an awkward spill down to the bottom. The walls mercifully hid his fall from view.

"Everything all right in there?" Jade called.

"Sure thing. Toss me my backpack." She did not reply, but the black canvas pack came flying through the opening a moment later. He caught it and turned to inspect the opposite corner wall.

Protected to a greater degree from the elements, the inner walls in this particular room were in better condition than the outer walls. The plaster was still intact in several places, including the bottom corner opposite the window.

Using a small metal detector, he scanned the target area, and was pleased at the resulting squeal that indicated something substantial lay behind the wall on the bottom left, a foot above the floor. Had he not gotten a hit, he would have tried Jade's radar unit, but he was satisfied.

From his climbing gear he pulled out a spike and small hammer, and began chipping away at the plaster over the area where the detector had found something.

He felt guilty at damaging a historic site, but he told himself that the damage would be minor, and the result might be of greater historical value. The plaster came away in half-dollar sized chips, and soon he had uncovered a stone two hand-widths square. His heart raced as he noted how different this stone was from the others around it. All the rest were thin, rectangular slabs like those he had seen everywhere else. This one was out of place.

He scoured the surface of the stone, rubbing away the last of the plaster. His fingertips found something strange. Something was carved into the rock! Using the spike, he scratched at the surface. When he was finished, his breath caught in his throat as he stared at it. It was a clover with a cross in its center.

With renewed vigor he worked the space around the stone. It was not fitted as tightly as the other stones. The space around it was filled with plaster. He had cleared the area around it and was about to pry it free when he heard Jade called a quiet warning. He stopped and listened.

He soon heard two elderly voices, one male and one female, engaged in friendly conversation with Jade. He could not understand the words, but by their tone, it was doubtless small talk that was trying her patience as much as it was his. The conversation finally came to an end, and he waited for Jade to give him the go-ahead, but she did not speak. Should he call to her, and risk discovery? After a count of twenty, he called her name softly, but no answer. He dared not climb up to the window, not without knowing who might be outside. He made up his mind to finish the job as quickly and quietly as possible.

The stone came free with surprising ease. He placed it on the floor with care, and scratched the hard, dry surface of the core. The mixture of mud and rock crumbled at the first touch. An inch below the surface he struck something solid. Hastily he cleared the dried mud from around it, and pulled it forth into the light.

It was a metal box, seven inches square and four inches deep. The clover and cross of Fray Marcos was engraved in the surface. It was neither hinged nor lidded, but a careful inspection of the bottom surface showed that it had been soldered closed. They would have to take it somewhere else to open it.

With a pang of regret he wrapped it in a poncho and stuffed it into the bottom of his backpack. He flipped the stone over to hide Fray Marcos' cross, and slid it back into the wall. Quietly he gathered the loose sand and plaster and sprinkled it around the far corners. At a casual glance, he doubted anyone would notice what he had done, and how often was someone likely to enter this room?

Just as he was wondering what to do about Jade, he heard her call to him.

"Are we clear?" he asked. At her confirmation, he climbed up to the window, and held the backpack out through the window. "Careful. It's heavy," he cautioned. Her delighted smile was almost as great a reward as finding the box. His good mood was dampened only slightly when he saw that Saul stood nearby, keeping watch. He managed to climb out of the window more gracefully than he had entered, and in a matter of seconds they were headed back through the ancient site.

"Sorry I ditched you," Jade said. "Those old people invited me to walk with them, and I couldn't very well stand in one place all that time without raising their suspicion. Saul showed up a few minutes later and I told them he was my husband." Saul smirked and Jade grimaced.

"So," Saul said, sounding annoyed that Dane had succeeded where he had failed, "what exactly did you find?"

"I don't know yet," he said, "but I've got a feeling it's something good."

Chapter 9

Bones had no particular desire to finish the dig. Isaiah had made it through the surgery successfully, but remained in what the doctors described as a "shallow coma". They assured him this was normal, and in fact a healthy way for a person with a brain injury to recuperate. This was not the sort of vegetative state from which patients did not come back; it was simply the body's way of healing.

Not completely reassured, but encouraged, he decided to go back to the dig. It was Isaiah's project, and he felt an obligation to see it through to the end. And perhaps he could pick up some clues to his cousin's attackers.

The dig site had changed much in the four days since Isaiah's attack. The ground around the rock overhang was roped off in squares and digging was well underway. But the dig lacked the pleasant air of people doing what they loved. Everyone worked in sullen silence. Only two of them even looked up from their work to greet him with curt nods. He headed to the rock face where a man in khakis and a starched pink oxford cloth shirt stood with a clipboard in hand, scowling at whatever he was reading.

"May I help you?" he said in a sour voice, not looking up from his clipboard.

"No, but I can help you. Your bald spot is getting sunburned," Bones said.

The fellow jerked his head up to scowl at Bones. One of the diggers snickered.

"Thank you. I shall attend to that right away. What can I do for you?"

"I'm Dr. Horsely's cousin, Uriah Bonebrake. I was helping him with the dig."

"I see. Well, I am sorry to tell you that we have all the help we need. I appreciate your visit, and will thank you to leave without further disturbing our work." He turned his back on Bones and walked away.

"Wait a minute. This is Isaiah's dig," Bones protested.

"Not anymore." The fellow sounded disgustingly pleased with himself. "Dr. Horsely's financial backers have placed me in charge. I will thank you to leave my dig immediately."

"Who are these backers, mister…?"

"Doctor. Doctor William McLaughlin. And my backers are none of your concern. Now, if you will please excuse us, we have work to do. The Jesus picture is only the beginning."

"The Jesus picture? Have you established that's what it really is?"

McLaughlin was offended by the question. "Of course that's what it is." He turned and walked away before Bones could question him any further.

"Pompous ass," one of the diggers said in a hushed voice. Bones sidled up next to him. "All he cares about is fame." The man was tall and angular, with an expression of permanent disdain on his sunburned face.

"How about his backers?" Bones asked casually. "They after the fame as well?"

"Hardly. I don't know who exactly they are. No one on the dig knows. But I know they're Mormons. They want it to be true."

"What's that?" Bones asked.

"The Jesus thing. Mormons believe Jesus came to America and appeared to the people here. They would love to have the archaeological record support that." He spat in the dust. "They're going to spin this their way. No consideration of anything else. Oh, he has us going through the motions of excavating the site, but he's not at all interested in the artifacts. He wants more Jesus pictures." He spat another gob in the dust, and kicked it with the toe of his boot. "Anyway, how's Dr. Horsely?"

"He's stable," Bones said. "Still not come out of the

coma, but the doctors aren't too concerned yet. They say he'll wake up when he's ready. He's going to freak when he finds out what McLaughlin is doing to his dig."

"No kidding. Well, I'd better get back at it before McLaughlin jumps my case again. He and Orley got into it yesterday. You should have seen it. That old farmer was warning him away from that barn of his with the sick bull. McLaughlin couldn't care less about the barn or the bull, but he can't stand to be told what to do…"

Bones didn't hear the rest of the story. He suddenly remembered the last thing Isaiah said before going into surgery. *Orley doesn't have a bull.* Grinning politely as the fellow finished his story, Bones shook the man's hand and walked away. Feeling dazed, he wandered back toward the farm until he came to the barn.

It looked no more remarkable than it did the first time he had seen it: a small, sturdy wooden structure built against the side of a hill, though he had to admit that it was unusual to construct a building directly against a rock wall. He paused two steps from the door and looked around. No one was in sight.

"Mr. Orley!" he called. "Hello?" He didn't truly think the old man was around, but no need taking chances. "Anyone here?" He noticed that the door was padlocked. He pressed his ear to the wood and listened. Silence. If there was a bull in there, it was dead. He walked around the left side of the barn. Near the back, the ground had washed away, leaving a hole a yard wide and eight inches deep under the wall. Bones looked around again, then cleared away the rocks and loose. When he could make the hole no deeper without a pick and shovel, he dropped to the ground.

He lay down on his back and squeezed into the opening. He had to exhale and relax his muscles in order to get his chest and shoulders through, but he made it with only a few scrapes. He climbed to his feet in the dim barn, brushed himself off and looked around.

It could not properly be called a barn. It was more of a

storage shed; a simple wooden building with various tools and implements strewn about. Old bales of straw were stacked to the ceiling against the back wall. Bones pulled one down, covering his face with his sleeve against the thick cloud of dust that kicked up from the old, dry bale. There was no back wall- the shed was three-sided and abutted the rock face. That was interesting. He moved a few more bales out of the way, then, half out of intuition and half out of impatience, he took hold of the two bottom center bales and yanked.

The middle of the straw wall tumbled down, one of them bouncing hard off his shoulder. Dust burned his eyes and nose. He leaned down, plugged one nostril and blew the other out, then repeated with the other side. Dane hated what Bones called "the farmer's handkerchief", and Bones took pleasure in disgusting his friend from time-to-time. As he was wiping his eyes he was surprised to feel cool air on his face.

A four foot-high fissure, three wide at the base, split the center of the stone wall. This was getting more interesting all the time. He fished the mini maglite out of his pocket and ducked down to explore the opening.

The narrow beam of light shone on a long, narrow tunnel only a few feet high leading back into blackness. Never the one to ignore his curiosity, he made up his mind to explore. He had to crawl, holding his light between his teeth. The floor was smooth stone, and cold on his hands. He had gone about thirty feet when the passage opened up into a room with a ceiling high enough for him to stand. He played his light over the walls. What he saw made him whistle in surprise.

The room was roughly rectangular with a fire pit in the center. The walls on either side of him were adorned with pictographs much more impressive than what they had found outside, the likes of which he had seen only in pictures of southwest Indian ruins. There were spirals, handprints, and images of animals. They were beautiful and remarkably well-preserved. But it was the opposite wall that took his breath.

A large circle, about a foot in diameter, was carved into the wall near the top. Seven straight lines descended from it, each ending in what looked like a hand.

On the left side of the wall, below the row of symbols, was a scene reminiscent of the "Jesus" picture he had discovered a few days before. It was clear, however, that this was not Jesus. The bearded man led a line of men in Spanish military uniforms, and others dressed in robes. These particular cave paintings were clearly were not done by the natives who had carved the pictographs. Though not surprised, he felt a bit of disappointment at the knowledge that this was not Christ. The feeling, though, was quickly replaced by the excitement of knowing that there was definitely a mystery here.

The men were pictured moving through various scenes with landmarks behind them that probably would have borne significance to someone familiar with the region. On the right side, near the bottom, was a scene depicting the same men bearing heavy sacks, climbing what looked like a giant staircase. The final image was that of a distinctive-looking peak, though one that was unfamiliar to Bones.

Near the base of the wall, a square niche was cut into the stone, similar to those in a kiva. Something glittered in the light.

A closer look revealed a golden disc about seven inches in diameter, with an image much like the one on the wall carved on the front. Intrigued, he turned it over. Fine writing spiraled in from the outer edge in an ever-tightening circle.

"Hebrew?" he whispered? "This is crazy." He took out his cell phone and used the camera feature to snap some pictures. Although his was one of the better phone cameras on the market, it still took several tries to get a few decent shots. He took care to replace the disc just like he had found it. He then took a picture of the front of the golden circle as it lay in the niche.

He backed up to the fire pit in the room's center and took pictures of the walls. Suddenly aware that he had spent a long time in this place, he shone his light around the room one last time. Satisfied that he had seen everything, he turned to leave. Dropping to his hands and knees, he crawled only two feet before the beam of his maglite shone on twin shotgun barrels leveled at his face.

"Back it up." Orley's gruff voice growled from the darkness. "Move slow and stay where I can see you."

Bones did as he was told, crawling backward into the room, his options racing through his mind. He was fast, and would stand a good chance of disarming Orley, but he'd have to injure the rancher in order to do so. He didn't want to do that if he could help it. For the same reason, he dismissed the .22 in his ankle holster. Besides, his instinct told him that the man was not a threat.

A flame blossomed in the darkness. Orley held a zippo in his left hand. He kept the shotgun trained on Bones with his right. "I didn't figure on it being you. By the way, you can take that pissant little flashlight out of your mouth."

Bones chuckled and tucked the light into his jeans pocket.

"This place is something."

Orley did not answer. He scrutinized the cave, his usual sour expression in place. "Well hell. You weren't gonna' take the disc?"

"Not me," Bones said. "My people aren't like that. I think you know that as well as I do." He stared at Orley, hoping he was right. If not, Bones would have to make a quick move for the shotgun. "I didn't take anything but pictures."

The silence hung between them in the semi-darkness for what felt like a minute before the rancher spat on the floor and lowered his gun.

"I reckon I do believe you at that. You ain't so bad for an Injun."

"And you're not too bad for a fat white man," Bones said, chuckling. Orley returned the jibe with a curse and a grin. "What is this place, anyway?" Bones asked.

"I don't rightly know. I found it near twenty years ago. A storm came through, one of them gully washers. Washed away enough of the rock to uncover this place. I've tried to figure some of it out, but I ain't too good at that kind of thing. I tried to keep it a secret, but once the government started pushing me to open up the other ruins, I knew this place would get found. If it has to be found, I reckon I'm glad it was you."

"Why do you say that?" Bones was flattered, but confused.

Orley was about to reply when a loud clatter came from the entrance.

"Mr. Orley?" a voice called. The speaker's tone of voice sounded taunting, as if the man, whoever he was, knew precisely where the rancher was.

Orley whirled around, peering back in the direction from which he had come. "It's them! Take the disc and..."

"Who is 'them'?" Bones asked.

"The Dominion. Now shut up and do what I tell you. Take the disc with you. There's a way out up there," he gestured over Bones' right shoulder to the dark corner. "It's narrow, but you can do it. Go!"

Bones wasn't foolish enough to argue. He grabbed the heavy gold disc and shoved it into his shirt. Three long strides brought him to the corner. He ran his hands up the wall, his fingertips finding purchase on a small ledge. He pulled himself up, digging his steel-toed boots against the rocky face, reached out with his right hand and found the narrow passage. Clambering up, he twisted onto his left side and scooted into the crevice.

"Don't come back no matter what you hear," Orley said.

Feeling more guilt than he had thought himself capable of, Bones slithered forward, now understanding how sausage was made. He had never had much fear of tight places, for which he was now thankful. The cold rock sucked the heat from his body. He continued forward in the darkness, wondering how long this passage was and whether it would narrow to the point that he could not get through. His shoulders were almost touching the sides. One thing was sure; Orley had never crawled through this tunnel, or at least not in many a decade.

He heard muffled voices, then a shotgun blast. He froze as the staccato report of small-caliber handguns echoed down the narrow tunnel. One more defiant shotgun blast, a pause, a single shot, and it was over. Bones remained motionless for the span of a three heartbeats, entertaining the irrational notion that he should somehow wriggle backward, take the bad guys by surprise, and save the day. Common sense won out over guilt almost immediately, and he continued his trek, cursing Orley for his stubbornness and himself for not being a hero. He was certain the rancher was dead. Now he needed to save himself.

He crawled for what seemed like an hour, all the while wondering when bullets would ricochet down the passage. Had they killed Orley immediately? Did he tell them about Bones escape route? Would they find it themselves? None of it mattered. All he could do was keep going.

The tunnel curved, and for a brief moment panic threatened to overwhelm him as the walls closed in on him, but he was soon able to wriggle free and move on. Still grappling with guilt over leaving Orley behind, he was distracted by a pale sliver of light in the distance. Energized, he scurried ahead on hands and knees.

A gentle slope climbed toward the light, and the tunnel gradually widened. Suddenly aware that he had no idea where he would be emerging, or who might be waiting on the other side, he slipped his .22 from its ankle holster and quietly moved ahead. Dry air tinged with the aroma of sage and dust assaulted his nostrils. The tunnel ended in a narrow crack about seven feet high and a foot wide at its broadest point. Sage and scrub covered the entrance. Bones could see little through the cover of foliage, but the way appeared clear. His pistol at the ready, he moved forward.

Emerging on the slope of a dry, narrow gulch and carefully making his way down into the parched defile, the sun scorching his face after the relative cool of the cavern, he thought about the layout of the passage through which he had come, relative to the ranch, and guessed that he was due northeast of the dig, on the other side of the hills that backed Orley's barn and lined the eastern edge of his property. He couldn't be far away as the crow flies, but with gun-toting archaeologists, or whoever the hell they were, so close by, things felt decidedly unsafe. And what was the "Dominion" of which Orley spoke? He needed an answer.

Absently he ran his hand across his stomach and felt the disc underneath his shirt. He had actually forgotten about it. He withdrew the weighty gold circle and examined it in the sunlight. Its gold surface flashed in the brilliant light, displaying the spiraled writing in sharp relief. It was one of the most beautiful artifacts he had ever seen, and a complete enigma. What was a Hebrew artifact doing in Utah? "I hate puzzles," he muttered.

Flipping open his cell phone, he checked for coverage, and was relieved to see that he had one bar. No way he was going back for his rental. He'd call the agency and report it broken down. He didn't have any personal items in the car anyway. Who to call? He thought of Emily Dixon, the television reporter. She had been loads of fun for about five hours, and then the obvious fluff between her ears had significantly detracted from her appeal. He needed someone sharp, someone who might know about the Dominion, someone with the guts to dive into what might be a dangerous situation.

A broad grin spread across his face as he called information and requested the number for the Deseret Bugle.

Chapter 10

Shouldn't we open this thing in a lab?" Saul asked, leaning over the makeshift work table Dane had created in his hotel room. A white sheet draped over the study table, plus all the lights they could garner, comprised his work area. The three of them wore gloves and dust masks they had picked up from the local home improvement store. All in all it was a poor excuse for a scientific environment, but Dane had his reasons for doing this privately.

"What lab, Saul? And even if we managed to find one around here, who's to say it would remain a secret? I don't know who those guys in the helicopter were, but I'll assume they're no friends of ours until I have reason to believe different."

"I agree," Jade said in a distracted voice. Her attention was focused on the box Dane had recovered from the wall at Chaco Canyon. Working with a set of tiny chisels and hammers, she gradually chipped away at the solder that had held the box closed for, they hoped, a half-millennia. "Help me out here, Maddock."

Dane took hold of one side of the box and, following Jade's instructions, they worked the lid free. It came loose reluctantly, but in short order the box lay open on the table. Ancient fabric enshrouded whatever was inside. Jade lifted it free, muttering soft curses as the dry linen crumbled at her touch. Saul laid out a square of clear plastic to catch the debris. Jade turned the bundle over, laid it on the plastic that covered the table, and unwrapped it.

A shiny black object about half the size of Dane's fist lay inside. It was black rock, carved into an eighth of a sphere.

"It looks like someone cut a grapefruit in half, then quartered the half," he observed. "Weird."

Jade held it up to the light. "Onyx," she whispered. "I'm almost certain." Dane and Saul both leaned forward for a closer look. The rounded top was perfectly smooth, with an odd lip running along the curved bottom edge. Jade turned the artifact over, and took a long, deep breath. Faint lines were etched into the bottom surface. They were worn and difficult to discern, but they were definitely letters of some sort. They gazed at the artifact for a long while before Jade laid it gently on the plastic.

"What do you think?" Dane asked, puzzled by the odd piece. He had never seen such a thing, though his background in marine archaeology was not the best preparation for this project.

"I think the artifact has been cut. Possibly into quarters based on the shape of this piece. Look at the straight edges. You can see markings as if someone sawed it. It's mostly smooth, but lacks the perfection of the other sides. So..." she paused.

"So Fray Marcos has gone to the time and effort of setting us on a scavenger hunt through the American Southwest. Is that what you're thinking?"

"It's the only thing that makes sense, considering what we know so far. Marcos chopped up the artifact and hid the pieces, or had someone hide the pieces, in various locations. The shield provides us with a map of sorts."

"Find the pieces, put them together, and it leads us to Cibola," Dane said. The prospect was exciting. "So what we need to do now is figure out where the next piece is hidden."

"Got it covered," Saul said, his perpetually sour face even more puckered, if that was possible. He returned shortly with the briefcase in which they kept the pictures of the shield along with their maps and notes. "I have to tell you," he said, spreading the photographs on the bed, "I've given this a great deal of thought, and most of these images are a mystery to me. I also wonder if we need to visit them in any certain order."

"If we're collecting pieces of this artifact in order to reconstruct it, I don't imagine it would make any difference what order we found them in." Dane rubbed his chin, feeling the stubble that announced evening was fast approaching. One of these days he would grow a beard. "There has to be some key to understanding the instructions. Chaco Canyon was a lucky guess. The place had a distinct shape. I don't relish the idea of roaming the desert southwest looking at every landform and ruin that resembles these icons.

"These two," he indicated the images that lay on the center of the cross, and on the left, "could be two of I don't know how many different peaks. And the images on the right, at the cross point, and at the top look like ruins, but which ones and where?"

"How did we find this artifact?" Jade asked. "The solstice was important, and so was the number seven. Can we use either of those to help us?"

Dane's mind was turning over an idea at a rapid pace. The number seven was tumbling around in his thoughts. There was something he had come across in their research. Something to do with travel and direction.

"Are you planning on telling us what you're thinking?" Saul snapped. He stood with his hands folded across his chest, leaning toward Dane to emphasize the two inches by which he was taller than Dane.

"The roads," Dane said, ignoring Saul for what felt like the thousandth time since Jade and her assistant had crossed his path. "Remember? The Chacoans built a series of roads leading out of the canyon. They were special because they were so straight and well-engineered."

"That's right. There were seven of them," Jade said, her voice indicating cautious interest. "What are you thinking?"

"Six of them scatter out in various directions and don't go very far," Dane said. "But the one in the center shoots straight up, and it's much longer than the others. It stands out to me. I'm suddenly wondering if it points at anything in particular."

Saul leapt to the charts, obviously not wanting to feel left out. He sorted through them until he found the one with the ancient roads. "Is this the one?" he asked, pointing at the center avenue. Dane nodded. Saul took his time, checking orientation and marking the roads on a larger map. Finally satisfied, he laid a ruler along the edge of the road and drew a faint line in pencil. The line ran out of New Mexico and into Utah. With his finger, Saul traced the implied path of the ancient road. "All of this is barren land. It doesn't seem to intersect any of the known sites. In fact, it pretty much covers empty land all the way to..." he stopped.

"Sleeping Ute Mountain," Dane and Jade said at almost the same time. They looked at each other, and Jade grinned.

"Look at the image in the middle of the cross. It's not the entire mountain, but compare it to..." she paused as she sifted through her papers until she found a silhouette of the famed mountain. "This picture. What do you see?"

"It's the foot of the mountain," Saul said. "That's why we didn't recognize it. The outline of the entire mountain we'd have recognized, but not such a small section." He stared at the pictures Jade held up, then looked down at the spot where his finger touched the dot marked *Sleeping Ute Mountain.* "Does this mean the artifact is hidden on his foot?"

"I don't know," Jade said. "I don't know that something could be hidden there. I feel like there should be something more specific. We're onto something, but we're missing a critical piece."

Saul picked up his laptop that he had left running on the bedside table, and clicked on the icon for internet access.

"We have the number seven connection. I guess now we need the solstice connection." His frown quickly turned to a smile. "Aha! There's a flat area up on the mountain where the Utes hold sacred dances, get this, in conjunction with the solstice! That's got to be it!"

Something did not ring true for Dane, but he didn't have a better idea. "Can we get up there?"

"It says you have to have permission from the tribe, and be escorted to the top," Saul replied. "We can get around that, can't we?"

"I've never been there," Dane said. "I don't know what's around there or if we can even get close to it."

"Let's try and do it the honest way," Jade said. "I'll make some calls tomorrow and see what I can arrange. If we can't work it out, we'll decide what to do next."

"What? You're going to ask some Ute bigwig if you can take a shovel and metal detector and maybe dig up their sacred dance floor? Yeah, that's really gonna' work," Saul sneered.

Jade pressed her palms to her temples. "Saul..."

"I know. The decision is yours. But I'm registering my objections, okay?" He shut down his laptop and snapped it closed. "I'm gonna' grab something to eat, then hit the sack. I assume we're heading out early tomorrow?" He didn't wait for Jade's answer, stalking out of the room and closing the door just hard enough to make it obvious that it was intentional.

"I feel like I'm teaching Junior High," Jade groaned, falling down on the bed. "Maybe if this all works out, if we can solve the mystery, I won't need the backing anymore."

Taking a chance, Dane sat down on the bed next to her. He pulled her hands away from her head, and began massaging her temples with his fingertips. Her satisfied groans sounded like purring, and set his nerves on an excited edge. Forcing himself to go slowly, he massaged her scalp, her neck, then her shoulders. Gradually the tension drained from Jade's face, and was replaced by a satisfied smile. His fingertips trailed down her sides, stroked her stomach, and slowly made the climb up her taut belly. She breathed deeply. He ran his hands up her sides and across her chest. Propping on one elbow, he stroked her cheek and leaned in close, his lips close enough to feel her breath...

...His ears close enough to hear her snoring.

Chuckling, he carefully rolled off the bed and let himself quietly out of the room. Would his luck with women never change?

Chapter 11

Dane rose early and enjoyed a long, quiet jog in the dim light of dawn. He did his best thinking when he was on the move, keeping his body and mind in sync. Something about Sleeping Ute Mountain did not seem right to him. He couldn't put a finger on it, but he had always been one to listen to his instincts, and right now they were telling him that something was just a little bit off. Returning to his room, he unwound with a hot shower, then sat down to do a little research. By the time Jade appeared at his door he was on to something, but she was in no mood to hear about it.

"Saul is gone," she said, handing him a slip of note paper. "He left this at the front desk for me. I'm going to kill him."

Jade, the note read, *I rented a car. Had some things to take care of. Don't worry about me. I'll call you this afternoon and we'll reconnect. Saul*

"He isn't answering his phone. All of his things are gone."

"Did he take the artifact?" Dane asked before he could stop himself. Though constantly annoyed with Saul, Jade was often touchy about criticism directed toward her assistant.

"Of course not," Jade snapped. "It was in my room." She dropped heavily into one of the leather padded chairs, picked up the remote and turned on the television. "Do you mind?"

Dane wasn't much for TV at any time of the day, but given the mood she was in, this was not the hill he wanted to die on.

"I guess we should go on as planned," he said. "Saul did say that he would catch up with us later. We can find rooms near Cortez and..."

"Hush!" Jade said, holding up a hand. She had stopped on a local news program. Behind the reporter was an image of Sleeping Ute Mountain.

"...morning Ute Tribal Police arrested a man for trespassing on restricted tribal land. The suspect was reportedly trying to gain access to a sacred dance floor on Sleeping Ute Mountain. No motive...."

"Bloody hell!" Jade articulated the words as only an incensed woman can. She turned off the television and dropped the remote onto the table. "One guess who they arrested. What an idiot."

"I guess there's no point in me suggesting that maybe it wasn't him?" Dane asked with an utter absence of sincerity. He had disliked Saul almost on sight, and nothing the man had done since then had convinced him otherwise. This stunt was exactly what Dane would expect of the man.

"Not if you want me to continue respecting your intelligence," Jade said. "In one fell swoop the moron has killed any chance of us checking out the dance floor."

"I'm not sure we'll need to," Dane said. Jade's expression was unreadable, so he hurried on with his explanation before it became a book he didn't want to open. "I didn't feel right about the dance floor. There's nothing to indicate that particular area was used for solstice dances at the time of Fray Marcos. Also, it's not just solstices and equinoxes that are significant. I think the sun itself is important. Remember the sunbursts on the shield, and the fact that the first piece was hidden in a place where the sun's rays actually strike on the solstice?"

"I'm listening," Jade said in a flat tone that hopefully indicated abating anger and rising interest. She sat with her arms folded beneath her breasts, her legs crossed, tapping her foot in fierce rhythm.

"I did some searches on the terms 'Sleeping Ute

Mountain,' 'solstice,' and 'equinox.' I had to do some digging, but I found a likely spot. It's called Yucca House."

"Never heard of it."

"Neither had I. It's a site that's fallen into ruin. The National Park Service maintains control of it, but it's out in the middle of nowhere with no facilities or anything, just an occasional ranger making a drive-by. Anyway, it lies between Mesa Verde and Sleeping Ute Mountain. From there, you have a perfect view of the foot of Sleeping Ute Mountain." He thought Jade sat up a little straighter. "Supposedly, if you stand in the right place on the date of the equinox, the sun sets right on the tip of the Sleeping Ute's toe."

"It sounds... promising," Jade said. Her toe had stopped tapping and she was now gripping the arms of her chair and leaning slightly forward. "It's not like we have anywhere else to go at the moment."

"Remote location," Dane added, his convictions strengthened by her interest, "few visitors, and best of all; it's never been excavated."

"All right," Jade said, sounding unconvinced. "Let's give it a try."

Saul parked the car in a dense thicket of cottonwood and snakeweed, killed the engine, and double-checked the topographical chart he had printed out at the library. This appeared to be the right place. He took a long look around before exiting the car. He was crazy to try this, but it was necessary. If the Ute police caught him twice in one day, no way would they let him go again.

The rustle of cottonwood leaves in the sparse breeze put him to mind of a rattlesnake lying in wait. How could such an open, empty space seem so sinister? He had no time for such thoughts. He needed to hurry.

He hadn't believed it when he found it on the map: three hills, almost perfectly round, like the lobes of a clover, and a butte where the stem would be. And the place was perfectly positioned! This had to be it.

He crested the closest hill and gazed down into the valley. It was beautiful, as so much of this land was, but didn't look like much. Lots of scrub, yucca, juniper, and oxeye sunflowers. A flash of movement caught his eye and he dropped to a knee, though there was nowhere to hide up here. He relaxed as he realized it was a lone pronghorn deer wandering past.

He trotted down the hill and began picking his way through the tangle of flora. As he walked, he saw the remains of low walls, piles of stone, and a few overgrown holes that likely had been kivas. That was encouraging.

At the center of the valley, the ground dropped off in a circle forty feet across. His heart leapt. This once had been a massive ceremonial kiva. The roof had long since collapsed, but hopefully...

Choosing a spot where the remains of the roof had piled against the edge, forming a ladder of sorts, he clambered down into the ancient center of worship and moved to the center, careful not to turn an ankle on the loose rock. He squatted down and started clearing away the debris when the ground suddenly seemed to churn and something brown and black burst forth from the hole he had created. Scorpions!

He snatched his hand away and stumbled backward, landing hard on his backside. Seven or eight of the angry creatures scurried out across the rocks and vanished into the cracks and crevasses among the loose piles of stone . They were huge! Each one was at least five inches in length. He was no expert, but he thought they were called desert hairy scorpions. They ought to be called desert harrowing scorpions after that surprise.

He got to his feet, breathing a deep sigh, brushed himself off, and even more cautiously returned to the hole he had created. He really didn't want to get stung, but he had to do this. He would regret it if he didn't.

Slowly, one rock at a time, he cleared a hole about a

yard in width. He bit his lip when he saw only hard, dry earth underneath. But he couldn't be wrong. It had to be here. If it wasn't in the center, he'd have to go back for the metal detector and inspect the whole place, and who knew how long that would take? He pulled out his pocketknife and scraped at the hard-packed earth. The blade caught on something. He continued to scratch the surface, revealing something round. This was it! Ten minutes of digging and clearing rewarded him with precisely what he had been looking for. A clay seal bearing the sigil of Fray Marcos de Niza!

Not wanting to waste time working the seal loose, he picked up a heavy stone, raised it above his head, and brought it crashing down onto the seal. The ancient clay shattered, falling into the dark hole that had been the sipapu—the ceremonial hole in the center of the kiva. He reached into the sipapu and his hands closed on a metal box. He had found it!

The pitted, dirt road bounced their rental, jostling them as they drove.

"Ow! My coffee," Jade sputtered, dabbing at her pants with a napkin. "Cheap gas station lids. When we get back to civilization, the first thing I'm going to do is find a Starbucks."

"Sorry," Dane said. "I don't know how you can drink that stuff in this heat." The arid southwest climate was not as oppressive as the humidity of the Caribbean, but the feeling of perpetual dehydration was wearying. They came to a fence line with a gate blocking the way. "Are we in the right place?" he asked, bringing the vehicle to a stop. "This looks like a ranch or something."

"It says here that the road crosses private property," Jade said, consulting the directions she had printed off the web. "You don't need permission. Just close the gate behind you. I got it." She slipped out the door and strode into the hot midday sun.

Dane watched as she walked to the gate and swung it open. He loved the way the sun played off her glossy black hair and lithe, athletic figure. Best of all, she was smart. Bones might like them dumb, but not him.

"Sometime today would be nice," Jade called, waving him on. Grinning, he stepped on the gas and pulled through the open gate. Jade secured it behind them and hopped into the cab. "It is seriously hot out there." She picked up his water bottle and uncapped it.

"Hey, what about your coffee?"

"Are you crazy? It's too hot for coffee. Besides, caffeine dehydrates you." She rolled her eyes at him as she took a drink.

Dane shook his head and grinned. There was no point in trying to win.

They arrived at the site a short while later. There was no parking lot. The dirt road simply faded into flat, open ground, ringed by post and wire fences. A ranch lay off to the right, and a brown sign with white lettering directed them through an empty horse corral to the main gate on the other side.

Mesa Verde lay in the distance, clearly visible in the clean, clear air. Dane looked out at the fabled Anasazi settlement, and wondered what it was about that place that seemed to tug at him.

"Jade, have you checked any of the shield symbols against Mesa Verde structures? I mean, why wouldn't it be one the Seven Cities? Seems like an obvious choice to me." They arrived at a small gate flanked by a brochure box and a dented, green garbage can on the left and a faded brown National Park Sign. He gave the sign a cursory glance, and helped himself to a brochure before opening the door and motioning her through.

"I have done some checking," Jade said. "The problem is that it's such a large settlement, and the images on Fray Marcos' shield are so small. It could be any little corner or section of a cliff dwelling. As to why it wouldn't be Mesa Verde, I suppose because it's too obvious. I'm still working on it., hoping to find a likely location."

Dane followed her through the gate. He felt a little strange securing the gate behind them in this desolate place, but he supposed it was there for a reason.

"Have you checked out the solstice angle?"

Jade looked back over her shoulder at him, crossed her eyes and stuck out her tongue. "Yes, I've checked. There aren't any structures that are specifically designated as solstice markers. In such a big place, there might be some structures that fit the bill, but..." She shrugged.

"Needle in a haystack," Dane said. The thought didn't discourage him. In fact, the challenge made him even more determined to solve the riddle. Men who were easily discouraged didn't make good marine archaeologists. The countless hours going back-and-forth on sonar sweeps saw to that. "So, where is this place?"

"Right here." Jade pointed to a series of overgrown mounds ahead of them. "Not what you expected, I take it?"

"Hardly," Dane said. The site was surprisingly large, but there seemed to be nothing still standing, except a single wall running along one side. "All of these mounds... is this it?"

"This is it," Jade said. "Really, Maddock, don't you read your own research? The largest one is Upper House." She indicated a mound in the center of the complex, then handed him a computer printout. "Here's a sketch drawn by William Holmes, the man who initially discovered the site. Of course, much of it is speculation. The site was already in ruins when he found it."

"Oh," Dane said, scratching his head. "I stopped reading at the solstice part. Okay Boss, where do you want to start?"

"Honestly, I think it's going to be kind of arbitrary. I thought we'd scout it out, then get the metal detectors and see if we can come up with anything that way. I still can't believe Saul took off with the ground penetrating radar."

"It was almost worth it to see the look on your face when you found it missing," Dane said. He had not believed so lovely a face to be capable of such contortions. "You looked like something between Plastic Man and the Hulk."

"Do you always say the wrong thing, or is it only with me?" Jade lowered her sunglasses to peer at him like a schoolmarm. "No wonder you're not married." She must have noticed something in his face because she immediately forsook the mock-disapproval and laid a gentle hand on his arm. "I just stepped in it really deep, didn't I?"

"My wife died a few years ago," he said "Look, it's okay," he continued as Jade smacked herself on the forehead hard enough to leave a mark. "You didn't have any way of knowing. I don't really talk about her."

"Oh my..." she blushed furiously. "Dane I am so sorry. Here I was accusing you of saying the wrong thing and I make the blunder to end all blunders."

"Like I said, you couldn't have known. I really don't talk about it much."

"Tell me you accept my apology and I'll feel a little bit better. Not much, but a little."

"Aplogy accepted. Now how about we get to work?"

They spent the next thirty minutes clambering over and around the heaps of rock that had once been a thriving Anasazi settlement of some size. Try as he might, though, Dane could not see how to even begin their search. It looked like an old quarry.

The midday sun was sweltering. They sought refuge in the thin shade of some scrub growing atop the remnants of what had been the largest structure in the settlement. They shared the tepid water from Dane's canteen and stared out at the distant hills, hazy in the hot air.

"Do you miss her?" Jade asked, staring out at the ruined site.

It took Dane a moment to realize of whom she was speaking. "Every day," he said.

"Does the hurt ever go away?" Something in her eyes told him she had a very personal reason for asking.

"Not exactly." He let the word hang between them, thoughts of Melissa seeming to choke off further words. Finally the tightness in his throat subsided, and he was surprised at how normal he sounded. "But it dulls with time. At first you can't stand to think about it, but you can't think of anything else. Little by little, you distance yourself from it. After a while it's only the little things that get to you; a certain song, a favorite place, a little gift you gave her that you thought she'd thrown away. Then it all comes back, if only for a little while."

"I know what you mean," Jade said. She exhaled loudly and sprang to her feet. "Well then," she said, a forced cheerfulness in her voice. "I think the most likely place to start is down by Lower House. I saw an overhang that looks promising." She picked her way through the rubble toward high house without waiting for him.

When Dane caught up with her, Jade was on her hands and knees crawling into a shady opening at the base of the rock pile that, according to the brochure, had once been an L-shaped Puebloan dwelling with a large central kiva, the round, sunken building that was the center of Anasazi worship. He dropped down alongside her, peering into the darkness. The air was cooler, though not by much, but still it was a stark contrast to the sun blistering his back.

"It looks to me," Jade said, "like this part of the structure has actually held together. If we can scoop out some dirt, we might be able to get inside. I think I see an open space back there." She flicked on a tiny flashlight and directed the beam to the back of the overhang where the blackness was complete. She lay down on her stomach and scooted forward.

A flicker of movement caught Dane's eye. Lightning fast, his hand shot out just as an angry buzz filled the small space. He grabbed hold of the rattlesnake's tail and with a flick of the wrist, slung it out into the sun. The fat, gray-brown viper beat a hasty retreat into the rocks and scrub, rattling furiously all the while.

"Oh my..." Jade backed out of the overhang and rolled over onto her back, where she lay spread-eagle, her eyes closed and her breath coming in gasps.

"Are you all right?" Dane asked. "He didn't get you, did he?"

"I'm fine," she said, still breathing rapidly. "Not my first rattler, but my closest call." She took a few deep breaths, gaining control of her breathing, before sitting up. "Western Diamondback?" she asked.

"I think so," Dane said. "We don't get too many of those in the Caribbean, but I watched Wild Kingdom when I was a kid."

"How did you manage to grab that thing?"

"Fast hands and poor impulse control," he joked. "I caught sight of him when you turned on your flashlight. He was coiled to strike, but he was turned so that I had a clear shot at his tail. Probably wasn't the safest way of handling a snake, but at least I went for the less-dangerous end."

"I can't believe I was so careless," she said. "I'm just so mad that we wasted our time coming out here. It seemed so promising." She pulled the folded printout of Holmes' map out of her front pocket. She opened it and scrutinized it for a moment before balling it up and throwing it on the ground. "I give up," she said. "Let's get back to semi-civilization. Maybe Saul is back, and I'll have someone to take out my frustrations on."

"Wait a minute," Dane said, picking up the crumpled map. Something had taken shape in his mind when she had opened it up moments before. He smoothed it out and laid it on his lap. "Got a pen?" Wordlessly she handed him a cheap ballpoint with a chewed cap, and sat back with her arms folded across her chest and a look of skepticism painting her face.

"Look at how the site was originally laid out." He drew a faint outline around the layout as he spoke. "Notice how the general layout makes a three-lobed shape. And if you tie in this square ruin at the bottom…"

"A clover," Jade said, her eyes wide in amazement. "But wait a minute. This place would have been here before Fray Marcos's time. It would have to be a coincidence."

"Yes," Dane said. "But imagine you're Fray Marcos or Estevanico, looking for places to hide pieces of this… puzzle or whatever it is. You don't want it to be too easy, but you also want to make sure someone will eventually find the clues. What better place to hide one of the pieces than in a village that is shaped like Marcos' personal symbol?"

"Which would explain why such a small place as this would be a likely spot," Jade said. "I like it. But where do we look?"

"If I draw a line right down the center," Dane said as he drew, "see what it looks like when I cut a horizontal line right across this well in the middle?"

"It's a perfect cross!" Jade said. "But couldn't it be another coincidence?"

"It could," he agreed. "But there's only one way to find out for sure."

They made their way to a low spot that was, to the best of their estimation, the site of the small kiva. With great care they began moving aside the jumbled rocks. After twenty minutes of tiring work, he was surprised to feel a cool draft on his face. He dropped to his belly and scooted down into the hole they had made.

"There's a tangle of interlocking roots holding up all of this rock," he said, dragging a heavy stone away to reveal open space underneath. "I think the kiva is intact down below us!"

"No way," Jade said, sliding up alongside him. "Just like the well where we found the breastplate." She took out her flashlight and shone it into the hole. Its slender beam sliced through the darkness, illuminating stones that had not seen sunlight in centuries. "Hard to believe it wasn't filled up with debris. I just assumed it wouldn't be worth inspecting when I saw the pile of rubble."

"If we can clear a large enough hole for me to fit through without bringing the whole thing down, I'll drop in there and see what I can find," Dane said, sliding back from the hole and climbing to his feet.

"I'm going too," Jade said, standing and brushing the dirt and bits of rock from the front of her clothing. "I'm not letting you have all of the fun. This is much too cool to miss."

"One of us has got to stay up here with the rope in case something goes wrong," Dane said. "If we're both down there and the roof comes down…" He did not need to finish the sentence.

"In that case," Jade said, "I should be the one to go down there. I'm lighter, so there's less chance of me bringing something crashing down. And if there is a problem, you'll have a much easier time pulling me up than the other way around."

Dane wanted to argue, but her logic was impeccable. Besides, he had seen her in action, and she was far from helpless. Still he did not like it.

"I see your point," he said. "I just think I should be the one to go down there. We don't know what we're going to find."

"And why should you be the one to take the risk?" she asked. Her voice held a note of challenge. She folded her hands across her chest. "And you had better not say it's because I'm a woman."

Actually, that was exactly what Dane had been thinking. He knew it was irrational, but it was the way he had been raised. He also knew Jade would not find it an acceptable reason.

"Suit yourself," he said. "Just promise me you'll be careful."

"Thanks, Galahad," she said, smiling. She put a hand on his cheek in a gesture that was somehow both condescending and affectionate at the same time. "I promise I'll be careful."

They began clearing way the rubble, until there was enough space for her to wriggle through. They secured a rope to a nearby boulder and doubled it around the base of one of the larger scrub brush for added strength. Dane took hold of it and held tight while Jade squirmed backward through the hole and slid down into the darkness.

The oppressive darkness seemed to press down on Jade. She shone her light on the ceiling above her. The mass of earth and stone seemed to strain against the roots that bound it, seeking to pour down upon her. It seemed more threatening than the well in which she had dove. Somehow, the water had felt like a safeguard. Here, it was painfully obvious that nothing would protect her should gravity finally win this centuries-long battle.

"You're wasting time, Jade," she chided herself. She let the light play across the floor and then around the walls, searching for a clue. Maddock had better not have brought her on a wild goose chase. She continued to search, occasionally brushing dirt off of a likely-looking stone, hoping to find something, but to no avail.

She paused, dropping to a knee and looking around. What might she be forgetting? Solstices were important. What was the connection between solstices and kivas? The axes of kivas were usually built on solstice lines, which meant the solstice sun would shine on…

She turned her light toward the heel stone that hid the tunnel through which the shaman would enter the kiva. Could it be?

She first inspected the heel stone, but found nothing. Now for the tunnel. The Anasazi had been a small people compared to modern-day humans. The tunnel was going to be a squeeze. Holding her flashlight in one hand and her knife in the other, she squeezed into the opening and scooted forward. Inch by inch she wormed her way back into the darkness. *If I get stuck, there's no way Maddock will hear me call for him.*

She finally reached the end of the tunnel. Above her, where the shaman had once climbed down into the tunnel, was another hole filled with a precariously loose clump of stone and debris. The wall in front of her would have been in direct alignment with the sun, if not actually illuminated by it, so she started there. She started scraping away at the rocks in front of her. Nothing on the first one. Nor the second. Maybe…

A dull, dragging sound like a burlap sack being dragged across a rough floor filled the hole and she looked up in time to see the ceiling cave in on her.

Dane checked his watch. It had only been three minutes, though it seemed longer. No word yet from Jade. He strained to listen, but could hear nothing. After a couple more minutes he called down.

"Everything okay down there?" He hated not being down there with her. "Jade?"

No reply.

"Jade, what's going on down there?" What had happened to her? It wasn't so far to the bottom that she would not be able to hear him. "I'm coming in after you if you don't answer me." He suddenly had a vision of the rope giving way during his descent, leaving them both trapped at the bottom. But what choice did he have?

"Hold your horses, Buddy!" Jade called back. "I had to… I'll explain when I get up there." Another long silence, then "Go ahead and pull the rope up."

"You want me to pull you up?" he asked. "Are you hurt?"

"No, Maddock. Just pull up the rope." Her voice had the quality of a wife wearied of her obtuse husband. He remembered Melissa speaking to him in that tone many times, usually involving bright-colored laundry and the wrong temperature water. Duly chastised, he started hauling.

Whatever was on the end of the rope was light and came up easily. He hauled it out of the hole: a metal box like the one they had found at Chaco Canyon.

"You did it!" he called. Quickly untying the knots that held the box in place, he dropped the rope back into the hole so she could climb out.

Jade was covered in dirt, her face grimy, but her eyes were positively aglow. She immediately set to untying the rope.

"The interior of the kiva was still intact, just as we thought," she explained. "There was a tunnel. Shamans would use it to make a dramatic entrance while the room was smoky and the worshipers frenzied. It made them look like they were appearing out of nowhere." She finished coiling the rope and headed back toward their vehicle, still lecturing. "I followed it to the end. The box was sealed up in a recess behind a rock like the one you described from Chaco. I had to scrub away the dirt to find the right stone, and managed to bring a chunk of the ceiling down on me. It scared me more than anything, but I finally found a rock that had the symbol carved in it."

"Glad you're okay," Dane said, looking her over just to make certain. "I wonder how many researchers have been in that room, never dreaming that if they just did a little scrubbing they'd find something amazing," Dane said, holding the plain, metal box as if it were a priceless treasure.

"Lucky for us, this site doesn't seem to have gotten much attention," she said. "Let's get out of here before someone shows up. I can't wait to see what's inside this box."

Chapter 12

And you're sure he said "Dominion?" Amanda Shores turned back to the desktop computer in her office at the Deseret Bugle. The desk was cluttered with notes, a framed picture of what looked like Amanda and some friends in college, and a coffee-stained paperback fantasy novel. A framed graduation certificate from Colorado State University hung above the desk next to a small white board.

No boyfriend pictures is a good thing, Bones thought.

"Yep," he said, picking up the picture to get a closer look. She had been cute in college, but was definitely better-looking now. "The Dominion. Orley said it like some movie voice-over, like I should know what he was talking about. Ever heard of it?"

"I think so," she replied, her attention fixed on the screen. She tapped a few keys and sat back. "Take a look."

Bones scooted the rolling chair closer. The website to which Amanda had surfed was royal blue with a beehive logo in the top, left corner. The heading read, *The Deseret Dominion.*

"The Deseret Dominion, also known as simply, 'The Dominion,' is a para-political organization that supports independence for the former state of Deseret," Amanda explained. Seeing his blank stare, she continued. "In 1849, settlers in Utah proposed the formation of the state of Deseret. The proposal was basically for most of the land acquired in the Mexican Cession of 1848 to be included in the new state: all of present-day Utah and Nevada, and parts of Colorado, New Mexico, Wyoming, Idaho, and Oregon, and large chunks of California and Arizona. The United States didn't act on the proposal right away and the provisional government actually existed unofficially for two years before the Utah territory was created."

"So this… Dominion," Bones said, "thinks it can start a new country inside the US?"

"It's complicated," Amanda replied. "Officially it's a small political organization that lobbies for Mormon interests. Take a peek beneath the surface and you'll find all sorts of interesting things: rumors of training facilities for paramilitary troops, chemical weapons facilities, religious nuts... Who knows how much of it is true?"

"So you think these are the guys Orley was talking about?" Bones asked. "Why would they care about a farmer and an archaeological dig?"

"That picture you found. They're calling it the 'Jesus Image.' Anything in the historical record that could help support the Book of Mormon would be of interest to the Dominion."

"So they went after Isaiah to shut him up," Bones said, realization dawning on him, "because he wouldn't say that the image was of Jesus. But why would they go after Orley?"

"I don't imagine they were after Orley," she said. "But instead, they were after whatever was in the cave. Or maybe to keep what was in the cave from coming into the public eye. Those pictures you took suggest we're talking about a Spaniard rather than Jesus."

"I've got to do something to make sure Isaiah is safe from these guys," he said.

"I'll wager he is safe," Amanda said. "First of all, they haven't come back to finish the job. Also, they've gotten him off the project. The new foreman is probably their man, and if Isaiah comes out against him publicly, he'll just look like the envious professor who is angry because he didn't get to finish the dig he started."

"I hear you," Bones said, "but I still think I'll talk to Isaiah about getting out of town. How about Orley? Have you found anything out about him?"

"Whoever followed you two into that cave didn't try to hurt him. They subdued him and took him to a hospital.

They claimed he had a fit. I also found out he's been transferred to a psychiatric hospital for evaluation. They can't hold him for long unless they can find something wrong with him. Problem is…"

"If the Dominion has connections in the hospital, his evaluation might not be the most honest or accurate," Bones finished.

"And," Amanda added, "they would have the drugs and know-how to question him in great depth. Anything Orley knows about that cave, the Dominion will learn sooner or later."

"My to-do list keeps getting longer," Bones said.

"Would you like to share it with me?" Amanda asked. "Maybe I can help."

"My list mostly consists of people I'm gonna' kick the crap out of," Bones said. "What you can do is help me find out exactly who to punch first."

"I can do that," Amanda said, her eyes glistening with excitement. "No one's ever really investigated the Dominion. Most of their critics are raving conspiracy theorists, but if Orley is correct, this is something worth pursuing."

"It could be dangerous," Bones said. "If we're right about this, they've already come after two people."

"I know," Amanda said. "But I want to do it anyway."

"All right," Bones said. "See if you can find out who it was that brought Orley to the hospital. They could be our link to the Dominion. Also, see what you can dig up about the guy who's taken over Isaiah's dig. Even if he's not one of them, we might be able to find out who's pulling his strings."

He removed the golden disc, now wrapped in cloth and hidden inside a plain, brown paper bag, from his jacket pocket. "So what do you think we do about this?"

"It's a tough call," she said. "The Dominion has members everywhere: in government, in business, even in universities. It's hard to know who to trust. We need someone we can complete rely on who has a background in local Native American history."

A sudden thought struck Bones. The girl who was working with Dane might fit the bill.

"I think I know of someone who can help us out on that end," he said. "I'll also send the cave pictures and pictures of the disc to a friend of mine. He's sort of an über computer geek. If anyone can make something of the writing, it's him."

"Sounds good to me," Amanda said. "What do you want to do first?"

"First, we break Orley out of that hospital."

Chapter 13

Do you really think this is going to work?" Amanda whispered, peering across the dark parking lot at the glass-paneled entrance of the Central Utah University Neuro-psychotic Institute.

"No, I just thought it would be cool to get you arrested," Bones said. "Relax. It's going to be fine. I've got a feeling this won't be the first time you've bluffed your way into somewhere you weren't supposed to be."

"True, but I look like a tramp in this," she said, looking down at her tight, black leather miniskirt and fishnet hose.

"You say that like it's a bad thing," Bones said, leaning back to avoid her playful slap. "Seriously, you look great and you'll definitely get the interest of the guy at the front desk."

"What if it's a girl at the front desk?"

"You know, that never actually occurred to me," he said. "I guess you'd better hope she likes chicks. Either that, or you're going to have to put on the coveralls and I'll wear the skirt and hose."

"Let's just get this over with," Amanda said. She slid gracefully out of the car and set off across the parking lot in a purposeful, yet delicate, walk. Bones watched as she disappeared into the lobby, kicking himself all the while for not making sure the person on duty was a guy. Amanda would just have to wing it.

He told himself he was being overly cautious. This was a university mental health center, not a prison or a military installation. But if the Dominion was holding Orley, they might have extra security. Then again, what reason would they have to think someone would be coming after Orley? He was banking on lax security to get them through.

He gave Amanda one minute, then retrieved the toolbox from the back seat and hurried to the door. Careful not to be seen, he peered into the lobby. Score! The kid at the front desk couldn't have been more than twenty-five and from the look on his face, he'd never seen a girl dressed this sexy outside his favorite websites.

Amanda and the rent-a-cop spoke briefly, with Amanda doing most of the talking and the kid doing most of the mouth-agape, dumbstruck nodding. Finally he gave a halfhearted shake of his head, at which point Amanda bent *way* over his desk and said something that must have done the trick. He removed his headset, stood and looked around before slipping out from behind the desk and leading Amanda down the hallway to the left.

Bones slipped in the front door and headed in the direction Amanda and the guard had gone. He moved silently- he told everyone it was an Indian thing, but actually it was just lots of practice- and soon he could hear Amanda somewhere up ahead. Good girl! She was sticking to the plan, acting the brainless babe coming to visit her sick uncle. The guard should be leading them to Orley's room.

He paused at a cross-hall, not sure which direction to go. He heard an elevator down the hall to his right, and he stole a quick glance around. Amanda stepped inside and the guard turned and headed back in Bones' direction. *Crap!* This wasn't the plan! He needed to get to the elevator in time to see at which floor it stopped, or he'd have a hell of a time finding Orley's room.

The footsteps came closer.

He looked around for somewhere to hide. He could deal with the kid if he had to, but he hated to involve someone who was just doing his job and had no idea what was going on. The only nearby door was the ladies' room. The light was on, but at this time of night there was probably no one in there. He took a deep breath and ducked inside.

The first stall was occupied.

Hoping whoever was inside would not see his boots, he moved to the far wall and made his way to the last stall.

Shutting himself in, he sat down on the toilet tank, toolbox on his lap and his feet on the seat. *Hurry up, Lady!* He checked his watch. Amanda was definitely off the elevator by now. He pulled out his phone to text her. No signal.

Just then a cell phone rang in the other stall, sounding like a fire alarm in the quiet room, and nearly eliciting a curse from Bones.

"Hello? Oh, hi! I've been meaning..." She dove into a lengthy conversation that left Bones fuming. He tried his cell phone again. Nothing. *I need to find out who her carrier is,* he thought. Perhaps he could slip out while she was talking. He didn't know where he would go from there, but he could at least start looking.

"I've got to go," the woman said. "We've got this problem patient up on the fourth floor. A grumpy old rancher who keeps telling us he's been kidnapped. Totally paranoid. He's due for another sedative in about five minutes."

"Fourth floor," Bones whispered too low to be heard. "At least I caught one break."

Bones had no trouble finding Orley's room. He just followed the sound of profanity.

"...putting no needle in me!" The rancher's familiar voice lifted Bones' spirits. He liked the tough old fellow and was glad he had not been hurt. The fact that Orley believed he was being held against his will only served to confirm his and Amanda's suspicions.

"Mr. Orley, you need something to help you calm down," the woman from downstairs was saying. "Your niece..."

"I done told you I don't know this girl!" Obviously Amanda was in the room with them. Bones took a peek around the corner just as Orley turned toward him. The rancher scowled, but then his eyes widened as he realized who Bones was.

"It's okay," Bones mouthed, hoping Orley would understand that he and Amanda were there to help. Thankfully, Orley relaxed and quieted down.

"This will only take a moment, and then you'll feel much better," the nurse said. In short order she had given him the injection.

Orley looked at Bones as if to say, *You'd better know what you're doing.* Bones gave him the "thumbs-up" and ducked into the bathroom just inside Orley's doorway. He hid in the shower until Amanda came to tell him the nurse was gone.

"Let's get you out of here," Bones said to Orley as he hurried into the room. He helped the wobbly man to his feet.

"Damn stuff's already gettin' to me," Orley mumbled. Amanda found his clothes and helped him get dressed.

"What's going on here?" A muscular man with a square chin and a shaved head stepped through the door. He wore a white hospital coat and held a clipboard, but Bones could tell this was no doctor. "I haven't discharged this patient."

"My uncle wants to walk a little," Amanda said. "He doesn't feel comfortable wearing the gown, you know."

"He can barely stand," the man said. Orley's knees were weak from the sedative. "Put him back in the bed now." He took two steps before Bones' presence finally registered. He glanced at the coveralls and toolbox, turned away, and then jerked back. Their eyes met and recognition shone in his face.

Bones swung his toolbox up at a tight angle, catching the fellow on the side of the head. The man had good reflexes, and was able to turn away from the blow, catching most of the force on the back of his head. He spun away, but recovered his balance quickly.

The man drew a pistol from the pocket of his coat, but Bones was ready. He swept a vicious crescent kick at the man, sending the gun flying across the room, and hurled his toolbox at the surprised man, who managed to dodge it.

Bones leapt forward, landing a quick jab, and following with a right cross that just missed. Lab Coat Man bounced a punch off Bones' solid abs, and struck with a knife hand that whistled past Bones' throat.

A meaty fist appeared seemingly out of nowhere, catching the man clean on the chin, and he crumpled noiselessly to the floor. Bones turned to see Orley slumped against Amanda.

"That's all I got left," the rancher said. "Get me the hell out of here. There's always at least two of 'em around."

They helped the stumbling rancher into the hall and back toward the elevator. Orley was heavy—years of ranching had turned him into a veritable chunk of muscle. Those muscles were not of much help, though, as the sedated rancher struggled to keep his feet under him.

"Hold him," Amanda whispered, shifting the weight to Bones' side and ducking out from under Orley's arm. She disappeared around the corner and returned with a wheelchair.

"Nice," Bones whispered. "I think I'm going to keep you around."

"Like it's up to you," Amanda replied with a wink. "Give him to me and let's get him out of here. Head for the elevator."

Bones took a moment to get everything situated, took the wheelchair and headed down the corridor. Reaching the cross-hall he made the left that would take him to the bank of elevators. He heard footfalls behind him.

"Hey! Where are you going with that patient?"

He glanced over his shoulder to see a man in a security uniform round the corner at the far end of the hall. This was not the rent-a-cop from down the hall. This guy had every bit of the military bearing that Lab Coat Man had.

"What did you say?" Bones shouted. He quickened his pace and was careful to keep his body between the wheelchair and his pursuer. "I didn't hear you!"

"Stop!" the man yelled and began trotting toward

Bones. Good. The fellow wasn't overly concerned yet. "What the hell are you doing taking a patient out of here anyway?"

"He's being checked out. The nurse asked me to help her with him." He looked back over his shoulder. The man was closing the distance quickly. Bones kept the dialogue going as he passed an empty nurse's station. "She was blowing chunks. You should have seen it. I think she had pizza for dinner."

"I'll take care of the patient," the man yelled. "Just leave him there for me."

Bones stole one last glance at the elevators, only ten feet away, and saw that all of them were on the first floor. The man was no more than fifty feet away.

"Suit yourself," Bones said. He turned and shoved the wheelchair through the nearest open door, a patient's room, and ducked into a nearby stairwell. As the door swung shut behind him he heard a crash as the wheelchair spilled its contents: the toolbox he had hidden under a blanket. By now, Amanda and Orley were hopefully making their way out through the basement service exit they had discovered in the hospital floor plan they'd reviewed before attempting to retrieve the rancher. Angry voices told him he'd at least created a small diversion. He hoped he hadn't hurt any patients in the process, but what could he do? If anyone was injured, at least they were already in a hospital.

He jumped ten or so stairs and landed with a resounding thud on the landing. Ignoring the pain that surged up his legs and spine, he turned and leapt down the next flight. A sign read *Second Floor*. They would expect him to go all the way down to the ground floor. He slipped through the door and hurried down another glistening white hallway, similar to the one above.

A middle-aged nurse with graying brown hair and a smudge of chocolate frosting on her cheek stood up and peered with alarm over the nurse's station desk as he ran by.

"Big mess upstairs," he huffed. "No nurse on duty,

either. You might want to get up there."

"But I'm not..."

He was gone before she could finish her sentence.

Bones tightened his grip on the .22 he held hidden under his sleeve. He really didn't want to shoot anybody. Under any circumstance it would be difficult to explain why he was kidnapping a patient. Considering the political clout the Domain apparently wielded, it would be doubly hard to justify putting a bullet in anyone.

He made a right turn and dashed down the empty hallway to the back of the building where he came to a break room with a huge plate glass window overlooking the back parking lot. Amanda sat parked directly under the window in the old van she had borrowed from her uncle. The magnetic "Patton Plumbing" sign Bones had stolen off a parked vehicle they passed along the way completed the ruse nicely. They'd mail the sign back to the rightful owners, and have the rental company pick up the car in which they had arrived. They'd rented it under a false name so it wouldn't trace back to either of them.

He was about to head to the back exit when he heard footsteps in the hallway. He had not bought himself as much time as he'd hoped. He took a long look at the window.

"Oh, what the heck?" he whispered. "Let's just hope it's not heavy-duty safety glass."

He picked up one of the break tables, a heavy, round job with a formica top and black metal trestle, and heaved it into the window. The table rebounded with a crack and a thud, crashing to the tile floor, but the damage was done. A hole gaped in the middle of the window and a web of cracks spreading three feet all around. Hoping he'd judged the distance correctly, he got a running start and leaped, shielding his face as he smashed through the glass.

There was a moment of groin-tingling free-fall, and then he crashed with a metallic thud onto the roof of the van. Amanda yelped and stuck her head out the driver's window.

"Where did you…"

"Just drive!" he yelled. He grabbed the front edge of the van roof as Amanda hit the gas. The van surged forward, then sputtered and lurched to a halt. Bones tried to dig the toes of his boots into the pitted, dented surface, but to no avail. He slid forward and tumbled down the windshield and over the hood. He slowed enough to get his feet under him as he dropped to the asphalt.

"Sorry!" Amanda said. "I forgot the transmission on this thing sometimes…" The staccato crackling of gunfire rang out, and bullets whizzed past the front end of the van.

Bones returned fire, sending two well-aimed shots through the remains of the second-floor window. The van had rolled forward far enough to make for a difficult angle, and he had no idea if he'd hit his target, but it bought sufficient time for him to take the wheel from Amanda and hit the road.

"You have to baby the gas a little or else it stalls," Amanda said.

"Yeah, I sort of figured that out." He checked the rear-view and side mirrors and saw no pursuit. He doubted it would last.

He was right.

Headlights appeared behind them, growing fast as the vehicle sped toward them. Bones had no doubt it was their pursuers. He cut off the van's headlights and hung a right down the nearest street, careful not to tap on the brakes, lest the brake lights give them away. He stood on the gas, praying no one would pull or walk out in front of him. The odds were slim this time of night. He took another right, this time the van felt like it was going up on two wheels. Orley, lying on the back floorboard, groaned as he rolled over.

As they zoomed down another deserted street, Bones spotted an old white van nearly the twin of the one they drove. He slammed on the brakes, bringing the van to a halt.

"Why are we stopping? Are you nuts?" Amanda shouted.

"Here," Bones said, reaching out the window and yanking the magnetic sign off the door. "Slap this baby on that van. With any luck it'll slow them down." When she was finished he whipped the van around the next corner just in time to see headlights from the direction they had come. He sped up, hoping they had not been spotted. They flew down the darkened street with no sign of pursuit. The false trail had apparently bought them some time.

Bones made three more turns before he was satisfied they had left their pursuers behind. He slowed the van and turned the headlights back on.

"Can I breathe now?" Amanda asked, releasing her vise grip on the armrest. "I've never been shot at before."

"I think we're good," Bones said, still keeping a wary eye out for pursuit. "How's Orley?"

"Still doped. It isn't safe to take him home. Where should we go?"

"Considering we're both probably on hospital security video," Bones said, "I vote we get out of town."

Chapter 14

So your friend Bones is on his way here and he's bringing what?" Jade's attention was fixed on the e-mail they had received from Dane's friend, computer geek Jimmy Letson, and she was only halfway paying attention to what he'd told her.

"He says he's found a gold disc with some kind of weird writing. He also has a bunch of pictures he took of cave paintings. He thinks you might be able to help him out."

"Did you tell him we're kind of busy here?" she asked, turning over another page. "Jimmy says the writing is something like Hebrew, but not quite. As if it's an older form that grew out of something else. He's identified a few phrases, and thinks given enough time he'll be able to make some sense of it."

"What do you make of the two artifacts we've found so far?" Dane turned the new piece over. It was almost the twin of the first one they'd found. Put together they made a quarter of a sphere. He wasn't certain, but the writing seemed to flow across from one to the other – they seemed to be a match. "Do you think maybe there are eight of them, so it makes a sphere?"

"I don't know," Jade said, still focusing her attention on the papers. "There are only six symbols on the shield, which makes me think there are six pieces."

"Six pieces, but seven cities," Dane mused. He stroked his chin, feeling the stubble of a day's growth. "Yucca House was quite ordinary, and not even a city. Chaco Canyon qualifies as a city, but not golden."

"What are you getting at?"

"Just wondering what's at the end of the rainbow."

"Meaning?"

"I mean that obviously all seven 'cities' are not cities of gold or treasure. If your theory is correct, and all six locations point to a seventh, then is that where we find whatever it is Fray Marcos was hiding? And if so, what is it?"

"I wonder that myself," Jade said. "The only legend I've uncovered is that of the Moorish treasure and the religious artifacts, although the idea of an eighth-century crossing of the Atlantic, followed by going halfway across America to hide something seems a bit far-fetched."

"I've seen crazier. Trust me," Dane said. "What do you…"

"Hey! It's another e-mail from Jimmy," Jade said. She took a moment to read the contents, printed it off, and handed it to Dane. "He's managed to get what he thinks is a translation of the writing on the first piece." She handed him the paper from his computer guru friend and stood back with her arms folded across her chest and watched him read.

Dane and Jade,

This is weird stuff- an unusual variation of Hebrew. Here's my best stab at the translation with the help of a professor friend.

'In the sepulchre, in the third course of stones. Under the tomb. In the chain platform. This is all of the votive offerings of the seventh treasure, the tenth is impure.'

Doesn't look like too much. Sorry I couldn't help more.

Jimmy

"He's right," Dane said. "It doesn't look like much. What do you make of it?"

"Nothing yet."

A knock at the door interrupted her. Dane answered it and was surprised to see Saul standing in the doorway. He was covered in dirt, but otherwise looked no worse for the wear.

"What the hell, Saul?" Jade's soft voice was razor sharp, and her eyes were ablaze. "You take off with my equipment, you don't let me know where you are…" She stopped there, her hands in the air, looking as if she couldn't decide whether to scream at him or strangle him. Finally, with an exasperated sigh, she waved him into the room and stalked out past him.

Saul watched her go before turning to Dane with a sheepish expression on his face.

"Guess I'm not on the invite list for her next soiree," he said.

"Not likely," Dane replied. He had no idea how to take Saul, but the guy at least seemed contrite. "She's pretty stressed out, though. We have a translation from the artifacts we've found, but it doesn't seem to mean anything."

"You found another one?" Saul sat heavily on the corner of Jade's bed. "And you have a translation?"

"Yeah," Dane said. He felt a little strange telling Saul this, but he supposed there would be no harm. The translation was close to nonsense; at least, it was of no use to them being incomplete and out of context.

He handed the sheet to Saul who read it over silently, shook his head, and read it aloud.

"*In the sepulchre, in the third course of stones. Under the tomb. In the chain platform. This is all of the votive offerings of the seventh treasure, the tenth is impure.*" He looked at Dane, his expression unreadable. "It sounds like a treasure hunt. What could it be?"

"No idea," Dane said, though his mind conjured possibilities, each more far-fetched than the other, that set his heart pounding. He supposed he was just a kid at heart.

He loved the thought of unraveling a mystery.

"Who did the translation?" Saul was staring at the paper again, as if some secret were buried between the lines.

"A friend of mine," Dane said. "Computer guy. He had some help."

"And he's certain of the translation?"

"As certain as he can be," Dane said, feeling a touch of defensiveness rising. "He's reliable, and very thorough."

"No doubt," Saul said. He gave Dane a long, measured look, and opened his mouth to speak when a loud knock drew their attention. Dane knew who it was immediately.

"Bones!" he said, swinging the door open. His friend grabbed him in a rough embrace and slapped him on the back.

"Maddock! Good to see you. How's the latest adventure?" Before Dane could answer, a short, attractive brunette with the high cheekbones that spoke of native blood stepped up behind Bones. "This is Amanda," he said. "I think I mentioned her to you."

"Absolutely," he said, shaking hands with Amanda. "Dane Maddock. Good to meet you."

"Bones told me plenty about you on the drive here," she said, smiling.

"Half of it's not true and the other half's a lie," he replied. Remembering Saul, he turned and introduced him to Bones and Amanda. Dane had told Bones of his discomfort with Jade's assistant, but Bones greeted Saul politely as they shook hands. Dane was about to ask about the find Bones had made in Utah when Jade re-entered the room.

"Oh, hi," she said. Obviously her anger at Saul had distracted her. "Sorry. I'm Jade Ihara." She offered her hand to Bones, who surprised Dane by neither hitting on her nor saying anything remotely inappropriate. He simply shook her hand and introduced himself and Amanda.

The two women shook hands politely, but eyed one another as if they were sizing each other up. After an uncomfortable pause, Jade invited them to sit.

"What's the latest with Isaiah?" Dane asked. "How's he doing?"

"Better. He's in Denver staying with friends while he recoups. He wanted to go back to the dig, but it's not his anymore, so…" Bones shrugged.

"So, where is the rancher guy you had with you?"

"Dropped him off with some relatives in Grand Junction," Bones said, settling into a chair opposite Dane. "I think he's going to be fine. He's a tough old fellow."

"That's good," Dane said. "So tell me about what you found in the cave."

Bones reached into his jacket pocket and extracted something wrapped in cloth. He removed the cloth with great care, and laid the golden disc on the table. Bones had already described the disc to Dane, but seeing it was amazing.

He turned it over in his hand, narrowing his eyes the writing that spiraled around the golden circle. It was like nothing he'd ever seen before. Or was it?

Jade slid her chair against his and leaned in close. Her soft hair brushed his arm and her soft intake of breath seemed to tingle in his ear.

"Dane, she said. "The writing! Do you think it's the same?"

She didn't need explain what she meant by the same. It definitely looked to him to be the same writing they had found on the artifacts: a version of Hebrew. He couldn't say for sure, but Jimmy could find out for them.

"I think they are the same," he said. "It's one hell of a coincidence, though. Bones finding this disc and us finding the artifacts…"

"It can't be a coincidence," she said. "They have to be connected somehow. We've got to get this translated."

"I've already sent it to Jimmy," Bones said.

"Did he tell you anything?" Jade asked, her eyes sparkling with enthusiasm.

"Yes. He told me he already had a real job, and if we keep dumping all this crap on him he was going to start charging us for it."

Jade groaned and sank back in her chair. "I hate being stuck waiting around like this. I want something to do."

"Bones told me you were trying to identify some symbols on an artifact." Amanda said. 'Perhaps a fresh set of eyes would be of some help."

"Why not?" Jade said without much conviction. Dane wondered what had gotten her so down all of a sudden. The possibility that Bones and Amanda's find could help them in their search had him feeling good about their prospects.

Jade brought out a high-resolution picture of the breastplate along with a set of papers. Each paper had an image from the breastplate at the top and a list of notes, thoughts and possibilities were jotted below.

"We've solved these two," she explained, indicating the moon-like icon that represented Chaco Canyon and the jagged promontory that was the foot of Sleeping Ute Mountain. "We believe that each has some association with solstices or equinoxes. We've also found Fray Marcos's personal symbol, a cross inside a clover, at each location. Dane noticed that the layout of the second site, Yucca House, was clover-shaped as well."

Saul grunted in surprise and everyone turned to stare at him.

"What?" Jade asked her voice still cold with anger at her assistant.

"Well," Saul said, hanging his head, "I guess now is as good a time as any to tell you. I figured out another of the clues."

"Which one? Where?" Jade asked.

"This icon here," Saul said, pointing to the image that reminded Dane of the palace of an evil sorcerer. "It's Ship Rock. It's not shown from the angle that most people see in photographs, but it's definitely Ship Rock."

"Heck, I could have told you that," Bones said, rocking

back in his chair and grinning. "It looks like Dracula's castle. It's wicked cool."

"Bones, I e-mailed you a picture of the breastplate several days ago," Dane said. "Why didn't you say something?"

"I didn't know *then!*" he said, still smiling. "But I saw that thing in the distance as we were driving down here, and that's the first thing I thought of just now when Jade showed us the picture."

Jade buried her face in her hands. For the first time, Dane noticed that her knuckles were scarred—probably from field work.

"We drove down that long stretch of highway with Ship Rock in our sights and never once did I even think about it. All I had my mind on was Yucca House and wondering where Saul had gone, and I didn't even notice it."

"It doesn't matter now," Dane said. "What's important is we know where to find another piece of the puzzle."

"It's not that simple," Saul mumbled. "When I got caught trying to get onto Sleeping Ute Mountain they took me in for questioning, but let me go after I convinced them I was just a flaky New-Ager trying to have a spiritual moment. While I was there, a photograph on the wall caught my eye. It was Ship Rock from the perspective you see on the breastplate.

"I thought about trying to climb it, but then I considered the solstice connection. I remembered that white settlers used to call it "The Needle" and wondered where the shadow of the most prominent point would fall at the various solstices. I found a library with internet access and started poking around with satellite images until I found a promising location: a formation of three hills and a butte that made a clover shape. I didn't have any way to perform the calculations necessary to test my theory, so I figured I'd check it out."

Everyone was silent. Even Jade was now listening

attentively, her previous anger abated.

"When I got there, I found a kiva right smack in the center, hidden by scrub and yucca. The roof was gone, of course, but when I cleared away the rubble, I found that the sipapu, you know, the ceremonial hole in the center, had been sealed. Or rather, it once had been sealed. The seal with Fray Marcos's symbol was lying broken off to the side. Anyway, there was a box like the one Maddock found at Chaco. Empty." He shrugged as his tale came to an end. "Somebody else found it. Probably the same guys we saw before."

Jade swore and covered her face with her hands.

"Well, at least we have two of the pieces," Dane said.

"May I see the ones you already have?" Amanda asked.

Jade brought Amanda the pieces, and Amanda laid them on the table, pushing them together to form a quarter of a sphere."

"You know what this looks like to me? One of those Egyptian beetles."

Dane stared at the piece which now was looking oddly familiar to him, but he could not name the shape.

"A scarab," Jade breathed. "Most are ornate, but this one is plain. That's why it was not readily obvious to us what it was."

"I see it now," Dane said, feeling both excited and confused. "The ridges around the bottom are the legs." He thought for a moment. "There are six symbols on the breastplate, which means that the scarab was cut into six pieces. When we find them all, we'll have the entire message. Or at least, we'll have five out of six pieces. If Jimmy translates it all, I'll bet we can still make something of it." He paused, mulling over this odd discovery. "But why would someone take a scarab—an Egyptian artifact, write some lines in Hebrew on it, cut it up, and hide it in America?"

"The legend does say that they hid treasures of religious significance," Jade said. "And there was frequent interaction between the Hebrew kingdom and that of the Egyptians. Perhaps this scarab was a part of that treasure."

"Weird," Bones said. "It's not how I imagined the cities of gold." His face tautened. "Wait a minute…"

"What?" Dane asked.

"Dude, does this mean we're going after another Bible treasure?"

"Whatever it is," Jade interjected, "we need to keep up the search. We've already lost one of the clues. I don't want to slow down and risk missing any of the others."

"Do you have any ideas on the other locations?" Amanda asked, mulling over the icons.

"Nothing definitive," Jade said. "This one," she indicated a tower-shaped structure, "is not distinctive-looking, but it could be one of a number of structures at Mesa Verde."

Bones whistled. "Talk about a needle in a haystack. That place is huge. How many ruins are there?"

"Oh, about six-hundred cliff dwellings and four thousand or so archaeological sites," Jade replied. "But I've scoured the maps, and it's the only likely location. Plus, I've used the solstice connection to narrow the search, and I have a few ideas." She smiled. "Shall we pack?"

Chapter 15

"And you want me to climb down there?" Dane gazed down into the sheer-sided canyon. Set beneath a deep overhang, Square Tower House looked remote and inaccessible. "Isn't there a service road? How do the rangers get down there?"

"I told you," Jade said, sighing. "There isn't one. They use ropes and ladders to get down there. Unless, of course, you want to try the Anasazi handholds."

Dane shook his head. "That's something Bones would go for. I'll take the rope." He paused and looked her up and down, admiring the snug-fitting faux ranger uniform she had cobbled together. The boots, khaki shorts, NPS t-shirt, and Mesa Verde cap looked good on her. Of course, she made everything look good.

"You know that getup would be more believable if you had not shaved your legs," he kidded. "You know-- go natural like the ranger women."

"Shut up and get going," she said, giving him a shove toward the edge.

"You did put up the sign, didn't you?" Dane asked, knotting a rope in a bowline around his waist.

"Of course," she said. "*This Trail Closed For Maintenance.* It should fool tourists, maybe even a really lazy ranger. Now hurry." She took hold of the safety rope he had secured around his waist, wrapped it once around the base of a nearby tree, and secured it to a larger one. She would play the line out as he descended. He probably wouldn't need it on the way down. He would be sliding down the other rope they had hooked to the same tree. Where Jade would really come in handy would be on the way back up, when her added strength would help him with his free climb up the rope. It was the most unsafe, ridiculous-looking rock climbing setup he'd seen since he was a stupid teenager, but they didn't have the time or equipment for real rappelling.

Donning his climbing gloves, he got a good grip on the rope, hooked it around his ankle, and slowly backed over the rock face. Jade kept tension on the rope as he worked his way down. He was an experienced climber, and the first several feet made for an easy descent. The rock soon curved back beneath the hill, forming the overhang. His boots began to slip, telling him it was time to change tactics. The drop was just over one hundred feet, but it looked farther from this vantage point. Much farther.

"Okay! I'm going down!" he called.

"Go for it!" Jade shouted back.

He kicked free of the wall and immediately the hands of gravity yanked him downward. The rope burned his thighs and palms through his clothing and gloves as he shot downward. He squeezed tighter and his descent slowed a little. He felt the jolt from the balls of his feet to the base of his skull when he hit the ground. His foot tangled in the rope and he sat down hard, rolling a little on his hip to minimize the impact.

"Some action movie star I'd make," he muttered, looking around for spectators he knew were not there. He untied the safety rope and hurried over to Square Tower House.

Overlooking the ancient Anasazi ruins, Square Tower House loomed four stories high, set against the back wall like a lone skyscraper. He navigated through the remains of foundations and walls, worn smooth by wind and time. He soon found himself at the base of the tower. His destination was the top room, where, according to Jade's research, was a window through which the sun struck a peculiar outcropping on the day of the summer solstice. It wasn't the most definitive clue, but it was worth checking out. He hoped the climb would not be for nothing.

He entered the ground floor room of the tower. It was less than five feet high, and cramped. The walls were blackened with soot from ancient fires, but here and there he could make out traces of the stucco-like substance the Anasazi used to cover their walls. Where it had chipped away he could still see evidence of the fine stonework. There was a small hole in the ceiling through which he could gain access to the upper levels. He wasn't tall, but his shoulders were broad, and they made for a tight squeeze. With difficulty, he worked his way up to the top level.

Reaching the fourth floor, he stood, forgetting the low ceiling and banging his head. How small had these people been? Of course, Bones claimed the Anasazi were actually aliens who built fancy cliff dwellings then flew away, inadvertently leaving their pet chupacabras behind. He was pretty sure his friend was joking, but was not one-hundred percent certain.

Where to begin? He looked out the front window and got his bearings, and then scanned the small room. Square Tower House sat on a south-facing cliff. Sunken as it was in a valley, sunrise and sunset would not be visible to the structure. Most likely, the solstice marker would have been based on the mid-day sun, meaning the center of the far wall. He used his knife to scrape away the ancient plaster. Once again he felt guilty at damaging an ancient structure, but hoped the end result would reveal a prize of such historical importance that it would atone for his acts of minor destruction.

The plaster came away in sheets, and soon he was looking at the bare, ancient stone. The building blocks were much larger than those of Chaco Canyon, but they were pieced together with the same precision. For a brief moment he wondered if Bones was right about aliens building this place. It was almost unthinkable that primitive people could create such an architectural marvel. He ran his fingers across the surface, feeling the joints where the stones fit together so neatly. He could find no indication of a compartment that would hide the next piece of the puzzle. Scratch this site off the list. No point in making the climb without giving it a good effort, though. He moved closer and scraped away at the stone. Something caught his eye.

In one spot, the consistency of the stone was somehow different. It dipped in ever so slightly and the stone felt grittier. His fingers traced the indentation like a blind man reading Braille, and they looped around in an oval pattern. He scraped away at the stone with greater intensity and soon uncovered a clover-shaped engraving that had filled with the ancient plaster, thus making him miss it at first glance. Given that Mesa Verde was abandoned a good three-hundred years before Fray Marcos and Estevanico made their journeys, whoever had secreted something here must have plastered over the stone himself. He obviously didn't want the clues lost forever, but neither did he want to make it too easy. But to what were these clues leading?

He worked the stone loose and was rewarded with a box exactly like the others they had found. He slipped it into a drawstring backpack and replaced the masonry as best he could. Peering out the window, he scanned the buildings and ledge for signs of rangers, but he could see no one. He felt a momentary pang of regret that he could not stay and admire the spectacular scenery for a while longer, but time was of the essence.

Climbing down was much easier than climbing up, though squeezing through the small holes was just as uncomfortable. He made his way quickly back to the ropes which still hung where he had left them. He gave the climbing rope two tugs-- his signal to Jade that he was ready to make his way back up-- but there was no answering tug. He tried again, but still no answer. She might have walked away, or encountered some tourists and had to do her ranger improv. He didn't want to entertain the possibility of anything more serious. He let two minutes tick away on his watch and tried again. Still nothing. He checked his cell phone, though he knew he would have no reception at this remote location. Sure enough, there were no bars showing. He tried the call anyway-- a remnant of his upbringing by a father who believed in leaving no stone unturned and no detail unattended. No dice. He debated calling her name, but a gnawing feeling of unease had crept up his spine, and he now felt that something was wrong. If so, circumstances might dictate that announcing his presence would be a bad idea.

Dreading the climb he was about to make, he took both ropes and scrambled up onto a nearby boulder. He pulled the safety rope taut and cinched it around his waist. Without Jade to take the slack out, it wouldn't keep him from falling should he lose hold of his climbing rope, but by starting higher than ground level, it would break his fall before he hit the ground. Of course, it could break his spine as well, but he was confident that if he lost one rope, he could grab the other before he went tumbling. With no more preparations to make, he donned his gloves, grabbed the climbing rope, and swung out.

He had scarcely begun his climb before something went wrong. A vibration like the plunking of a guitar string ran down the climbing rope and he dropped about a half-inch. He knew what that meant.

"Oh no!" He hastily grabbed the safety rope in his left hand, transferring as much weight as he could. The climbing rope shuddered again and he grabbed onto the safety rope with his other hand. He hung there catching his breath. Something had caused the climbing rope to fray. A few more seconds and it would have snapped completely. It was a brand new 11mm rope and should not have frayed under any natural conditions. That left the possibility that someone had tampered with it. And if they had tampered with the climbing rope...

The realization struck him just as the safety rope to which he now clung gave an inch. Cursing roundly he slid quickly down the rope. He reached the limit, forgetting he had shorted it to keep from falling, and found himself spinning like a wind vane ten feet above the rocky ledge. He had only a moment to consider the absurdity of the situation when the rope parted, dropping him like a sack of potatoes onto the ground. His breath left him in a sudden rush. He rolled over onto his back, his mind ticking off the curses his body lacked the breath to articulate.

His mind raced with possibilities as he recovered his breath. The likelihood that even one of the ropes would have broken was remote. But for both of them to not only break, but to just happen to break at the same time? Not a chance. Which meant foul play, and that something likely had happened to Jade. He scanned the rocky face above, seeing nothing amiss. Self-preservation dictated that he either find a place to hide until he felt certain that whoever did this was gone, or that he climb all the way down into the canyon and search for a new way out. Neither one would work, though, because of Jade. He had to find out if she was all right.

It would take an experienced climber to make his way back up to the top. They wouldn't expect him to climb out on his own, but he was a skilled climber. He didn't relish the idea of a free climb, but he had no other acceptable choice. Then he remembered what Jade had said earlier. The Anasazi always carved hand and footholds in the cliffs in order to access their homes. All he had to do was find them.

His search seemed to take forever, scanning the weathered cliffs, inspecting each crack and shadow, but when he finally found the first shadowy concave space in the rock, his watch showed that only six minutes had passed. Perhaps he'd be doubly lucky and his hidden enemy had given him up for dead. Without further consideration, he set to climbing.

The ancient holds were eroded in places, some of them no more than shallow pits. He moved as quickly as he could, taking more time where the holds were almost gone. He did not look down, but instead kept his eyes on the top of the cliff. What would he do if someone appeared above him? Hope it was someone on his side, he supposed.

He made steady progress until he was about halfway up

when the next handhold simply wasn't there. He paused, squinting his eyes against the sun's intense glare, and searched for it. His hands burned from scrabbling up the rock, and his muscles were knotted from the awkward contortions the climb had forced upon him. Where was the next hold? It was not long before a memory crashed down on him. The Anasazi coded their hand-holds. If you didn't start with the correct hand and foot, you could get just far enough along to get...stuck.

Keeping his body pressed as close to the rock as possible, he turned and looked back, seeking a way down. He could see the way he had come, but his feet and hands were all wrong and the intervening space too broad to permit him to move backward. He was in trouble. He certainly hoped Bones was faring better.

Chapter 16

Bones scanned the ruins of Sun Temple. Even now it was an amazing sight. The remains of two towers stood inside a D-shaped double wall.

"It doesn't look like a clover to me," Saul said, his constant scowl fully in evidence.

"No but we need to check it out anyway," Bones said, wondering how he had gotten stuck with Saul as a partner. "The marker is supposed to be at the southwest corner." He indicated the direction they should go and led the way.

The walls were short and thick, the craftsmanship amazing. Sun Temple had never been completed, so Bones was skeptical about what they might find, but Jade had insisted they leave no stone unturned, so to speak.

Arriving at the southwest corner, they found a heavily eroded stone with three circles carved against a blurry-edged, diamond shaped background. Bones knelt and ran his fingers across the surface of the marker up to the point where it curved into the wall. He didn't see anything here that would indicate Fray Marcos had chosen it as one if his hiding places.

"This is it, huh?" Saul said, putting his hands on his knees and leaning forward to gaze intently at the stone. "It looks a little bit like two planets crashing into a sun."

"It does a just a bit, doesn't it?" Bones looked all around the stone to see if he was missing anything. He didn't see anything that indicated a hidden compartment or Marcos' symbol. "I don't suppose the three circles could be the leaves of a clover?" he asked, somehow knowing it was not so.

"Doesn't look like what we've found so far," Saul replied, the doubt clear in his voice.

A movement caught Bones' eye. Someone was moving

beyond the farthest tower. That in itself was not strange, but it was the way they were moving—as if they were trying not to be noticed.

"Keep looking down at the rock like you're interested," he whispered to Saul. "Don't do anything else unless I tell you,"

"I hear you," Saul said. He didn't offer any argument or ask questions. Maybe the guy wasn't as stupid as Bones had believed.

He kept an eye on the far tower. There were two men moving slowly around the back of the chest-high structure. They were facing the back of the tower as if admiring the architecture, but it was obvious to Bones that they were watching him just as much as he was watching them. Their appearance was wrong as well. They wore casual clothes like any tourist would wear, but they were neatly pressed and their shirts were tucked in. Their haircuts were perfect. Everything about the way they looked made it seem they had checked in at the office before dropping by the ruins. Their bearing was not that of civilians. Their backs were too straight and they moved with too much purpose to be sightseeing.

Bones turned the lay of the land over in his mind. The men stood between them and the parking lot. The surrounding area offered little cover.

"Are you packing?" he asked Saul.

"Am I what?"

"Carrying a gun."

"Oh, no," Saul replied. "Why?"

Just then, the two men rounded the tower and moved toward Bones and Saul in a fast walk. They separated, each drawing a weapon and ducking low as they approached.

"Because I think we're going to need a little firepower."

Fatigue gave way to a bout of dizziness as Dane baked in the sun on the face of the cliff above Square Tower House.

Sweat ran into his eyes, but he scarcely noticed. He had considered and dismissed a dozen or more ideas, each more reckless than the next. He had just about settled on trying to slide down the cliff and hoped he survived the fall, when he began to hallucinate. At least that's what he thought was happening when a rope suddenly appeared six inches from his nose.

He blinked twice, but could not dispel the image. He thought of thirsty men in the desert seeing mirages, their minds willing them to believe that which they most desperately sought was before their eyes. But he wasn't that far gone. Tired, aching, and frustrated to be certain, but not on the verge of death.

"Maddock, are you going to grab on to the stupid rope or not?" Jade's voice sounded tired and a bit hoarse, but it was her. Looking up, he could see the outline of her form against the bright, blue sky. Hoping this really wasn't a hallucination, and that he was about to grab a handful of empty air, he reached out and grasped the rope.

"It's the rest of what wasn't cut," she said. "I've got it secured to the base of a tree, but I think I'm strong enough to help you up. But you've got to hurry."

Shaking off thoughts of ache and fatigue, Dane transferred his weight to the rope and started working his way up. Up above, Jade hauled on the rope. At first she seemed just to be dragging him across the rocky face, adding to his cuts and bruises, but then he saw a handhold. She had pulled him back over to the ancient egress. Keeping the rope twisted around his arm for safety, he scrambled up the ancient notches and quickly found himself face-to-face with Jade. What he saw made him grind his teeth in anger.

Her face was bruised, her lower lip split, and her clothing was ripped and dirty. She looked away, as if embarrassed to meet his eye.

"I don't know who they were," she said before he could ask. "They know we're after an artifact, but they didn't seem to know what it is. I didn't tell them." She kept her back to him, hastily gathering the rope and looping it around her hand and elbow.

"Why didn't they come down after me? Or wait 'til I got to the top and take it from me?" Dane asked. "If they wanted the artifact, cutting my ropes wouldn't help them."

"I convinced them you had just called up to me to tell me that it wasn't there, and that you'd be coming back after you put things right. They slapped me around a bit to make sure I was telling the truth. They finally knocked me unconscious. I assume they cut your rope to slow you down and then took off for Sun Temple."

"You sent them after Bones?" he said, unable to believe what he was hearing. "How could you…"

"No! They asked me about Sun Temple. I didn't say anything, but they seemed to already know about it, and that Bones would be there." She looped the last of the rope around her arm and finally turned to face him. The sight of her injured face brought a surge of guilt.

"I'm sorry," he said, taking her by the hand and heading off at a trot down the path. "I'm worried about both of you. Now, let's go find somebody for me to take out my anger on."

"You really think this is going to work?" Saul whispered. They had dived into a nearby kiva and were now squirming their way through the passage that connected it to another kiva on the far side of the ruin-- closer to their car, and hopefully behind the guys with guns, whoever they were.

"It might if you'll shut up," Bones muttered. It galled him to possibly be leaving the artifact behind, but he felt that he had little choice. He might have done something bolder had Maddock been with him, but all he had was Saul, and the research assistant didn't seem like someone to be counted on in a throw-down. Besides, this was the second narrow tunnel he'd had to squeeze himself through in the past week, and it was getting on his nerves.

His shoulders pressed against the edges. Bones was much too big for Anasazi architecture. Saul was a good-sized fellow in his own right, though his bulk was spread around a little more evenly.

"Maybe they're more concerned about the artifact, and won't notice us leave," Saul whispered.

"Maybe. Maybe not," Bones whispered, though he doubted the men would give up so easily. "Either way, I told you to shut up."

Saul lapsed into sullen silence, broken only by the occasional grunt as he squeezed through a particularly narrow section of tunnel. They finally reached the end of the tunnel. Bones hoped Saul had enough sense to remain quiet while he checked things out. He peered out into the kiva, and along the rim as far as he could see. No one was there. He closed his eyes and let his ears take precedence as his grandfather had taught him when he was a boy. He heard a whisper of dry wind through stunted trees, but nothing else. This sparse southwestern wilderness was so different from the forests of North Carolina where he was raised. He heard no birds singing, no scrabbling of squirrels in the trees. No gentle rustle of a nearby stream. But most important, no voices or footfalls. Of course, they could be waiting out of sight for him to appear. He drew his Glock and sighed. He would have to take his chances.

"I hate these roads," Dane muttered as he whipped around another tight curve. There was no direct path to anywhere in Mesa Verde. All the roads twisted, turned, rose, and fell along with the land. And there were just enough tourists to make things maddeningly slow. He whipped around an RV and stepped on it, barely making it around before a mini-van, horn blaring, appeared from around the curve ahead of them.

"Maddock," Jade groaned. "If you're going to drive like this, I probably should have just let those guys kill me.

Traffic accidents are so… messy."

"Tell me about it once Bones is okay," he said. He fished into his pocket and pulled out his cell phone. He flipped it open and glanced to see if he had a signal. He did!

"Maddock!" Jade shouted and grabbed at the wheel. "Keep your eyes on the road!" He had let the car veer precariously close to the edge of a steep-walled canyon.

"Sorry," he said, this time keeping his vision focused in front of him as he punched up Bones' number on speed dial.

Bones peered over the edge of the kiva. As he had hoped, the two men had made their way to the far side of the ruin, and now seemed more interested in the sun marker than they were in finding Bones and Saul. The gray-haired man knelt in front of the stone, while the redhead stood with his back to them, looking out across the canyon as if he believed his quarry had gone over the edge.

Bones leaned close to Saul, who had exited the tunnel and was hunched down beside him.

"They're not looking," Bones whispered. "We'll crawl over to the other side of the kiva, and I'll check again. If they still aren't looking, we'll slip over the wall and back to the cars as quickly as we can without making any sound. Got it?

Saul nodded, and together they crawled across the floor of the ancient Kiva. When they reached the other side, Bones dared another look, and was relieved to see that neither of the men was looking their way. He nodded to Saul, who quietly climbed out of the kiva and began crawling toward their car. Breathing a sigh of relief, Bones hoisted himself up over the ledge.

Just as his cell phone rang.

He cursed under his breath and took off, bending at the waist to present a smaller target. Saul followed behind, moving faster than Bones would have believed him able.

Something buzzed past his cheek and smacked into a nearby stone, spraying his leg with shards of rock as the sound of a gunshot reached him. He zigzagged, then hurtled the wall that surrounded the site. Bullets continued to fly as they dashed through the stand of trees and burst into the small parking lot. Saul rushed up to their rented Aztek, but he had not seen what Bones had seen.

"Keep going! They've flattened our tires!" He drew his Glock and fired off two rounds in the general direction of their pursuers.

Rather than following the road, where their pursuers could easily overtake them in their own car, Bones cut through the forested area of pine and blue spruce that separated the circular parking area of Sun Temple from the Mesa Top Loop Road. There was no way that on foot they could beat these guys to Square Tower House and meet up with Maddock and Jade, but maybe he could raise them on the phone and meet them halfway, or at least get some much needed backup. His phone rang again, and he saw that it was Dane on the other line.

"Maddock! Where are you?"

"Headed up the drive to Sun Temple. Are you all right? I tried to call you just a minute ago…"

"Yeah, and you almost got me killed. Thanks for that!" Maddock started to reply but Bones cut him off. "Listen to me. The bad guys are at the Sun Temple. They're either in their car coming your way, or they'll be chasing us through the woods on your right as you come to the loop." A bullet trimmed a branch from a nearby tree. "Okay. That would be the latter."

"Can you outrun these guys for a little longer? I'll turn around and meet you on the loop road."

"Can do," Bones huffed. "I don't know if Saul is going to make it, though. Gotta' do what we gotta' do. See you there. And don't call me back." He snapped the phone closed, pocketed it, and grabbed Saul by the arm to encourage him along.

"Saul, I need you to keep running pretty much straight ahead as fast as you can. Can you do that?" He kept talking as Saul nodded. "Weave around trees when you can, but don't deviate too far from the direction we're going. Dane and Jade are going to meet us. I'll catch up with you."

The news that help was on the way seemed to give Saul renewed energy. He took off at a faster clip. Bones ducked behind the first thick tree he could find, dropped to the ground, and waited.

The guys were making no effort to be quiet. Their footfalls pounded on the hard, dry earth, and soon they came into sight. He waited for them to sprint past before coming out from behind the tree. *Two of them, one of me. Gotta' make it count.*

He took careful aim and fired.

The redhead went down, clutching at his hip. He wasn't nearly dead, but he was out of the running, as it were. Bones immediately snapped off two more shots at the second guy, but the fellow was quick. At the sound of the first shot, he had veered to the left and dove behind a tree. Bones quickly ducked out of sight before the man could return fire.

Bullets struck the ground where Bones had just been standing. He fired a few rounds at the tree where the guy had ducked, and caught a glimpse of him scrambling away. He fired another shot and the man took off running in the opposite direction. Mission accomplished. Now for the next part of the plan.

Dane whipped the car around the curve, keeping his eyes open for Bones and Saul. He caught a glimpse of something moving in the woods to his left, and then Saul staggered out onto the road. Dane hit the brakes, the screech of rubber on pavement filling the air, leapt out, and ran to meet Saul, who leaned heavily on Dane's shoulder as they headed back to the car.

"Where's Bones?"

"Don't…. know," Saul gasped, opening the back door and half-falling inside. "Sent me ahead… Heard shots and somebody yell."

"I've got to go back after him!" Dane yelled, drawing his gun. "Jade, take the wheel and get out of here if anyone shows up."

"Maddock, you can't…"

Just then a figure appeared at the edge of the woods. His casual clothes did not look nearly as sinister as the Taurus semi-automatic in his hand. He caught sight of Dane and hesitated for a moment before raising his weapon. The brief pause gave Dane the time he needed. He brought his Walther P-99 to bear and squeezed off two quick shots. The man reeled backward, firing blindly as he stumbled into the safety of the woods. Dane dropped to a knee and kept his pistol trained on the spot where the man had vanished, but he did not reappear. He was debating whether or not to pursue him into the woods when the screech of tires caught his attention.

A black Pathfinder skidded to a halt next to their car, and a familiar face appeared in the window.

"Need a ride, pardner?" Bones shouted over the cacophony of heavy metal music he was cranking.

"Bones, what did you do?"

"Stole their car. Crazy Charlie taught me how to hot wire when I was in seventh grade. Sweet ride, huh?"

Dane couldn't keep himself from laughing at his friend's shenanigans. "Let's just get out of here."

Chapter 17

Amanda closed her laptop and took a deep, calming breath. She definitely had something here. She could feel it. The next step was to convince the others that she wasn't crazy. She fished her cell phone from her purse and punched up Bones' number.

"Yo, ho! What up?"

"That is, without a doubt, the rudest greeting I have ever received," she said, her voice not matching the smile on her face. "Try again."

"Sorry, let me try again. You have reached the voice mail of Uriah Bonebrake. I'm sorry I cannot…"

"I forgot your real name is Uriah!" she said with a laugh.

"What? You think my mom named me Bones? Ah, forget it. What's up?"

"I think I've come up with some promising leads," she said. "Where are you guys?"

"We just ditched a car I stole," he said. She couldn't believe the calm in his voice. *"Now we're cruising out of the park and headed to Durango to meet up with you."*

"Great! Meet me outside the library. And try not to steal any more cars while you're at it."

"It really wasn't my fault. They shot at me."

"Sure," she said. "What happened to your rental car, anyway?"

"That's another reason I had to steal their car. They were bad guys. You wouldn't have liked them."

"I don't know," she teased. "Were any of them cute? I might want an introduction."

"I wasn't attracted to them," he said. *"I shot one in the butt. He probably won't be able to keep up with you for a while."*

"I guess I could nurse him back to health." She

couldn't believe she was engaged in such banter with a man who had just casually admitted to shooting someone and stealing his car. Of course, after what she'd experienced in the short time she'd known Bones, the extraordinary was becoming ordinary. "Then again, that's too much trouble. I guess I'll hang on to you as long as your butt is intact."

"More or less," he said. *"Mine's always been a little flat. Maddock's the one with the booty."*

She heard a raised voice and laughter in the background.

"I don't think he liked that," she said. "Forget the anatomy. Did you find it?"

"Maddock and Jade did. It was in Square Tower House. They had a bit of trouble themselves, but we came out of it all right. You said you've come up with some leads. Entertain me."

"Some of it I can't really explain until you see what I've come up with. I can tell you that I'm almost certain one of the next places we need to go is called Hovenweep."

"Hovenweep? Never heard of it."

"It's actually pretty close to Mesa Verde. It's not very well known, but it's one of the finest known examples of Anasazi architecture."

"Keep titillating me with examples of Anasazi architecture, you naughty girl. So you were able to match it up to that little image on the breastplate? The image was kind of generic, wasn't it?"

"I matched the image to ruin at Hovenweep, yes. But I have another reason for believing I'm on the right track. That's the part I'll have to show you."

"Sounds good. We'll meet you at the library as soon as we can get there." He paused. *"Amanda?"*

"Yes?"

"Be careful."

The Elder reached for the phone on the first ring, then froze. It would not do to appear too eager… or apprehensive. He gave it two more rings before casually picking up the receiver.

"Yes?" he said, feigning disinterest.

"There is a Mister Anthon on the line for you," Margaret said, her nasal voice made even more annoying by the note of suspicion that rang clear. "He declined to give his last name."

"I'll take the call," he said, adding a sigh as if not interested in speaking to this semi-anonymous caller. The truth was, this was the call he'd been waiting for.

"What do you have to report?" "Anthon" had a real name, Jarren, but he was cautious about where and when he used that name. The Elder found his anticipation cooling as he listened to the report, until it finally froze in an icy block of frustration.

"You are telling me that not only did you fail to retrieve the artifact, but Mikkel was shot and your car was stolen?"

"That is correct. The Indian used a secret passage. They got out of the ruin before we could get to them. We chased them into the woods and he somehow got behind us. That's when he shot Mikkel. As for the artifact, it did not seem to be at the site. That woman Jade must have lied to us."

"If they have it, we will find out soon enough," the Elder said.

"Can you get us out of here? The park rangers were easy enough to evade, even with Mikkel's injury, but he can't go much farther."

"It would be easier to deal with were you still in Utah. I can send the helicopter to follow your GPS signal." Another failure. Another headache.

"Perhaps I made a mistake coming after them," Jarren said. "I could go back to letting them do our work for us. It has worked well for us so far."

"Maddock has been useful," the Elder replied with restrained patience. "He is clever and resourceful, and would also be the one to go to jail if he were caught. But we are getting close to solving the puzzle, and with this friend of his involved now… well, I don't need to tell you what might happen. Maddock needs to be eliminated before the final clues fall into place, and his friend might as well be dealt with while we are at it."

"Could we not simply let him find it, and then take it away from him?"

The Elder had to tread carefully here. Only he and a very few others knew what they were truly searching for, and if Maddock found it first… well, he simply could not think about that possibility.

"Maddock has become a threat. What were the odds that he and this Bonebrake would turn out to know one another and in fact join forces? If they manage to put their knowledge together…" He shook his head. "We must take great care in eliminating both of them. And then we will complete the search on our own." It was important to avoid drawing attention just yet, but once they had it in their hands, no one would be able to stop them.

"I understand," Jarren said. "I will, of course, make it look like an accident." He paused. "Elder, with all due respect, do you still believe our source is reliable?"

The Elder's cell phone vibrated and he glanced down to see that he had received a text message. What he read made his frustration melt away. "Yes," he said. "In fact, I have just received further proof of the reliability of our source."

"How so?" Jarren asked, his increased interest clearly evident the tone of his voice.

"When you and Mikkel are picked up, I am going to have them take you directly to a place called Hovenweep."

Chapter 18

Their surroundings grew more and more barren the closer they came to Hovenweep. The land was beautiful in its own way, with occasional sprinklings of rich greenery or bright desert flowers, but it was a parched, unforgiving landscape with little in the way of trees and even less water.

"Man!" Bones said from the front passenger seat. "I thought Kansas was empty, but this… Hey! Check it out!" He held the travel brochure up in front of his face and scrutinized it with an intensity and seriousness that said to Dane that his friend was being anything but genuine. "It says here that the devil's outhouse is just a mile or two away. We should check it out."

"What's the Devil's Outhouse?" Saul asked. "Some sort of rock formation?"

"No, dude. I mean this hot, dry, empty bunch of nothing must be where the devil comes to take a dump. We might even bump into him if we're lucky. I wonder how regular he is…"

Everyone chuckled but Saul, who pursed his lips and folded his arms across his chest. His severe, dour expression now filled Dane's rear-view mirror in a most unpleasant way.

"I kind of like it out here," Dane said. "The sea is pretty desolate sometimes, and there's a heck of a lot more sameness on the water."

"Not at spring break," Bones said, still reading the brochure.

A sign directed them to Hovenweep National Monument. The small visitor's center was visible from far across the desert terrain. Several police cars, lights flashing, took up a large portion of the parking lot.

"I wonder what's up." Amanda said, leaning forward to

peek between Dane and Bones. "Whatever it is must have just happened."

"Maybe it'll be newsworthy," Bones said. "Give your editor a scoop?"

"I can't imagine something down here would newsworthy at home, but you never know," she said. She had told her editor just enough about what Bones had found at Orley's ranch, plus a few hints about the Dominion, to convince him to let her accompany Bones to follow up on the mystery.

"I guess we'll find out," Dane said, pulling into an empty space and shutting off the engine.

The heat blasted him like a furnace as soon as he stepped out of the vehicle. It was even hotter than Chaco Canyon had been, and not a breeze stirred the air. "Now I know how pottery feels," he said.

"You get used to it," Jade replied. "It's humidity that I hate. Makes you feel like you're drowning in the air. Around here it's the proverbial 'dry heat'."

No one was on duty in the visitor's center. They looked around for a while before finally concluding that everyone must be at the scene of whatever incident had brought out the police. Dane left a twenty under a paperweight on the counter and they made their way into the park.

The brick path gave way to a primitive trail that wound down into a narrow, twisting canyon, thick with sun-baked rock and desert flora. Amanda clambered up onto a nearby boulder and scanned the canyon.

"Where to, hot chick?" Bones asked.

"I'm not seeing…" Amanda's voice trailed off as she spoke.

"I thought you said you knew this was the place," Jade snapped. "You said you were certain of it. But you won't show us whatever 'proof' you claim to have." The two had argued in the car on the way to Hovenweep. Jade had already researched and subsequently eliminated this site from consideration, the architecture of the ruin with the only known solstice room in the park did not match any of the images on the breastplate.

Amanda slowly turned and stared down at Jade, waiting for a moment to make sure the other woman had finished. "It is very rude to interrupt people, Jade. Didn't your mother teach you that?"

A slender young woman in a NPS uniform appeared on the trail behind them, cutting off Jade's retort.

"May I help you?" she asked, shading her eyes against the sun as she looked up at Amanda, who remained atop the boulder, hands folded across her chest. "Are you looking for a specific ruin?"

"Yes, actually," Amanda said, hopping down. "I'm Amanda Shores from the Deseret Bugle. I'm sort of combining business with pleasure on our trip. The article I'm writing is on Anasazi solstice markers. Do you have any structures in the park of that sort?"

"Well," the woman said, taking off her brown, mesh ball cap and running her fingers through her coppery hair which she wore in a loose ponytail. "Tracking the solstice and equinox was fairly common among the Anasazi. A room would often have a small window, and the family would follow the course of the sun by marking where it struck the wall on the opposite side. Some buildings were constructed in such a way that the sun would strike a specific place on the solstice, like a corner.

"In this park, Hovenweep Castle is about the only one that fits the bill. But you can't go there." The woman's hazel eyes flitted from person-to-person in Dane's party. Her mouth was drawn in a tight, nervous frown.

"I didn't realize it was closed to the public," Amanda said.

"It isn't. I mean… it is today. I…" The woman closed her eyes and shook her head. "I apologize. I'm a little out of sorts." She took a deep breath, looked up at them and started again. "Someone vandalized it just a short while ago. In fact, they broke open the wall in what is called the Sun

Room. It's where the solstice is marked. I guess your question just threw me off."

Bones muttered something inaudible and Jade made a sound that could have been sympathy but sounded more like annoyance. Dane took a deep breath and released it slowly, taking control of his rising anger. Had there been any doubt before, it was now certain that someone else was on the same trail. And whoever they were, they had somehow gotten here first.

"Did they take anything?" Saul asked.

"There isn't really anything to take," the ranger replied, frowning. "The ruins have been empty for a long time. Strange, though. They booby-trapped it." She didn't wait for them to ask what she meant. Their quizzical expressions must have been enough. "Whoever it was placed some very large rocks above the doorway, held up with some posts, then tied a trip wire between the posts. The ranger who first investigated the damage didn't see the trip wire in the dim light."

"Is he all right?" Amanda asked.

"We think so. He'll need a few stitches in the back of his head, and he might have a concussion. Anyway, back to your question. You might be interested in the solstice marker at what we call the Holly Group. There is a sandstone wall with a number of carvings: a snake figure, two spiral circles, and some others. Nearby rock formations cause daggers of light to appear on the wall. It actually marks the summer solstice and the spring and fall equinoxes."

"Are you familiar with a ruin that looks like either of these" Amanda showed the woman a paper with the remaining undiscovered symbols from the breastplate.

The ranger scrutinized the paper, holding it close and staring intently. She broke into a sudden smile and tapped a picture of what looked like a cylinder floating on a rough sea.

"Yes! This ruin is in the Cajon group. It's a fascinating

example of Anasazi architecture. They constructed a round tower atop three very uneven boulders, yet the masonry is perfect. It's a very impressive structure, but the Cajon Group is more than eight miles from here, and not readily accessible, so it doesn't receive nearly the attention it deserves."

"Does it have a solstice room?" Dane asked, suddenly excited.

"Not a solstice *room*," she said, "but there is a solstice connection. There a set of three buildings. On every solstice and equinox, the shadows of two of the buildings meet at the corner of the third building, as if the shadows are pointing to something. Few people know about it because it isn't a true solstice marker or sun room. It might be something interesting for you to write about." She turned a hopeful smile to Amanda.

"Thank you so much," Amanda said. "I think it will be perfect."

The road leading to the Cajon group took them along a winding, heavily-rutted dirt road. It seemed much farther than the eight miles the ranger had told them it would be. They traveled in silence, knowing that whoever was after Fray Marcos' secret had somehow gotten ahead of them, and might even be waiting for them at their destination.

Dane wondered if they were even on the right track. He hoped so. It felt right, but this whole thing had been nuts. One close shave after another. How long could their luck hold?

They came upon a simple wooden sign that read, Cajon Group. Please do not leave the trail or climb on the ruins. He chuckled. Fat chance they'd be following those guidelines. He scanned the ruins for signs of their adversaries, and found them blessedly empty.

It was a small settlement. The remains of a few lodges ringed a small reservoir. While the ruins might not have been as impressive to a tourist as, say, Mesa Verde, Dane found them appealing because they had not been reconstructed by modern archaeologists, like Cliff Palace at Mesa Verde had been. What remained was in its original state, and clearly illustrated the fine craftsmanship that had been involved in its construction.

"I see the tower," Jade called, pointing across the ruin. "I'm going to go ahead and check it out." Without waiting for a reply, she strode away at a fast walk. Saul hurried after her.

Dane started to follow, but Bones touched him on the shoulder.

"Let's talk for a minute while we walk," he said in an uncharacteristically soft voice. "Try to act nonchalant, though." He nodded toward Jade and Saul as they picked their way across the rocks toward the tower.

Dane slowed his pace and fell in beside Bones and Amanda, but kept his gaze ahead of him. "What's up?" he asked.

"I'll make it quick," Bones said. "It's too big a coincidence that these people found out about Hovenweep at the same time we did, and actually managed to get here before us."

"What are you saying?" Dane asked.

"If I have the story correct," Amanda joined in, "they were at Chaco Canyon, Mesa Verde, and Hovenweep. But they weren't at Yucca House."

"True," Dane said, knowing where she was going with this and wishing he could disagree.

"And Yucca House was the only place Saul didn't know about because you figured it out while he wasn't there," Bones said.

"So you think Saul is a mole," Dane said. "I hear what you're saying, but Jade trusts him. Doesn't like him all that much, but trusts him."

"You've got to admit it makes sense," Bones said. "It would explain how they know where we're going. What I don't get, though, is what these guys need with us if they have all these resources at their disposal?"

"They need Jade," Dane said. "She's spent years researching the history and legends surrounding Cibola, and she's gotten farther than anyone before toward solving the mystery. She found the breastplate, which is more than anyone else can claim. Saul is a necessary evil- he comes with the financing."

Amanda made a "huh" sound that said she considered this merely to be further confirmation of what she already believed.

"I'm not completely sure why she needs me," Dane said. "I guess I was in the right place at the right time. I know why she wanted me to help with the well. It was a dangerous dive."

"Maybe she thinks you're 'hawt'," Bones jibed. "My sister always said you were a cutie, Maddock."

"Your sister scares me," Dane said. A former Marine, Angelica Bonebrake was nothing like her name. Hot-tempered and easily offended, she'd been in more barroom brawls than Dane and Bones combined. She was now fighting in a mixed martial arts organization under the name "Demonica" Bonebrake.

"I'd have to say that you've probably been very helpful to her," Amanda said. "You have some background in treasure hunting, and you helped her in Argentina. Why wouldn't she want you around?"

"I suppose," Dane said. He sort of hoped Jade wanted him around for more reasons than that, but he felt like a high school kid even thinking that. "So what do you want to do about it?"

"Don't tell them where the next site is until we get there," Bones said.

"That's not going to be easy," Dane said. "I don't care what we tell Saul, but Jade is technically in charge of the search. She's not going to like it."

"If Amanda is correct, we're going to need some

special gear for this next leg. We'll just play it all mysterious and maybe we'll think of something better while we're on our way to pick up what we need. Worst case scenario, we just out-and-out lie to both of them."

A triumphant cry interrupted their conversation. Dane turned to see Jade emerge from one of the ruins, a box tucked under her arm. When their eyes met, she smiled and raised the box above her head. "Got it!" she called.

Dane gave her the thumbs-up. He couldn't help but notice that Saul wore an expression that was anything but joyful. He glanced at Bones and Amanda who, by their expressions, had obviously noticed the same thing.

"Looks like he couldn't get his cronies here in time," Bones muttered. "Of course, I've been keeping an eye on him ever since we found out someone had gotten here before us."

"You missed all the fun!" Jade said as she and Saul joined them.

"Well, you know," Dane said, "I've gotten two of them already to your one. I figured it was your turn."

"Thanks. You are such a gentleman," she said with a sly grin.

"What can I say?" Dane grinned, his eyes locking with hers for a split-second.

"I don't know about you," Bones interrupted, "but I say we bolt before the bad guys stumble upon us again." He turned and headed away without explanation.

Dane looked from Jade to Saul and back to Jade again, shrugged, and followed his friend.

Back in the car, the focus was on the newly-discovered clue. Jade opened the box with great care to reveal another part of what they were now certain was a scarab.

"I can't wait until we've pieced this puzzle together," she whispered, more to herself than the others in the car. "I want to know. I *have* to know."

Dane expected Saul to ask about the next site, but he was strangely subdued. He gazed thoughtfully at the piece in

Jade's hands, saying nothing.

Dane looked toward the front of the vehicle. His eyes met Bones' in the rear-view mirror, and they both shrugged. It felt so strange, acting as if things were fine, all the while waiting for Saul to betray them. They settled into an odd silence as the barren land flew by.

Chapter 19

The silence did not last. As soon as they stopped for the equipment they would need for their next excursion, Jade and Saul had both raised questions, particularly when they saw what Dane and Bones were renting.

"All right," Jade said. "You've kept us in suspense long enough. Where are you going and why do you need diving gear?"

Amanda glanced at Bones, then to Dane. Seeing him nod, she began her explanation.

"I know that at one time you considered the possibility of the shape on the breastplate being more than just a symbol—that it could be overlaid on a map and give you the locations you sought."

"We tried that," Jade protested. "It didn't work. Some places were nowhere near any ruins."

"I know," Amanda said, her voice calm and patient. There was no sign of her usual annoyance at Jade's interruption. In fact, the longer the conversation stretched out, the longer it would be until she was forced to reveal their next destination. "When you lay it out over a modern map, it doesn't work. But…"

"But Fray Marcos didn't have a modern, scale map." Jade's voice was little more than a whisper, and her eyes faded into a distant gaze as she sunk into thought. "So if it were an overlay, it would be for a map from his day. What an idiot I am!" She snapped out of her reverie as quickly as she had faded into it. "You found a map from Fray Marcos's time?"

"A reproduction," Amanda said. "I wasn't even looking for one. I spent the morning in the library searching for hints of old legends that might give us a clue, but no luck. I gave up and was on my way out the door when I looked up, and there on the wall was a reproduction of a very old Spanish map of the region. There was a brass plate on the frame indicating it was a reproduction of a map that had been drawn by... wait for it... Fray Marcos de Niza. Best of all, there were symbols sketched all over it, including those from the breastplate."

"And they let you examine it?" Saul asked. From the tone of his voice, he seemed genuinely interested, and not the least bit annoyed that he had neither made the discovery himself nor been let in on it earlier.

"Yep," Amanda said. "I showed the librarian my press credential and a few bits and pieces of the research I had with me. I told him I was looking into Spanish contact in the region, and he was happy to take it down for me and let me examine it. Of course, he kept looking down my shirt the whole time I was examining it, so it wasn't like he was just being helpful."

"You should have punched him," Jade said.

"Hey, it got me the chance to look at the map and..." she dug into her bag and withdrew a rolled paper, "he made a copy for me. It's not to scale, but it's a pretty decent size." She unrolled the paper to reveal the map she had described.

Dane leaned forward as if drawn by some magnetic force toward what could be the key to the mystery. He reached out a hand toward the moonlike sketch of Pueblo Bonito that he had first recognized. He hesitated before his finger touched the paper, remembering that it was only a copy. Amanda had traced the outline of the shape on the breastplate, and he followed it from place-to-place until it stopped on their next stop.

"Rainbow Bridge," Amanda said. "Fray Marcos had all the right places on his map, but his distances and relative locations were way off. That's why the overlay wouldn't work on an accurate map."

"That's very, very good work," Jade said, her tone indicating a newfound respect. "But I still have two questions. Is there a solstice marker at or near Rainbow

Bridge, and why do we need dive equipment?"

"There's no solstice marker," Amanda replied. "But once I knew we were looking at Rainbow Bridge, I found that, years ago, the shadow of the arch pointed directly into the window of a nearby ruin on the day of the summer solstice."

"But there aren't any ruins in that direction," Saul said. "I checked into that a long time ago. There's only…" his voice trailed away as the color drained from his face.

"Lake Powell!" Jade shouted. "That's brilliant! When the lake was created the water covered countless ruins. No one really knows how much history lies beneath the water." She turned to Saul. "I'm feeling dumber today. How about you?"

"I couldn't believe they were able to find diving gear out here. I never even thought of Lake Powell."

"But why all the cloak and dagger?" Jade asked. "Why not just tell us?"

"I wanted the chance to explain it to you," Amanda said. "You know-- tell you the story, show you the map. If I had just announced we were headed to Lake Powell to find a submerged ruin, what would you have thought?"

"That you were wrong," Saul said. "It makes sense, though, the way you explained it." He turned to Jade, who nodded.

Dane glanced at his cell phone, ostensibly to check the time. He was pleased to see he had no coverage, as was the case in most of the places they visited. He'd have to keep an eye on Saul as they drove, but hopefully there wouldn't be many opportunities to contact the outside world.

Rainbow Bridge stood in stark relief against the cornflower sky. More than three-hundred feet high, and nearly as wide, it was the largest natural bridge in the world. Dane had never heard of this marvel of nature, but now he wondered how it was he had never learned of it. It was somehow magnificent in its simplicity. He continued to be amazed that someone who loved the water as much as he did could be charmed by this parched land.

"Sort of makes you homesick for St. Louis," Bones said, sidling up next to him and admiring the giant stone arch.

"How can you be homesick for somewhere you've never lived?" Dane asked, not taking his eyes off the bridge.

"Same way you can call a girl a 'friend' who was obviously much more."

"What?" Dane turned and looked at Bones in genuine puzzlement. "I don't get it."

"I've just realized how big a mistake you made with Kaylin," Bones said. "Don't get me wrong. Jade's hot and smart and feisty, but that's what you've got me for. Kaylin's the girl for you. You should call her."

"Besides the fact that this is a weird time to be talking to me about this," Dane said, "do you really think you're qualified to give me relationship advice when you've never stayed with the same woman for more than four months?"

"Exactly," Bones said. "I know more about women than you do because I've had relationships with about a hundred times more women than you. And my record is seven months."

"So tell me; exactly how long was your second-longest relationship?"

"Nine and-a-half weeks," Bones said. "But we packed a lot of living into that time, so it really counts as about four months."

Dane shook his head. He wouldn't even have this conversation with anyone else, but Bones had long ago earned the right to say whatever was on his mind. Of course, Bones said what was on his mind whether he had the right or not.

"Look, Maddock. You and I both know that the only reason it didn't work with Kaylin was because she was the first one after Melissa."

Dane was proud of himself for not wincing at the mention of his deceased wife's name.

"But why the hell are we having this conversation here and now?"

"Because it needs to be said and I might forget to say it later. You know how distracted I get sometimes. Seriously, I see there's something between you and Jade. Might just be potential, but it's there, and that's cool. But she's not the port where you want to drop anchor."

"You're not you when you're with her. Well, you're you, but not all of you. I don't know if it's because she's so smart, or exotic, or whatever, but I can already see that you take a step back when you're around her. You're like eighty percent of you when she's around. You're too badass for that. Besides, my girlfriend thinks she's a bitch, and I don't want you bringing her to the wedding." He turned on his heel and strode away. "Time to dive!" he called back to Dane.

"Whoa! What…? Did you say wedding?" He followed Bones away from the arch toward the lake where the rest of their party waited.

"Not so loud," Bones said. "I haven't let anyone in on this little secret of mine."

"Have you at least let Amanda know?" Dane kidded.

"She doesn't yet know that she's in love with me," Bones said. "But she'll figure it out. They all do eventually." Bones gave him an evil grin. "Just kidding. I do like her, though, and I'll probably keep her around for a while. It would make things a lot less tense if those two would get along. Maybe I could tell Jade we're engaged, and then she'd lay off."

Dane threw his head back and laughed, clapping his friend on the shoulder. There was no one quite like Bones, and having him here made everything better, even if he did occasionally cause Dane to ponder things he'd rather not think about.

The water was pleasantly cool, and Danes knifed through it like a dolphin at play. It felt so good to be back in fins and a mask, even if it was only for a brief lake dive. In no time, he and Bones had crossed the lake and were now treading water below the exact spot Amanda had indicated. They double-checked their tanks and valves, waved to the three who waited ashore, and dove.

The sun filtered through the greenish water in wavy beams of gold, putting him in mind of a jungle far away and a long time ago. He suppressed that unbidden memory before it was fully formed, and locked it back where his other demons were imprisoned. He supposed he'd have to exorcise them some day, but not today.

They worked their way along the face of the submerged canyon, their lights playing across the rugged surface. It was surprisingly free of silt and debris. The sunlight played out quickly, leaving them in a frustrating half-light that played tricks on their eyes and turned shadows into phantom doors and windows that vanished under closer scrutiny.

They reached the bottom and turned to ascend, spreading out to cover a new swath of rock. Bones hated this kind of methodical search, but Dane enjoyed it. There was something about the precise, leave-no-stone-unturned method that appealed to him. It amused him that he and Bones could both be former military, but so different in their approaches. Dane could have been a career officer had he wanted. Bones was fortunate to have avoided being kicked out of the Navy entirely. He'd been good at what he did, but lived on the edge of serious trouble.

Three passes later, Dane was growing concerned that they might not have sufficient air for what was becoming a lengthy search when his light struck something that was definitely not a natural formation. Swimming closer, he saw the keyhole-shaped doorway of an Anasazi dwelling. He blinked his dive light at Bones until he received a return signal, and waited as his friend joined him. They shone their lights in and played them through the small room. It wouldn't be much to search, but there were other problems. One concern would be the inevitable silt that would be stirred up as they entered. The other was the size of the doorway. Dane would be able to squeeze through, but not with his tank strapped to his back.

Getting Bones' attention, he traced the shape of the doorway, pointed to his tank, and drew his finger across his throat. Bone nodded and immediately helped Dane remove his tank. Once free, Dane took a breath of air, exhaled, and squeezed through the opening. They had not worn dive suits for what was to be such a brief dive in relatively warm water. The coarse rock tore his t-shirt and scraped his shoulders as he forced with way through. He managed to bark his shin for good measure as he swam inside. Once in, he turned back to the doorway, where Bones held his tank for him to take another breath.

The decades of silt that had blanketed the inside of the ruin now churned throughout every square inch of open space, limiting visibility to less than a foot. He began with the corners, feeling blindly until he collided with the far wall, working his way along the bottom edge. The right corner revealed nothing. The back wall seemed to be hewn into the rock of the canyon wall. There were no stones to break loose, and no sign of Fray Marcos's symbol.

He swam back to the doorway, startling Bones who jerked as Dane appeared from the storm of silt. As he took a few breaths, waiting for his heart to stop racing, he shook his head to indicate he had found nothing.

A search of the other corner was no more fruitful. Based on their relative locations, he knew the shadow of Rainbow Bridge would strike the lower part of the back wall, so he took time to swim slowly across the back of the room, scouring the wall with his fingertips, hoping to feel if not see the cross and clover he sought.

By the time he had crossed the room, his lungs were screaming for air and his head felt like it would explode. He had always been able to hold his breath longer than anyone he knew, even the other SEALs with whom he had served, but this time he had pushed himself to his limit. He turned and pushed off from the wall, shooting toward the doorway.

Red light exploded in his head as he crashed into the opposite wall. He involuntarily sucked in and had to suppress a cough as water burned his sinuses. He had miscalculated. The doorway could not be far, but where was it? He could see almost nothing in the cloud of particles that roiled around him. Had he overshot his target, or fallen short? His ears now rang from the combined effects of oxygen deprivation and the blow to his head.

Calming himself, he placed his hands on the walls and felt his way along. His body screamed for air, and it was all he could do to maintain control. It was a small space, he reasoned, and he would find the doorway soon.

His field of vision narrowed and the world was tinted red. He felt his lungs cramp, and he began to fade.

And then a beam of light sliced through water directly above him. Bones must have known it had been too long and shone his flashlight through the hole to serve as a homing beacon for Dane. Swimming up to the doorway, he felt a surge of relief as he bit down on the valve and felt blessed air fill his lungs again. It didn't take him long to feel revitalized and ready to renew the search. *Where to look next?*

He tried to visualize the position of the sun and the arch. Where would the shadow fall? The angle would be steep. Perhaps not the corner...

He remembered the dive he and Jade had made together in the well. Fray Marcos' symbol had been in the center of the floor. Of course, that had been a trap, breaking the seal to a drain. That wouldn't be the case this time. There was no way anyone could have had the foresight to know that these dwellings would someday be flooded by a man-made lake. In any case, it wouldn't hurt to check, and he was out of ideas.

A few more breaths, and he was back to searching.

With patient care his fingers probed the floor, searching every crack and indentation until he felt a circle. Hastily he scrubbed the area around the shape until he had uncovered a clover. This was it!

He needed two more trips back for air before he could finish the job, but soon he and Bones were headed back across the lake, another box secure in his dive bag.

Chapter 20

Dane and Bones sat in reclining pool chairs, soaking up the moonlight and the aroma of sage drifting on the dry breeze, barely suppressing the chlorine smell of the hotel pool. He trailed his finger absently across the condensation on his bottle of Dos Equis and pondered their next move.

"I suppose if I was a chick I'd say something like 'what are you thinking' or something equally annoying," Bones said. "Spill it, bro."

"We've hit a wall," Dane said. "We've found all the pieces to the puzzle we're going to find, but the clues don't lead us anywhere."

"Au contraire," Bones said, "they will eventually lead us somewhere just as soon as we figure out where the starting point might be."

"And therein lies the problem," Dane said. "And I can't shake the feeling that the other side might already know, and the only thing holding them back is waiting for Saul to get them the translation of the final pieces of the scarab."

"If that's the situation, the only thing we can do is get there first. At least we have a head start on them. We need to figure out the next step, and make certain that no more of Jimmy's translations fall into Saul's hands. This is going to be a race." Bones took a gulp of his Cherry Coke and belched the letters A through F. "I never make it to 'G'," he muttered. "So, have you thought any more about what I said this afternoon?"

"You mean about you getting married?" Dane said.

"No, about you and…"

"I know what you mean," Dane said, cutting him off in mid-sentence. He realized he had made a decision. "I've thought about it. Maybe it's not that Jade is wrong for me.

Maybe I just need to quit being such a wuss around women. Melissa wouldn't want me to spend the rest of my life moping around. If the situation was reversed, I'd want her to have a good life, and to keep being herself."

"I knew you'd get there eventually," Bones said. "And thank you for not making me say it."

"Thank you for making me figure it out. Matter of fact, I'm going to go talk to Jade." He rose from his chair, chugged the last of his beer, and made it all the way to H.

"Show off," Bones said.

"Anyway, I'll catch you later."

Dane knocked on Jade's door. He didn't know if it was the beer, his epiphany, or both, but he felt… different. Like whatever decision he made right now would be the right one.

You're not you when you're with her… you take a step back.

Bones was right. Jade was smart and sexy and a pain in the neck, but she wasn't too good for him.

Jade smiled and wrapped her lithe, brown arms around his neck, pulling him close.

"I was just about to come and get you," she breathed. "Your friend Jimmy just e-mailed me. He's been looking at the pictures Bones took and he thinks there's a connection to our mystery. He says he'll have something for us maybe by tomorrow. He's being a bit mysterious, but I get the impression he knows something already."

"Jimmy's like that," Dane said. He had taken the look in her eyes and the hug as happiness at seeing him, and he was disappointed to realize that she *was* happy to see him, but only because of the new development in the mystery. "He likes to drop the bomb on you, then step back and take his bows. This piecemeal translation has probably been driving him crazy."

"Well I hope he's…" Her gaze locked with his and her expression turned serious. "What's wrong?

"Nothing," Dane said. His heart pounded out a relentless beat and his stomach felt like frozen cement. If he didn't do it now, he'd never do it. "I just wanted to give you something." Before he could change his mind he cupped her chin in one hand, wrapped the other arm around her waist, drew her close, and kissed her.

He felt her stiffen and for a moment he thought he'd made a mistake of epic proportions, but then she relaxed. Her lips responded to his with a gentle insistence. Her fingers tangled in his hair and she drew away, kissing his cheek, his neck, his chest. He groaned and pulled her closer, pressing his body against hers.

She drew back long enough to help him out of his shirt before leaping fully into his arms, wrapping around him like a hungry parasite. For a brief moment, he was once again struck by her scent. It was like sage and cinnamon, and for some odd reason he found that quite remarkable. That was his last rational thought for some time, as he lifted her off her feet and carried her to the bed, where they collapsed into a writhing tangle of arms, legs, bed sheets, and discarded clothing.

He awoke in the semi darkness with Jade leaning over him, speaking softly. He grinned and stretched luxuriously.

"Aren't you tired?" he asked.

"Get up," she whispered. "I've gotten a message from your friend Jimmy."

There was something in her voice that brought him instantly awake. There was a sense of urgency, and an underlying strain that puzzled him. It must be because of Saul. If Jimmy had made a breakthrough, she'd want to follow up on it before Saul could find out.

"What is it?" he asked, rolling out of bed and searching around for his clothes.

"He's found a connection between our mystery and the discovery Bones made. I'll tell you about it in the car. Come on!"

He barely had time to get dressed before she ushered him out of the room, and hurried him to the car. Ten minutes later they were winging down the road, the aroma of cheap, gas station coffee assaulting his senses.

"So, are you going to finally tell me about this breakthrough?"

Jade paused before explaining.

"The writing on the disc Bones found was not exactly in Hebrew. Or, it was, but it was a cipher. Jimmy suspected as much when he first tried to translate it, so he set some computer programs to trying to crack it, and went back to our puzzle. The computer managed to crack the code late last night. The disc tells a very interesting story." She bit her lip, her eyes fixed on the road ahead.

"So, are you going to tell me or not?"

"Sorry," she said. "I'm just preoccupied." She paused again, as if deciding how to proceed. "Have you ever heard of Akhenaten?"

"Wasn't he some sort of Egyptian sun god or something?"

"No quite. Akhenaten was pharaoh from about 1350 to 1336 b.c.. You might have heard of his wife Nefertiti."

"Okay, but I thought she was a fertility goddess or sex symbol or something."

"Maddock," she sighed, "it's one thing to not know, but you don't have to advertise it. Anyway, Akhenaten is known as the heretic pharaoh, or the enemy, because he tried to convert Egyptians to monotheism. He declared that the sun disc Aten, from whom he derived his name, was the one true god. This didn't set well with the polytheistic Egyptian people, and when Akhenaten died, there was a backlash against everything associated with his rule. Buildings were demolished and all ties to his religion were severed. Even his remains and those of his family disappeared. Egypt returned to what they considered normal."

"Wait a minute," Dane said, remembering something Bones had once told him. "Wasn't he the guy with the weird body? He had feminine and masculine features, and some people think he might have had a disease?"

"Very good," Jade said. "You're smarter than I thought." Her laugh sounded forced. "There's a picture of him." She indicated a printout lying on the seat in between them.

The image was a familiar one, now that he saw it. The pharaoh was rendered with an elongated face and pear-shaped body.

"I remember him now. Bones thinks he's an alien."

"Oh, good Lord," Jade groaned. "Does Bones always connect everything to aliens?"

"Not everything," Dane replied, trying to lighten Jade's mood. "He's pretty sure the Loch Ness Monster, Bigfoot, and Elvis are earthlings."

"Lovely. At any rate, the symbol of Aten was a disc with rays beaming down, each with a hand at the end. Sound familiar?"

"Sure," he said, immediately remembering the image on the gold disc Bones had recovered. "So, Bones' disc has an Egyptian symbol on the back. Our puzzle is carved into a dismembered scarab, which is also Egyptian. Is that it?"

"Nope, there's more. The translation of the writing on the disc tells the story of the downfall of Akhenaten. He and his most faithful follower recovered the treasures of the temple at Amarna and fled into the desert, where they lived in exile in the Sinai for forty years. He continued to teach his monotheistic faith, and taught them ten laws for living, based on Spell 125 of the Egyptian Book of the Dead. They continued to revere him as the "mose" or "heir" to the throne."

"Whoa. Ten rules for living… the Sinai… mose… You mean Moses…"

"Moses and Akhenaten are one and the same, at least according to the writing on the disc. They eventually settled in what we know as the Holy Land. Aten became Yahweh, or "I Am," and the Jewish faith grew from the seeds planted by Akhenaten."

"Unbelievable." Dane was stunned by what Jade was telling him. Of course, the story on the disc could be completely wrong, but he had seen enough on his last foray into the Middle East to make him realize that anything could be possible. "So, you're saying that God isn't God? That he's just this Aten in new robes?"

"I'm not saying that at all. In fact, I'm not much for religion one way or the other. You could look at is as Aten being the beginning of understanding the true nature of God. A polytheistic, pagan people were discovering the underlying truth. Maybe Yahweh, or God, is the culmination of that spiritual journey."

"I hear you. Anyway, is there a connection to our scarab other than the fact that they're both Egyptian artifacts with Hebrew writing engraved on them?"

"You left out the fact that both are in the middle of the American Southwest, and based on some of the cave artwork, both are associated with Spaniards. But yes, there's more.

"Akhenaten, now known as Moses, wanted to develop a cultural identity apart from that of Egypt. He ordered the treasures hidden away, and appointed a sect of followers to be the keepers of the secret. This group, called the Essenes, recorded the secrets of the treasure on a scroll made of copper."

"The Copper Scroll," Dane breathed.

"It's been generally assumed that the Copper Scroll leads, or led, to the treasure of the temple at Jerusalem, but the Egyptian connection makes sense. Another Essene scroll, the Temple Scroll, gives dimensions of a temple that coincide nicely with records of the size of the temple at Amarna."

"And the connection to our mystery?" Dane still wasn't seeing the link, though he was fascinated by the story Jade was spinning.

"Jimmy also discovered that the writing on our scarab consists entirely of quotes lifted directly from the Copper Scroll."

"What? But…" His mind buzzed with conflicting thoughts. Why would Fray Marcos come to America to hide pieces of a larger treasure map that led to an Egyptian treasure hidden in Israel? What would be the point?

"This is where the cave art comes in. Legend has it that the Knights Templar found the temple treasure, and carried it back to Europe. Another legend, one given less credence over the years, holds that the treasure was brought to the New World and hidden away. The idea seemed absurd. Why would anyone do that? But if you believe the story on the disc, well…"

"There's no way they could have revealed to the world that Moses was an Egyptian pharaoh who worshiped the sun," Dane finished, the pieces now fitting firmly in place. "They couldn't bring themselves to destroy it, so they hid it in America. And that's why Fray Marcos left the clues. He understood how dangerous the secret was, but he wasn't willing to let it be lost forever."

"I think so too," Jade said. "The cave art depicts a group of Spaniards, transporting sacks of something a great distance. Obviously, someone thought this was worth recording. Fortunately for us, landforms in the pictures are very distinctive. Whoever made those images knew the place quite well. Jimmy was able to pinpoint it to a place in southern Utah."

"And our clue?"

"Snatches of phrases from the copper scroll, carefully selected to guide the seeker once they've found the site where the treasure is hidden. And you'll never believe the name of the place."

"Umm… Jerusalem National Park."

"Close," she said, turning to look at him for the first time. "It's called Zion."

Chapter 21

Bones re-read the printout of the e-mail from Jimmy. It was unbelievable. Could it possibly be true? Moses a pharaoh? The legendary Seven Cities of gold merely steps on a journey to a single, fabulous treasure? He checked his watch. It was early, but not too early to wake Maddock.

He rapped on the door that connected their rooms. Amanda groaned and turned toward him.

"What are you doing?" she moaned. "It's five o'clock."

"Solving a mystery," he said. "Get out of bed and I'll tell you all about it." He knocked again on Dane's door, but no reply. "I'm going to get Maddock, and I'll tell you both."

"Maybe he's in Jade's room." Amanda said, rubbing her eyes with her fists.

"Yeah, I'll check." Bones replied. He hurried out the door, but encountered Saul almost at once.

"Have you seen Jade?" Saul asked.

"Nope. You seen Maddock?"

"He's gone too?" Saul looked around, as if Dane or Jade might be hiding in the parking lot. "Oh crap."

"What's up?" His distrust of Saul notwithstanding, there was something in the man's voice that worried Bones. Saul met his gaze with a long, level look.

"Can I come in? There are some things I need to tell you. I wish I had done it before, but…" He shrugged and set his jaw, still looking Bones in the eye.

"Sure," Bones said. "Just let me make sure Amanda is decent." Amanda had dressed and was brushing her teeth, so Bones let Saul in. She joined them around the small table and waited for Saul to explain himself.

"I don't exactly know where to start," he said. "Have either of you heard of the Deseret Dominion?"

Bones shifted uncomfortably in his seat and looked at

Amanda, who nodded.

"Okay," Saul said. "The thing is… Jade works for them."

"What the…" Bones said, sitting up straight. "But we thought you…" *I stopped myself about three words too late*, he thought as Saul's eyes darted from Bones to Amanda and back.

"Me? Hell no. I'm working against them." He saw the skeptical expressions on their faces and hurried on with his explanation. "I didn't know at first. She seemed okay, but I got suspicious when I started noticing some of the calls and e-mail she got."

"What about it?" Bones asked, still not sure whether or not to believe Saul. "What made you suspicious?"

"I recognized some names." Saul hung his head. "My dad was in the Dominion. I thought he was out of it, but it's too big a coincidence that he put so much money into Jade's expedition and set me up to work with her. I guess he's still involved." He took a deep breath, but kept looking down. "Anyway, when those guys showed up at Chaco Canyon, I knew. I didn't say anything to Maddock, since I didn't really know him, but it was kind of obvious what was going on."

"And what exactly were you going to do about it?" Amanda asked.

"I had hoped to stop her from getting some of the clues. Maybe I could beat her to them. I thought that if I could keep her from passing complete information to the Dominion, I could keep them from doing whatever it was they are trying to do. I even tried to steal the breastplate from Maddock's boat back when this all started, not knowing Jade had taken it with her after all. Of course, I didn't have a plan for what I would have done with it. If nothing else, I was hoping that, when the time came, I could take the information and get there first. But since the first few pieces turned up, I haven't had a chance to do anything. It's like you've been keeping me…" He looked from one to the other, understanding dawning in his eyes. "Oh."

"We've suspected you. No lie. But I don't know," Bones said. "How do we know you're not the one in the Dominion, and you're just trying to get information from us?"

"Oh my…" Amanda's voice was cold with realization. "Bones, I'm so stupid. It never occurred to me before. Jade teaches at Central Utah University."

"And your point is?"

"When Orley was taken from his ranch, where did they have him?"

"Holy crap," Bones muttered. Orley had been at the Central Utah University Neuropsychotic Institute. Even had he been aware of Jade's affiliation with the university, it was unlikely he would have made the connection, but it did seem to fit with what Saul was telling them.

"That's one reason to believe me," Saul said, "but I have another." He dug into his pocket and produced something wrapped in a handkerchief. "The Dominion didn't get the Ship Rock piece. I did." He unfolded the cloth to reveal the missing piece of the scarab. "There you go. My cards are on the table. Maybe I'm nuts for telling you this, but now that we're at the end, and Jade's disappeared, I don't know what to think. I've got this crazy idea that she and the Dominion know where Cibola is."

"They do," Bones said. With numb fingers he slid Jimmy's e-mail over to Saul. The other man's eyes widened as he read. Bones was cold all over. How could they have been so wrong? And what about Maddock?

"He blind-copied this to you," Saul said. "So Jade doesn't know anyone else has the information. And we have the missing piece to the puzzle. If Jimmy can take care of the translation, we might have a small advantage."

"Saul," Amanda said, "what is it that the Dominion wants? What are they trying to achieve with all of this?"

"I don't know everything, and I can't be one hundred percent sure. It's a long, unbelievable story that I can tell you while we drive" Saul said. He sprang to his feet, almost toppling his chair. "I've made a scan of the artifact. We'll send it to Jimmy, find a car, and get the hell out of here. Maybe there's time to save Maddock."

"What do you mean, 'save'?" The disbelief that numbed Bones' senses was melting into anger.

"It's the endgame," Saul said. "Maddock was helpful, but Jade doesn't need him anymore. The Dominion won't let him live once they have the prize… if he lasts that long."

They didn't waste any time gathering their things. Bones grabbed Dane's belongings as well. We'll catch up with them, he thought. *Amanda was right. The woman is bad news.*

Saul was back in their room in five minutes with his laptop in hand and his backpack slung over his shoulder.

"I e-mailed the scan to Jimmy," he said. "They don't have cabs out here in the middle of nowhere, but I checked and there's a rental agency a couple of miles from here. We'll be their first customers of the morning." His smile was grim.

Bones looked up at the dark sky and imagined the time slipping away as Jade drove Dane right into the hands of the Dominion while the three of them hoofed it down the highway in search of a rental car. A single pair of headlights sliced through the darkness. As the vehicle drew closer, it slowed, then cut a sharp right into the hotel parking lot. Tires squealed and kicked up a cloud of the fine dust that coated the asphalt. His instincts told him that something was wrong. He grabbed Amanda and yanked her down as he ducked behind the nearest car. He opened his mouth to warn Saul, but he was too late.

A wet, slapping sound that Bones knew all too well preceded the muffled pop of silenced pistol. Saul grunted and staggered back. As if that first shot were a starter's pistol, a torrent of bullets sizzled through the air. Glass shattered, bullets ricocheted off of the brick wall, and Saul slid to the ground, his blood pooling around him, looking black in the dim light. The Dominion had arrived.

Trying to keep low and remain out of sight, Bones led Amanda along the row of parked cars. There were only four. The car that had zipped into the parking lot, a dark sedan, screeched to a halt. All four doors burst open and men leapt out.

The last car in the row was an old mini-van. "When I start shooting, you run," he whispered to Amanda. She nodded. He held his Glock in his right hand and with his left he reached into his ankle holster and withdrew the snub-nosed .22 magnum mini-revolver that he carried for special occasions. He placed his left foot on the front bumper and launched himself onto the hood. A second leap and he was on the roof. He opened fire, dropping the two closest Dominion men, who were still scanning the parking lot, and didn't expect an attack from above. The other two returned fire, their reckless shots well off-target. Lights were coming on inside many of the hotel rooms, but no one came outside.

Bones leapt down into the bed of an adjacent pickup truck and squeezed off two more shots, causing the men to hit the ground and roll. He was taking a risk exposing himself like this, but he had seen how few shots had hit Saul, and concluded that these were not soldiers. Hired killers they might be, but these sorts of toughs never found themselves in real combat situations. He'd take the battle to them. Lying flat on his stomach, he slid to the end of the truck bed, raised up, and peered over the edge. The remaining two men had vanished into the shadows. Where were they?

A spare tire lay loose in the bed next to him. Cautiously, he tipped it up on its side and gave it a shove. It bounced once and rolled across the darkened lot. Dull pops sounded and bullets sprayed the blacktop all around the rolling tire. Bones spotted muzzle flash from a dark corner near the ice maker, and squeezed off three quick shots. He heard a shout of pain and surprise. He had hit one of them.

He ducked and rolled out of the truck just as bullets tore through the side of the truck near the spot he had just vacated.

Staying low and keeping to the darkest shadows, Bones crept forward, keeping a sharp eye out for any movement. Which way to go? A loud crash behind him made him whirl about, dropping to one knee, both guns at the ready. Instead of someone about to shoot him, he saw a man sprawled face-down on the ground, a hotel maid's cart lying on top of him. Amanda came charging down a nearby stairwell.

"Their car is still running!" she shouted. "Let's go!" Sprinting past the stunned man, she took Bones by the elbow and tugged him toward the waiting vehicle.

Bullets zinged past Bones' heel. One of the guys was still alive. He fired toward the hollow sound of the silenced pistol, which bought them enough time to leap into the Dominion car, slam it into reverse, and hurtle backward through the parking lot, zigzagging as bullets whizzed past. One pinged off the roof and another shattered the passenger side mirror, but nothing hit the windshield. Every moment took him farther from danger. He kept half an eye out for his assailant to come after him. Bones wished he would try it, but the guy was at least bright enough to remain hidden.

He didn't bother to slow down or turn around when they hit the highway, but kept it in reverse and floored it, hurtling backward down the narrow, two-lane highway before taking it into a controlled skid and bringing the front end about.

"Do you like my fancy driving?" he asked as they barreled down the road.

"That," she breathed, "was closer than the hospital. I didn't know what I was going to do. I couldn't just run away and leave you there, so I went up to the second floor and tried to keep a lookout, but I lost sight of you. And then that guy came out of the shadows, and the maid cart was there, so I…" She broke off, burying her face in her hands.

Bones reached over and laid a hand on her shoulder. He hated it when women cried, and hated it even more when it was his fault, which was frequently the case.

"It's okay," he said. "I'm all right."

"You're an ass is what you are," Amanda said, slapping his hand away and sitting up straight. Anger had replaced the fear in her eyes, and Bones was stunned to see that she was not crying. This woman was something else. "You could have given me one of those guns and I could have shot him instead."

Bones was momentarily speechless. She wanted to do what?

"Forget it," Amanda said. "I know you're trained and you can probably shoot better on the run with your left hand than I can taking aim with both hands. I just wanted to help you. It sucks being scared for someone, and it's worse when you can't do anything for them."

"You were great," Bones said, trying to deal with the torrent of emotions that surged through him. "Tell you what. When this is all over, I'll take you sidearm shopping. I'll even train you."

"Promise?" Amanda's tone made it clear that she would hold him to it. "And you'll let me use it to shoot people?"

"Do you have certain people in mind, or just random people?"

"You know what I mean. If something like that," she tilted her head back in the direction from which they had come, "ever happens again, are you going to let me fight, or are you going to make me run away?"

"I…" His first instinct had been to tell her what she wanted to hear. He knew, though, that Amanda would detect his lie. She was the sharpest woman he'd ever known. Plus, for the first time in his life, the idea of lying to a woman really bothered him. "I promise that if it makes sense for you to… shoot people, I'll let you fight. But you're going to have to promise me that you won't argue if I tell you otherwise." He could tell she was going to protest, but he raised his voice. "I'm not old-fashioned about much, but your safety comes before mine. Always."

"Why? Because I'm a woman?"

"Because I like having you around. It would kind of suck if something happened to you."

· Amanda unbuckled her seat belt, scooted up next to him, and wrapped her arms around his neck.

"You really *are* an ass," she whispered, and laid her head on his shoulder. They stayed that way, silent and content as they hurtled through the darkness toward the unknown.

Chapter 22

The bouncing vehicle jolted Dane to full alertness. He scanned the barren landscape. Red rocks and sparse hills surrounded them, morning light casting their surroundings in a faint, golden hue. There was no road in sight.

"Sorry. Didn't mean to doze off on you," he murmured, rubbing his eyes. It was not like him to fall asleep like that, especially after the startling revelations from earlier. "Where are we?"

"We're close to Zion," Jade said. She sounded oddly subdued, so unlike her excited, almost manic behavior of earlier. Of course, she had been driving since early morning and was operating on very little sleep. "I had to go off-road a bit. This will take us in through the back door. Assuming, of course, you're up for a bit of a hike."

"Always ready," he said, though his head still felt thick from his nap, as if his brain was filled with molasses. "Just need to finish waking up."

"If you don't have any coffee left, you can have the rest of mine." Jade inclined her head toward the two Styrofoam cups in the console.

Dane swirled the contents of his cup before drowning the three remaining lukewarm swallows. One glance at the clock told him he had been asleep for only about a half-hour.

Jade brought the vehicle to a halt and hopped out before reaching into the back seat and grabbing a paper bag she had brought from the convenience store. Dane assumed it held bottles of water for their hike.

They started walking. There didn't seem to be any distinct landforms by which to pinpoint their location, but Dane trusted that Jade knew where she was going.

"There's a cleft in the rock over there." She indicated a

spot in the distance where a dark, vertical line cleft the sun-illuminated stone.

He had to turn sideways and exhale in order to squeeze through the narrow opening, but on the other side it widened enough for two people to walk abreast. The way was strewn with loose rock and choked with cactus, but the slope was gentle and the path straight.

He shook his head, trying to clear the cobwebs. The moment of alertness he had felt when he first awoke was long gone, replaced by a feeling of increased heaviness, as if his head was slowly filling with cement. He stumbled and barely caught himself before his face hit the path.

"You all right?" Jade asked. His sluggishness and heavy feeling made her words sound cold and flat.

"Yeah," he replied. "I think… I think I need to sit for a minute."

"There's an outcropping up here where you can get out of the sun. Come on." She took him by the hand and guided him like a child up to the sheltered overhang where she settled him against the bare rock. "Close your eyes," she whispered.

He fought to stay awake, but his eyelids drooped, and Jade faded from sight.

It was hot… dry… he was in the depths of a canyon. A winged, skeletal figure hovered over him, spreading its arms to welcome him into its deadly embrace.

"Aaah!" Red light flashed across his vision as he bolted upright and cracked his head on the low-hanging rock. "Stupid!" He rubbed his head and looked around for Jade, but there was no sign of her. He searched the defile, calling her name. No luck. Had she gone on ahead? Surely not, but who could say? Perhaps she had left a note in the car.

Utterly confused, he made his way back the way he and Jade had come earlier. Heat ripped up from the parched earth, the late morning sun hung angry in the sky. He rubbed a dry palm across his equally parched forehead. He was dehydrated. The single cup of coffee he had drunk hours ago was not remotely enough in this climate. On the positive side, he felt much more alert than he had upon arrival. His relief was short-lived, as he squeezed out of the rocky cleft to discover that their car was gone.

His mind raced. What had happened to her? She wouldn't have just left him. They must have found her, and she had hidden the fact that he was with her. That was the only possible explanation. So what was he going to do about it?

He considered his options, which were few. He didn't know how far it was back to the road, or exactly which direction they had come. For that matter, there was no telling how many back roads Jade had taken before leaving the road entirely. Were he to make it back to any sort of road, he wouldn't know where to go from there. The wide open spaces of the American southwest meant one could seemingly go forever without a glimpse of civilization. That had, for the most part, appealed to him until this moment.

The only thing that made sense to him was to keep on going. Jade had indicated that their destination was within walking distance. His limited examination of the map on the way here, and his estimation of the distance they had traveled provided a degree of confirmation. If Jade had been kidnapped, they would expect her to lead them to whatever waited in Zion. His only chance was to find her there. He checked his cell phone just in case, but he had no coverage, as usual.

His thoughts flew unbidden to a moment, years ago. He remembered the sound of Melissa's voice, the scream the crash… He had stood there staring numbly at his cell phone, knowing his wife was dead, and he could do nothing about it. It had been completely beyond his control, but this was not beyond his control. He would find Jade and bring her back. Setting determined eyes on the horizon, he set off.

It was not long before the intense sun led him to tie his

handkerchief over his head like a turban. The thin fabric was of little help in the heat, but it did serve to deflect the worst of the sun's rays. The wise course would be to find a bit of shade in which to wait out the hottest part of the day, and travel in the evening and at night, but he could not spare the time. He did not know exactly how far he was going, or where for that matter, but the fact that Jade had brought no water with them when they left the car indicated that she did not expect it to be far.

The shimmering waves of hot air seemed to resist his every step, as though he was swimming in molten lead. Sweat beaded on his forehead, and he wiped it off and licked it off his palm. I need to conserve every bit of moisture I can, he thought. He hoped it would not be far. He did not know what he would find when he caught up with Jade and whoever had taken her, but he was certain he would need every ounce of strength he could muster.

The path he walked was not truly a path at all, but a low area among the hills and mounds of rock, where water flowed through during the rare downpour that touched the desert with its brief, violent kiss. He came upon a bit of shade, and rested for a moment, leaning against the rough, dry rock. His eyes searched the grounds for any bit of vegetation he could chew on for moisture, but he found nothing.

He continued to walk. The baked stone beneath his feet seemed to melt the soles of his shoes, and he imagined he was walking in mud, though it was only fatigue that made him feel like his feet were sticking to the earth. He came around a sharp bend, where the ground fell away to a narrow cleft where rocks and debris choked the bottom of the passage. His eyes fell on dark sand, and his heart pounded a hopeful beat. He half-climbed, half-fell to the bottom, and tumbled to his knees. He burrowed deep into the sand, working his way deeper until… yes! Moisture!

He continued to dig until his fingers struck rock. He twisted his arm back-and-forth, digging a tiny well for water to gather. He scooped up a bit of dirty, tepid water and carefully poured it into his mouth. He resisted the urge to gulp the water, instead letting it trickle back into his throat, keeping the grit and sand on his tongue. The hole yielded no more than another thimbleful, which dripped onto his swollen tongue. The moist sand he patted onto his sunburned arms and face. It did not come anywhere close to making him feel refreshed, but the worst of the heat seemed to dissipate. Renewed, he scooped up a couple of small, round, pebbles and popped them into his mouth before continuing his trek.

His pace grew torpid as he trudged across the unforgiving land. Concerns over lack of water and directions lay thin above the underlying fear that he might already be too late. What would they do with Jade once they found whatever it was they were looking for? He couldn't permit those thoughts. She had to be all right. She had to be.

By the angle of the sun it was well past noon. He hadn't the energy to even consult his watch. For the first time, he felt hope wane. Had he missed a turn? Was there a sign of which Jade had been aware that he had not? His fatigue and thirst made it increasingly difficult to fight off despair. He needed something to drink. He remembered his survival training, and groaned at the most immediate possibility. He could drink his own urine. It would be disgusting, and he had nothing in which to collect, but it would keep him going a bit longer. He really didn't want to do that. What would Bones say if he knew? The thought of his friend made him chuckle, and his spirits lifted, if only a shade.

What about food? He supposed he could poke around under some of the clefts and try to surprise a rattlesnake. If he could find one, and if he could manage to kill it without being bitten, he could eat the meat… raw. Of course, he would waste vital time and energy in what might be a fruitless quest. He would push on a bit further before making that decision.

He glanced up at the hazy, blue sky, the waves of heat rolling up like breakers on the sea. A lone wisp of cloud drifted lazily across the horizon, taunting him with the thought of the dark, heavy-laden storm clouds that visited his home in southern Florida every afternoon. Not a chance of that in this arid clime.

Something glimmered on the horizon. In his state, he could not tell if it was anything more than a mirage, but he continued to move toward it. His head swam, but he kept moving. Jade… Melissa… Jade… He stumbled, but maintained his balance. He had to keep going.

And then something was moving toward him. A shadowy figure, little more than a dark outline against the sun-scorched sand. As it approached, the form took on a human shape. Hope welled inside of Dane. He was too tired and dehydrated to wonder if the person might mean him ill. Dane raised a hand in greeting, or tried to, but he could not lift his arm. His vision blurred, and an icy cool flowed down his back. Heatstroke. He stumbled to his knees as the figure drew forth. Dane had only a brief glimpse of a hideous, beastly face before he slumped unconscious to the ground, the silent scream dying in his parched throat.

Chapter 23

The members of the small party picked their way across the narrow spine of rock that led to the top of Angel's Landing. Jarren kept his gaze fixed steadily ahead, refusing to look at the sheer drop-off on either side. Even the spectacular view of Zion National Park was not sufficient to overcome his touch of acrophobia and the myriad of thoughts that coursed through his mind. He had scoffed at the sign at the trailhead warning hikers of the potential danger this path posed, but now he saw the truth. The long, steep hike, particularly the switchbacks, had been challenging but not dangerous. This stretch was different. The ground seemed to flee from them as they crossed the narrow stone path. He could now see how several hikers a year managed to lose their lives on this perilous course. Why would anyone other than a skilled hiker be foolish enough to try and cross here? It was not that he had any sympathy for them; stupid people simply pissed him off.

A golden eagle circled far above, its lonely call drifting down from the heights. Jarren looked up for a moment too long and found himself struck by a moment of dizziness. He hastily dropped his gaze back to his destination, from which he was now only a few paces away. Angel's Landing. How fitting that the Lord's work would culminate in such an appropriately named place. He could scarcely believe it when the Elder told him. What were the odds that the Spaniards, more than a millennium ago, would have chosen a place that would later bear such a name? Zion indeed!

He knew little about what lay ahead. Excitement coursed through his veins. He suspected there still remained much the Elder had not told him. His instructions were clear: allow Ihara to guide them to the treasure, secure it until it could be removed, and then eliminate her at his leisure. It was the other part of the instructions he found most puzzling. *If anything blasphemous is found, neither it nor word of it is to leave until I arrive. If that means eliminating your partners, so be it.*

He grimaced at the memory of that last conversation. What might they find amongst the temple treasure that could blaspheme the Lord? Was he truly to kill the two men who accompanied him? Since those were his instructions, he was grateful for the small group. Initially he had thought the concern over a large party drawing unwanted attention to be unfounded. This park did not have so many visitors compared to Mesa Verde or Grand Canyon. But, he supposed, a touch of prudence was not a bad thing, though it went against his nature.

He turned his attention to his companions. Thaddeus was solid. He had done a few tours of duty in the army before joining the organization. He was very good with his sidearm and fair with his knife. He was dangerous, but his skill did not rival that of Jarren, nor would he be expecting an attack. If needed, Jarren would eliminate him first.

Jacob, the other member of their party, was a small-town police officer. He was steady, but was best suited for roughing up drunken Utes and the smart-alecky college kids who biked the scenic trails of southern Utah. His most redeeming quality was his zealous dedication to the Elder and to their cause.

As they neared the safe haven of the top peak of Angel's Landing, he relaxed and let his gaze drift to Ihara's trim figure. She was a fine-looking woman. A shame she had to die. He forced down the thoughts rising in his mind. Their sacred mission deserved his full attention, untainted by these stray thoughts.

"Almost there," Ihara called out.

"How is it," he asked, "that the entrance has been in this place all these years, yet no one has found it?" The question had gnawed at the back of his mind ever since he learned their destination.

"We don't know for certain that it has not been found," she said, not looking back at him. "It's entirely possible that others have found the entrance, but without the instructions we found, I assume you can't find your way to the treasure. I suspect the Spaniards made it very difficult to find."

"Maybe the monster ate them," Thaddeus said.

Ihara laughed and shook her head. They had arrived at the summit of Angel's Landing. She stood looking around, a half-smile belying her oddly sad eyes.

"Something funny?" Jarren asked. He hated being left out of jokes, always assuming them to somehow be at his expense.

"A local legend," Ihara said. "Some sort of chupacabra creature supposedly lurks around these canyons, killing the occasional goat or tourist. There have been a few disappearances, probably hiking accidents, but locals like to blame it on the monster."

"They found a body," Thaddeus said. "Mauled."

"Coyotes, most likely," Jarren scoffed. "Superstition is the tool of Lucifer, spreading fear in the hearts of those lacking sufficient faith." Thaddeus scowled, but Jarren ignored him.

"If you say so," Ihara replied. She fished into her pack and drew out a notebook. "I want to make sure we get this right. The first clue reads, 'Pass under the tenth step leading to the east.'"

"Step?" Jacob asked, shielding his eyes from the sun and looking around. "But there are no buildings here."

"Must be a natural formation resembling steps," Ihara said, "or steps hewn into the rock in a place that's not readily visible. In any case, the cave paintings discovered at Orley's ranch definitely indicate the presence of steps coming down from the peak. Let's look around." They made a cursory inspection of the top of Angel's Landing, and then made their way around the edge, carefully inspecting the steep cliffs below for any sign of the mysterious stairs.

"Tell me," Ihara said, "why didn't we come in your helicopter? We could have gotten a better look at the cliffs, then been dropped off up here without the big climb.

"Not worth the risk of notice," he replied.

"That didn't stop you before," she said.

"It was not so great a concern then. As long as we found the missing pieces, it did not matter if others grew curious about why we were there. Once we found what we needed, it did not matter if the authorities poked around. They would find nothing. But this…" his sweeping gesture took in the entire panorama "…this is where the treasure is. We positively do not want undue attention drawn to this place."

"There's something else I don't understand," Ihara said as they walked along. Her foot slipped and he grabbed her upper arm, steadying her. "Thanks. Anyway, I was reporting in regularly. I was doing the job. Why did your goons keep trying to get ahead of me?"

"That was my decision," Jarren said. He wondered if Ihara knew that he was one of the "goons." Likely, she would not care if she gave offense or not. "Initially, I did not know if you could be trusted, so we moved on Chaco Canyon as soon as I learned of your plans. You proved yourself at Chaco when you found what we did not, and you reported in as expected. At that point, I was content to let you continue on your own. Closely monitored, of course. That is, until Bonebrake showed up. He had already given us trouble, and we could not take a chance with a wild card like him."

"You weren't worried about Maddock?" Ihara asked, shielding her eyes against the intense sunlight and looking down over the edge of the precipice.

"He had shown himself to be loyal to you, so we were content to let things move along as they were. Too bad cutting his rope at Mesa Verde didn't kill him."

"Right," she said, her voice tight. "Wait a minute!" She

whirled around to face him. "You recovered the Ship Rock piece, and that was before Bones showed up."

"What do you mean?" Jarren asked. He suddenly felt cold all over. What piece was she talking about?

"The piece you recovered from Ship Rock."

"You said you had all the pieces," he replied.

"I said *we* had all the pieces. I have five. You have the sixth. Please tell me you brought the translation with you. I was so distracted by… everything I had to do today that I just assumed…"

"Ihara, I don't know what you are talking about. We did not recover any of the artifacts, and you certainly never reported anything about Ship Rock."

"There wasn't time," she said. "Saul actually figured it out, and by the time he told us about it, you had already…" Her eyes widened in shock. "Oh… my…"

"What?" Jarren was not certain he wanted to hear the answer. He was completely sure, however, that the Elder would not like to hear whatever it was that Ihara was about to tell him."

"Saul figured out the Ship Rock clue and took off without telling us. He came back and said that you had beaten him to it. He must have kept the piece himself. I'll kill him!"

"I imagine that has already been taken care of," Jarren said, relaxing a little. By now, Saul, Bonebrake, and the woman would be long-dead.

"We need to find out whether or not the missing piece was among Saul's things."

Jarren grabbed his walkie talkie and called down to Ian who was waiting near the trailhead.

"Ryan, I need you to contact the team. Have them search Saul's and Bonebrake's possessions. There should be a small stone artifact…"

"Sir," Ryan's voice came back fuzzy but discernible, "the team has not yet reported in."

"What?" Jarren checked his watch. Too much time had

passed. Something was wrong. He quickly turned over the possibilities in his mind. Notify the Elder? No, that was the last thing he wanted to do. He needed to be certain before he told the Elder anything. There had been too many failures already. He couldn't hike back down and investigate it himself, and he certainly didn't want to sit atop this rock while he waited.

"You're going to have to go there," he told Ryan.

"Sir? My instructions were to remain here and..."

"Your instructions have changed. Get there and back as quickly as you can. You won't be able to communicate with us once we've found the entrance. Leave Jedediah to man the post, find out what happened to the team, and get back here as quickly as you can."

"What should I tell the Elder?" Ryan's voice quavered.

"Should the Elder contact you, which he will not, tell him that the last update you received from me was that everything was proceeding as planned. Otherwise, play dumb." Shouldn't be a problem for him, Jarren thought.

"Something wrong?" Ihara asked.

"Nothing you need to worry about. Let me ask you; do you believe we can find our way to the treasure without the missing clue?"

"I don't know." Ihara shrugged. "I assume every clue is important, but I don't see that we have any choice. Even if it was among Saul's things, we'd have to get it translated, and I don't relish waiting that long, do you?"

"Definitely not. We'll begin our search, and in the meantime, the others can work on searching for the piece. Worst case, we are unsuccessful and have to start again with the additional information."

"Suits me," Ihara said. She led them on a circuit around the top, before coming to a sudden halt, her eyes gleaming in triumph. "The solstice!" she exclaimed. "I'll bet they would have chosen a location that caught the sun most of the day. Somewhere where a rock formation could have cast a shadow..." She did not complete her thought, but hurried toward the edge and lay down flat, her head hanging over the edge. She looked for a minute, and then cried, "I see it!"

Jarren joined her on the cliff edge and lay flat on his stomach, his head hanging over the edge. He could see why no one had discovered it before. Down below them, the rock receded into a deep overhang. A deep cleft wound through the rock and vanished into the shadows of the rocky ledge. No one would be able to see this from anywhere other than where he lay. The floor of the cleft resembled large stairs. This was definitely the spot. They wasted no time in working their way down. Ihara did not wait for them, but counted down ten steps as her translation instructed, dropped to her knees, and began brushing away dirt and loose rock. She drew a long-bladed knife from the sheath on her belt and began probing the area.

"See anything?" Jarren asked, moving in behind her.

"Not…. wait a minute!" Her knife had caught in something. She carefully worked it to and fro, and then drew it back toward her in a straight line. "I think I've found an edge. Get your knife and help me." Soon they had uncovered a slab roughly three feet square. With Thaddeus's help, they pried the stone loose, and upended it to reveal a tunnel descending at a sharp angle and curving out of sight.

"What's this carved on the bottom of the stone?" Thaddeus asked. A shamrock with a cross in the center had been scratched into the underside of the rock.

"It's Fray Marcos' sigil!" Ihara gasped. "If we needed further confirmation, this is it. We are in the right place. Follow me!" Without another word, she thrust her legs into the hole, scooted forward, and slid out of sight.

"Ihara!" Jarren called, but she did not answer. "Hell," he mumbled. "We'll have to follow her. Jacob, you come down last, and be certain to replace that stone before you follow." Gripping his flashlight in his left hand and his pistol in his right, Jarren took a deep breath and plunged into the darkness and out of sight.

Chapter 24

"Angel's Landing. Strenuous climb. Narrow route with cliff exposures. Hazardous during…"

"Bones, I know how to read," Amanda snapped. "I'll be fine. Besides, I've got you with me."

"If you say so," Bones said. "Of course, it's not so much the climb, but who might be waiting for us at the top that worries me."

"Then you'll just have to look after me that much more carefully." She smiled, took his hand, and led him up the trail.

The trek thus far had been strenuous, though nothing either of them could not handle. Truthfully, Bones was more worried about Maddock than Amanda. The few times he had gotten cell phone coverage, he had tried to call his friend but failed to reach him. He had spoken with Jimmy, who had not heard from Maddock, but had managed to translate the final clues from Saul's piece of the scarab.

"One other thing I wanted to tell you," Jimmy said, "is that I made a mistake translating a piece of the artifact. Instead of 'the tenth is impure,' I'm fairly certain it should read 'the *ten* is impure.' Doesn't make much sense, but there you go."

Bones didn't have time to think about the subtle nuances of language. He wanted to find out what had happened to Maddock. Tough as he was, if Jade had surprised him by delivering him directly into the hands of the Dominion…"

"It might be all right," Amanda said, reading his thoughts. "You've told me before he's the toughest, most resourceful guy you've ever known. Besides, it might not be what you think. She seems to care about him. Maybe she's double-crossing the Dominion and he's helping her."

"I don't know," he said. He didn't know what to think. He just wanted to find his friend.

A young park ranger appeared from around a bend up the trail. He approached them, an easy smile on his face.

"Afternoon," the ranger said. He was short and stocky with light brown hair and a faint splash of freckles across his sunburned nose. He removed his ranger's cap and fanned his face. "Enjoying your hike?" he asked, a twinkle in his bright blue eyes.

"It's beautiful," Amanda said, "but tiring."

"Walter's Wiggles," the ranger said knowingly, nodding in the direction of the steep switchbacks they had climbed a short while ago. "It'll do that to you."

"We're trying to catch up with some friends," Bones said in what he hoped was a friendly tone. "Did you pass anyone on your way down? We're pretty sure they went on ahead of us." He gave a quick description of Dane and Jade.

"Sure!" the ranger said. "I definitely saw the girl. She's hard to miss! She was with, like, three guys, though."

"Was one of them my friend?" Bones asked, every muscle tense.

"Probably," the ranger said, shrugging. "I just noticed the girl." He arched an eyebrow at the sound of Amanda's muttered curse, but did not comment. "They're probably up at the top by now. Even if they don't wait around for you, you'll definitely pass them on their way back down. There's no other way off this rock."

"That's great," Bones said. He stood, ready to resume their hike, when a glint of gold on the ranger's chest caught his eye. "What's that you're wearing?"

"Oh, this?" Hanging from a leather necklace was a heavy gold cross with a wide loop at the top. "It's an ankh," he said. "Pretty realistic-looking isn't it?"

"It looks very old," Amanda said, leaning in for a closer look.

"Yeah, but I'm sure it's not," the ranger said. "I found it in a stream here in the park. A visitor must have dropped it. Kept it in the office for a year and no one ever called about it, so they let me keep it."

"It's pretty cool," Bones said. "Well, we'd better be going. Nice talking to you."

"You too," the ranger said. "By the way, I wouldn't stay too long. I think there's a storm coming. I can smell something on the wind. It's going to be a big one."

"We won't dawdle," Bones said. He and Amanda shook hands with the ranger and continued up the path. When they were out of earshot, Bones turned to Amanda and said, "Well, what do you know about that?"

The top of Angel's Landing was void of human life. They stood in the eerie silence, catching their breath from the last stretch of trail, which had required hanging on to heavy chains bolted into the stone in order to make the climb. There was no sign of Maddock, Jade, or the other men with whom the ranger had reported seeing her.

"If Jade put these clues in the proper order, we're looking for something that resembles steps," Amanda said, consulting her notepad. "I don't see anything that looks like steps around here."

"They must have found them." Bones took in every detail of the top of Angel's landing. "I'll find them."

"And how do you plan to do that?"

"I'm an Indian. I'm going to track them." He had been a skilled tracker in his youth, and the knowledge had served him well during his military service.

"Right." Amanda sounded skeptical. "You're going to track on rock."

"It's not all rock," he said. "Look over there." He pointed to a small patch of dirt that had gathered in a low spot on the rock. "See that curved imprint on the left side? That's the edge of a shoe. Whoever left it went that way." He led her across the rock, pointing out an occasional scuff, bent patch of dried grass, and even an occasional footprint, finally coming to a halt on the southeast edge of the cliff.

"End of the line," Amanda patted him on the shoulder. "Sorry. You did a good job on the tracking."

"Oh, it's not a dead end," he said, grinning broadly. Had they more time, he would have let the suspense build before explaining, but that was a luxury they did not have. "See this smooth patch here? Someone hung a rope over the edge and climbed down. Their weight, plus the rubbing of the rope smoothed out this patch. I'll bet if we get a good look down below…" He lay down on his belly and hung as far over the edge as he dared. He immediately spotted what he was looking for. "There they are!"

"Seriously?" Amanda hauled him to his feet and leapt into his arms, crushing him in a hug and almost sending them both tumbling over the edge. "You are amazing," she whispered in his ear before giving it a playful bite. "Okay, Mr. Indian, this time you get to be the cavalry."

They used a nylon rope he carried in his pack to reach the steps. Once they were down in the rocky cleft that hid the rough staircase from sight, they immediately spotted the tenth step where someone, obviously Jade and her companions, had uncovered what looked like a large, square stepping stone. Bones pried it up, revealing a tunnel down below.

"It looks like one of those playground slides," he said, peering into the round, curving tunnel. "Should be fun. Got your gun ready?"

"Got it," Amanda said. Bones had lent her his snub-nosed .22.

"Good. We'll go down as quietly as we can. Keep your flashlight turned off for the time being. Whoever is ahead of us will have lights of their own. We want to see them before they see us." He turned on his own flashlight and cupped his hand across it, spreading his fingers just enough to allow a sliver of light to illumine their path.

He had been correct when he compared the tunnel to a playground slide. It was smooth and round, corkscrewing in a sharp, downward spiral. Gravity pulled him inexorably downward, and he had to use his heels as brakes. *I hope my pants still have a seat when I get to the bottom*, he thought as he skidded downward. Their dizzying spin through the darkness seemed to go on forever, but finally, without warning, the tunnel dumped them out into an open space. He grunted as Amanda tumbled onto him.

"Where…" Amanda began, but Bones clapped his hand across her mouth and whispered for her to remain quiet.

They lay there in the deathly black silence, ears straining to hear any sound that might indicate danger. The roaring of his own blood filled his ears, and the rapid tattoo of his heartbeat seemed so loud that he was certain it would bring the mountain down on top of them. After a minute, he relaxed and let go of Amanda. He stood and helped her climb to her feet. Playing his light around the room, he found that they were in a cavern about fifty paces across. Vaulted passageways stood to their right, and directly across from them. The wall to their left was unnaturally smooth and regular. Amanda turned on her light and went over for a closer look.

"It's some sort of plaster," she whispered. "This must be how they brought the treasure in. Nothing of any size could have come in the way we did." She turned away from the wall and consulted her notebook. "Okay, the next clue reads, "under the black stone at the western entrance.""

Bones consulted his Pathfinder watch, which included an altimeter, barometer, thermometer, and a digital compass. "We're almost a thousand feet down. Still four-hundred feet above the canyon floor." He switched the watch from altimeter to compass. "And the western passageway is over there." He pointed to his right.

Directly in front of the passageway lay three paving stones similar in shape and size to the one through which they had accessed the tunnel: one gray, one reddish, and the third black. They raised the black stone to reveal a vertical shaft with handholds carved into the wall.

They descended another twenty-five feet and found themselves in a narrow tunnel with a squared-off roof. The ceiling was scarcely high enough to permit Bones to stand upright, and he had to resist the urge to duck as he walked. The pathway sloped down in a gentle incline. He kept moving his light back and forth, up and down, looking for any potential hazard.

"What are you doing?" Amanda asked in a soft voice. "That's driving me crazy."

"Looking for booby traps or falling rocks or whatever. I don't know. I guess I read too many pulp novels as a kid."

"What do you think would have happened if we had not known about the black stone and just gone down the tunnel?" she whispered.

"Hard to say. Might loop back around on itself, or maybe come to a dead end, or even something worse. The last time I was in a place like this…" He paused, forcing down the memories of what had happened then. "Never mind. Looks like we're coming up on another chamber."

This chamber was smaller than the previous one. Two massive caves, each flanked by ornate pillars hewn directly into the rock, gaped dark and forbidding directly in front of them.

"Okay," Bones said. "These are the clues Jade doesn't have. What's the first one?"

"Above the pillar of the northern opening of the cave that has two entrances. Okaaay."

"Both caves are set in the west wall of the chamber, so the northern opening would be the one to the left." They shone their lights on the cave wall above the pillars that stood on either side of the northernmost cavern. "I see something," Bones said. He had picked out a spot of deep blackness above the pillar to the left of the cave. Had he not been looking for it, his eyes would have passed right over it, dismissing it as nothing more than an irregularity in the rough stone. As he moved closer, he could make out a small shaft a few feet above the pillar. He began to search the wall for the best way to climb up when Amanda gasped and clutched his arm.

"Bones, look!" She pointed into the mouth of the cave. Thirty feet back, the passage was blocked by a pile of rubble. At the bottom of the pile of stone, her light shone on a human leg sticking out from beneath the mass of stone. "You don't think…"

They moved cautiously forward, their lights playing off the ceiling, but it appeared solid. Reaching the scene of the cave-in, Bones knelt and touched what was obviously a man's leg. It was cold. He hastily stripped off the man's hiking boot and wool socks, and placed his fingers on the dorsalis pedis artery atop the foot for a pulse, but there was none.

"He's dead," he said, rising to his feet and inspecting the pile of rock. "It's not Maddock. This dude's foot is way too big."

"Do you think they're all buried under there?" Amanda whispered.

"No way of telling," he said. "I don't think it would be a good idea to try to move this rock. That is unless…" He left the rest unspoken. *Unless we find the treasure, but don't find Maddock and the others.* "Let's just assume that one of the Dominion guys bit the big one. Score one for our side."

Something stirred in the darkness. The creature did not see it. Generations of its kind living in complete darkness had rendered it and those like it blind. It did not smell it… yet. It did not hear it, though its sense of hearing was easily its most acute. Rather, it felt something moving. The creature and its pack were one with these caverns, perfectly attuned to their environment. Not a stirring of dank air escaped their notice. And nothing moved in these halls of stones without alerting the pack with both the sounds and the vibrations that rang through the walls of stone. Yes, something was stirring.

The creature rose and moved down the tunnel toward the source of the vibration. Its stunted, muscular legs and low-slung, broad body slunk easily through crevasses that would deny passage to larger creatures. Its heavily padded feet made no sound on the cold stone, and it kept its razor claws retracted until it needed to climb… or to kill.

The source of the disturbance was closer now. The creature could discern sounds alien to its experience. Harsher than the tumbling of water through the underground river that snaked through its domain. Steadier than the staccato clack of a rock fall. This sound was new and enticing. It followed the sound with a single-minded purpose, until a cloying scent assaulted its nostrils. Yes!

The creature knew this smell. It had ventured outside the caverns only one time it its life. It had run down and devoured a small, soft thing that had squealed as the creature's powerful jaws snapped its back. The warm blood, so unlike the cold, slick things of the river that were the staple of the pack's diet. Yes, this was a warm blood smell.

The creature sent out a call to the pack. There were no words, nor were there sounds. There was simply a shared understanding among the creatures of the pack. The message was simple.

We hunt.

Chapter 24

A lukewarm dampness pressed down on Dane's face. He grabbed at it as he sat up, and his hand came away clutching a sodden, green dish towel. Where was he? He quickly took in his surroundings. Faded curtains permitted a hazy glow to fill the small room, revealing twisted covers and a moldy pillow on the small bed upon which he sat. Above him, a water-stained ceiling drooped like a low-hanging storm cloud, and below him threadbare carpet of burnt orange failed to entirely cover the cheap subfloor. The walls were covered in murky gray-brown paneling, and were plastered with sketches. He was no art expert, but dating Kaylin Maxwell, a professional painter, he had enough familiarity that he could that this artist, whoever he or she was, was a talented amateur. Dane recognized the peak of Angel's Landing from a picture Jade had printed out. There were other landscapes done in pencil or crayon, and all were pleasing to the eye. Others, however, were more sinister. Dark caverns filled with grotesque figures were rendered in broad, heavy lines of crayon. Something was chained over a river. And most disturbing of all were the shadowy renderings of a fanged creature with dead, black eyes, and glistening claws. The beast was always drawn in a night scene, and never in complete detail, which made it seem all the more malevolent.

A sliver of light appeared in the wall as a door opened. He tensed as a figure appeared in the doorway, the brighter light outside the door bathing its features in shadow.

"Wake?" A slurred voice asked. "Wake?" There was no malice in the odd voice. The figure stepped into the room, and the dim light from the window fell upon the most hideously deformed person Dane had ever met. He was a young man, perhaps about twenty years old, though it was difficult to tell. His right leg was six inches shorter than the left, emaciated, and was twisted so that his left foot was pointed to the side. His right arm was also noticeably shorter than his left, though both were heavily muscled. It was his face that was the most disfigured. His right eye was tiny and beady, and the left bulged so far out of its socket that it looked like it would pop out if someone were to clap the young man on the back. His nose was not fully grown, giving it a pig-like appearance. His lips curled back in a permanent smile, revealing a few twisted teeth. His patchy, brown hair was long and fine, and seemed to float behind him whenever he moved his head. Despite his horrific appearance, though, there was somehow an air of gentle kindness about him.

"Yes, I'm awake," Dane said.

"Dink!" The young man thrust a glass of water into Dane's hands, sloshing half of it onto his lap. "Dink mo."

Dane was parched, and he gulped it down. It was lukewarm and had a coppery taste, but he did not care. He finished it and was brought another, which he forced himself to drink more slowly.

"I guess you saved me out in the desert," he finally said to his Good Samaritan who had sat down on the floor and was staring happily at him.

"Eah!" He nodded vigorously. "Eah!"

Dane was torn between the urge to get back to looking for Jade, and the sympathy and gratitude he felt for the youth. In any event, he needed to figure out exactly where he was, and how to get to Angel's Landing from here. That was it!

"Did you draw these pictures?" he asked.

"Eah! Daw." The young man climbed unsteadily to his feet and pointing to various pictures and talking rapidly. Dane could understand very little of what he was saying. When he indicated the pictures of the creature, he said something like "Choo. Choo." It didn't look like any choo-choo Dane had ever seen.

"Is that place close by?" Dane pointed to the picture of Angel's Landing.

"Eah." A noncommittal shrug.

"Have you been there?"

"Eah!" This time the young man seemed very excited. "Eh dah, eh dah, eh dah." He pointed to the cavern sketches. "You see." He dropped to the floor, reached underneath the bed, and pulled out a shoebox, which he opened with great care. He took out a handful of smooth pebbles and handed them to Dane. "Got dah." He indicated a sketch of what looked like a twisting river running through a dark cavern.

"You found these in that cave?" His question was answered by a vigorous nod. He needed to connect with this young man, if only to learn the way to Angel's Landing. He made a show of admiring the smooth stones, turning them over in his hand and rubbing them between his fingertips. But he did not have to feign interest in the next object that came out of the box.

The young man dropped a golden ingot into Dane's palm. Dane was no Egyptologist, but as a marine archaeologist, he had enough knowledge of Egyptian artifacts that he easily identified its origin, and could tell that it was very, very old.

"Where did you get this?" he whispered.

"Dah." Again, the same picture.

"Is this a cavern and an underground river?" He stood and walked over to the picture.

"Eah!"

"And you've been inside it, and it's where you found this?" He held up the ingot.

"Eah. Eh dah, eh dah, eh dah." The boy stood and this time poked each cave drawing with his index finger. He held the open box right in front of Dane's face. "Fi dese too!"

Dane gasped. Among the collection of native rocks lay a golden ankh, several scarabs of various sizes, a few amulets, and some beads.

"Can you show me where you found these?" Dane whispered.

"Eah!" He dropped the box, its contents scattering across the floor, and bolted out the door. Concerned that he might be left behind, Dane hurried out behind him.

The young man was standing in a small, dark living room babbling to an elderly woman who sat in a wheelchair with a blanket draped across her lap. She turned to Dane and greeted him with a toothless smile. Beneath the blanket, her twisted legs came well short of the floor. Other than this deformity, she seemed to have escaped the young man's misfortune.

"I see you're awake," she wheezed. "Justin brought you back from the desert. Put you in his bed and kept damp cloths on you. He's a good boy."

"He is," Dane said. "I thank you both for your help. What can I do to repay you?"

"Nothing," the woman said in her coarse, faint voice. "I taught him to do right by others, but we don't see many others out here. We mostly like it that way. Our family's lived here for generations, but there's nobody left but me and my grandson. We sure don't see many people out walking in the desert without any water. What were you thinking?"

"It's a long story and it wouldn't make much sense if I told you," he said. "Ma'am, would you happen to have a phone I could use?"

"Afraid not," she said. "And them fancy cell phones don't do no good out here either."

"Can you tell me if we're anywhere near Angel's Landing?"

"The Land of Zion?" she croaked. "You're heaven-bound, are you? We're not too awful far, but I think Justin wants to take you somewhere."

"Eah!" Justin said, taking Dane by the hand and leading him to the front door of the house.

"You boys be careful," she said as they stepped out

into the blistering sun.

Justin led him through a twisting dry wash, up a rocky hill, and through snarls of cactus and gnarled pine, and down into a tiny box canyon surrounded by steep walls of red rock. At the far end of the canyon abutting a sheer cliff a small pool lay hidden behind a screen of juniper and sagebrush

"Eah." Justin said, pointing down into the water. "Go dah." He made a diving motion with his right hand, dipping it down and bringing it back up. "Sim."

Swim under there. Dane was growing accustomed to Justin's manner of speaking. He thought it over. Could this possibly be a way to the treasure? If they were close to Angel's Landing, who was to say Justin had not happened upon the treasure, or at least a small portion of it that had been carried away by the underground stream. In any case, there was no harm in checking it out.

"And the cavern where you found the treasure is in there?" He pointed to the cliff face.

"Eah." Justin nodded vigorously and again made the down-and-up motion with his hand.

"All right," Dane said. "Guess I've got nothing to lose. Thank you for everything, Justin. You're a good man." He gave Justin's shoulder a squeeze and turned away, but the youth grabbed his arm and pulled him back.

"Choo choo," he whispered. His eyes no longer danced with infectious good nature, but were serious. He looked Dane straight in the eye, as if trying to convey a message beyond his capacity to verbalize. "Choo choo." His voice took on a pleading tone. "Choo choo."

"Right. Choo choo." Dane said. "Thanks again." He pulled off his boots, tied the laces together, and draped them around his neck. Taking a deep breath, he leaped feet-first into the water. The icy jolt as he broke the surface felt like an invigorating boost of energy. With powerful kicks and easy strokes he swam down into the waiting shadows. A circle of absolute darkness tugged at him like a black hole.

As he swam toward it, he could see that there was indeed an opening in the rock. He swam through, an eager sense of hopefulness surging inside him. The waning light from outside faded away, and he fished into the thigh pocket of his hiking shorts and took out the mini dive light he always carried with him. He hadn't actually expected to do any diving, but he preferred a waterproof light in any case. He clicked it on, and the intense beam knifed through the dark, clear water. The water above him churned in a torrent of milky bubbles.

He broke the surface in a large cavern. A roaring filled his ears, and he saw that the pool in which he swam was fed by a dozen narrow cascades of water pouring in on all sides. At the far end of the pool, the cavern wall sloped gently upward to the yawing mouth of a tunnel, above which was carved the shamrock and cross of Fray Marcos de Niza. He had found it!

Chapter 25

Jade muttered a curse as the tunnel ended in a blank wall. She had realized this tunnel was a mistake as soon as the booby-trapped ceiling caved in on Jacob. Obviously the missing clue contained something more vital than she had assumed. They gave up the idea of digging out almost immediately. There was no way to make it through the mass of rubble. They continued on, their nerves stretched like piano wire as they watched for further traps, but all they found was a long stretch of tunnel coming to this dead end.

"Any ideas?" Jarren asked, letting his light play up the wall and across the ceiling.

"Put your light back up there in the corner of the ceiling." She thought she had seen something. She added her light to his and the twin beams revealed a gap in the ceiling where the rock had crumbled away. There was a passage above theirs! "Boost me up."

Jarren hunched down and Jade clambered up onto his shoulders. He was very strong, and had no problem lifting her up to the gap in the ceiling. She peeked through, shining her light back and forth. It appeared that this passageway ran directly above the one in which they had been traveling, but unlike the lower passage, it continued on. She hoisted herself through, and then turned back to the others.

"Who's next? I can help one of you through if you need it, then we'll drop a rope and haul the last person up."

"I'll give Jarren a boost up," Thaddeus said. "I'm lighter, so it'll be easier to bring me up the rope."

A few seconds later, Jarren's head and broad shoulders appeared in the hole, and he clambered through. Jade had already fished the rope out of her pack and was looking for a place to secure it. Finding none, she instead secured it around Jarren's waist and tossed the other end through the hole.

"Ready when you are."

"Just a minute." Thaddeus's voice was soft and urgent. "I hear something in the tunnel. I'll be right back." He drew his pistol, turned off his flashlight, and headed off down the passageway.

"There can't be anyone in the tunnel," Jade said. "Both ends are blocked off, and we didn't see any side passages.

"He's an idiot," Jarren muttered. "I ought to go down there, but in the dark, he'd probably mistake me for a gentile. I should just go shoot him myself and be done with him."

Jade wanted to laugh, but the sounds that suddenly burst out through the hole in the floor chilled her marrow. A shout. A single gunshot. A shriek of agony that died into a wet, choking squelch.

"What the…" Jarren sprang to his feet. "Wait here. I'll be right back." He untied the belt from around his waist, slipped feet-first through the hole, and dropped with a thud to the floor below.

Jade sat in the darkness, her heart racing. What had happened to Thaddeus, and what would she do if Jarren did not come back? She entertained the frightened thoughts for only a moment before steeling her resolve. She would find the treasure by herself. How many years had she dedicated to finding the truth behind the story of Cibola? She had joined forces with an organization she despised, and betrayed a man about whom she cared deeply in order to fulfill her personal quest. She had heard of treasure hunters catching "the fever" and she knew it was true about her. Cibola was her passion, her purpose, her very life. She could not go on until she had seen it through. Perhaps, when it was over, she could find Maddock and make him understand that what she had done, she had done to protect him. Drugging him was the hardest thing she'd ever done, but if it kept him from walking into the hands of the Dominion, it would be worth it. Whether he would even believe her, much less forgive her, was another question altogether.

The thoughts fled as Jarren returned. It was all she could do to help him get back up to the second level, but they managed.

"I take it you didn't find him," she said.

"I found this." Jarren held up a Taurus PT92 that she assumed belonged to Thaddeus. "And lots of blood." Only now did she notice the reddish tinge on the Taurus's grips.

"Nothing else?" she whispered, unable to believe he could have just vanished like that.

"There were smears of blood along the passageway as if he'd been dragged away, but after about forty feet the trail just vanished at the base of the wall. I swear, I searched that wall from tip to toe and didn't find any sort of passageway, trapdoor, not even a seam." His voice was dull and he sounded understandably shaken. "I don't know who is in here with us, but I don't believe Bonebrake did that."

"All we can do is go on," Jade whispered. She did not wait for an answer, but turned and headed down the passageway. They continued for another five minutes until the tunnel gave way to a narrow staircase that wound around the inside of a deep pit. Grotesque gargoyles ringed the upper edge of the pit, each contorted into a different, agonized pose, all holding out their hands in supplication.

"Ugly," Jarren observed, shining his light upon one particularly gruesome figure. "What now?"

"Obviously, we don't know for sure that we're in the right place, and we're missing the fourth clue, but the fifth clue reads, 'On the third terrace in the cave.' And that," Jade shone her light across the pit, "looks like the mouth of a cave to me." As they crossed the pit, Jade noticed that the clover and cross insignia of Fray Marcos was embedded in the very center of the floor in polished marble. "This is encouraging," she said. "We found this symbol everywhere one of the clues was hidden." She shone her light around the room and saw that the insignia was also carved on the wall where the stairs began. "I have a good feeling about this. Let's go."

Chapter 26

"Get as close as you can!" the Elder shouted over the whir of the rotors. He looked down at the surface of Angel's Landing, taking in every detail. There was no sign of his people or Bonebrake. They must have found the way in. Where was it?

"The wind has picked up." The pilot looked nervously at the roiling black clouds sweeping toward them. "And I think it's only going to get worse. Are you sure you want me to leave you here?"

"You have your instructions." The Elder grimaced as fat raindrops spattered the windscreen. "I will contact you when you are needed. In any event, I want you out of here before the local authorities are notified of our presence. Hopefully this storm is keeping people inside and you won't be seen at all."

"Yes, Elder." The pilot grimaced and took them down. Strong winds buffeted the craft.

"Hold it steady," the Elder said. The rocky peak seemed to grow larger as they hovered lower and lower, until they were almost touching.

"Now!" the pilot shouted.

The Elder leaped out, followed by twelve handpicked men, all armed with Kalashnikov RPK 74M light machine guns. It was perhaps overkill, but he was finished allowing Maddock and Bonebrake to make a fool of him. First it had been the call from Bradley, gravely injured, telling him that Bonebrake had killed three of Bradley's men and escaped in their car. That made the second time the Indian had managed to steal a vehicle out from under the nose of the Dominion. Unable to contact Jarren, the Elder had then called that fool Ryan, who pretended everything was all right before finally admitting he had been instructed to find an artifact among Saul's possessions. Apparently he had held something back from Ihara, and now she, Jarren, and their party were apparently lacking critical clues to the treasure. It had taken a simple hacking of Saul's e-mail to confirm it, and to obtain the translation of the missing clue. The icing on the cake had been when Jedediah reported seeing a man and woman matching the descriptions of Bonebrake and Barnes climbing the trail to Angel's Landing. Of course, he had made no effort to stop them. The Elder had given Ryan the task of killing Jedediah. A fitting punishment for them both, as Jedediah and Ryan were brothers. Then the Elder had killed Ryan. Ihara had supposedly taken care of Maddock, but he no longer believed it. Too much had gone wrong to trust in any of his underlings anymore.

A jagged fork of lightning sizzled through the air much too close for comfort, and a deafening thunderclap seem to shake the very stone upon which they stood. He turned and waved his arm at the pilot, who gave him the thumbs-up and maneuvered the craft up and away. The helicopter had almost cleared the peak when the world was ripped apart. A blinding flash, and an explosion as lightning shattered a dying pine at the cliff's edge. The helicopter, already heeling over from the heavy wind, was directly in the path of the explosion. Chunks of tree tore through the spinning rotors, shattering the blades and sending shrapnel hurtling out in all directions. One of the deadly missiles cleanly decapitated Reuben, who was standing next to the Elder, but he did not notice; he was watching his helicopter tumble over the edge of the cliff and out of sight.

Rage boiled inside him, but he was its master. He stared for a moment at the empty space where the craft had been, listening for the explosion as it hit bottom. The fiery fate of the craft seared his determination. He would succeed where the others had failed.

Dane clambered up out of the tunnel into a warm, dark chamber. A strong animal odor immediately assaulted him. It was a heavy, oppressive smell, like that of a great cat. He shone his light around the cavern. It was oval in shape, with many ledges, crevasses, and overhangs cratering the walls. A steady stream of water poured down from a crack in the ceiling above, pooling in a circular indentation in the stone floor, likely created by centuries of falling water. All around him was the smell of wild animal.

He inspected the chamber, finding small bones, mostly those of fish or snakes, and lots of scat. The droppings were long and cylindrical, and tapered at the ends like that of a wolf or mountain lion, but free of the bits of fur you would expect to see from an animal that ate deer and small rodents. He didn't know what these creatures were, but he had found their lair.

An angry snarl filled the cavern, and he whirled around to see three beasts out of a nightmare come hurtling out of one of the crevasses. He opened fire with his Walther, bringing down the creature in the lead. The other two beasts kept coming.

He leapt up onto a nearby ledge, turned, and pumped three more rounds into the second creature. Another shot went wild, and the third beast was scrambling up onto the ledge. Dane kicked him twice in the snout, sending him tumbling back to the ground. As it crouched, ready to spring, he put a bullet between its eyes.

He leapt down from the ledge and dashed toward the only tunnel that looked large enough for him to pass through. He hadn't gone ten steps when another of the beasts came hurtling down the tunnel right at him. He stopped and squeezed off three shots before bringing it down. Five bullets left in the clip. Jade had hurried him out of the hotel so quickly that morning that he hadn't even thought to grab any reloads.

The tunnel opened up into a yawing cavern. A stone bridge no more than three paces wide spanned the depths.

Dane didn't spared a glance at the darkness below, but dashed across, keeping his light on the ground in front of him.

He was halfway across when he again heard the snarling sound that told him the beasts were coming again. One burst out of the darkness ahead, and he fired once, twice, but the creature kept coming. A third shot and it fell mere yards from him. He had no time to breathe a sigh of relief because now the sound was behind him. He whirled about, bringing his Walther to bear.

The creature was hurtling through the air, its gleaming white fangs shining in the darkness. He fell backward, firing as he went down. The beast hurtled past him, regained its feet, and leapt again.

Dane regained his feet, and as the monster flew toward him, he let his Walther fall to the ground and struck out with his open hand, catching it below its snapping jaws, striking in the throat with all his might. Sharp claws raked his shoulder and he caught a whiff of fetid breath as he knocked it back. Before it could spring again, he kicked it hard in the side with both feet, sending it tumbling over the edge and into the darkness.

He allowed himself only a moment to recover and holster his empty Walther before regaining his feet and continuing along the path. Whatever lay ahead, he would have to meet it with his bare hands.

"What's our next clue?" Bones stood in the center of the pit, directly atop Fray Marcos's symbol, letting his light play across the faces of the gargoyles. He couldn't help but be amused at the way the moving shadows seemed to make them come to life.

"If you'll stop playing for a minute, I'll tell you," Amanda said. "Under the stairs in the pit." She turned and shone her light back toward the stairs they had just descended. "Under the stairs…"

"This is the other clue Jade doesn't have," Bones said. "If she made it this far, she probably went down that passageway over there, which means we're ahead of her." He inclined his head toward the tunnel on the other side of the pit. There was no way of knowing whether or not any of Jade's party had survived the cave-in, but he held out hope that Maddock was alive and well, and somewhere in this warren of dark tunnels.

"I just don't see anything 'under' the stairs," Amanda said. "They hug the edge of the pit. It's just solid stone. Maybe one of the steps comes up, or something."

"Could be," Bones said. He decided they should take the systematic approach. "Tell you what. We'll start at the bottom. You check each step, I'll work my way along the wall."

The steps had been carved into the natural rock, and everything about them seemed solid. He ran his hand across the smooth surface, seeking an imperfection, a recessed area, anything that would indicate a doorway. He was just beginning to think they were in for a long day when his light fell on a sight they had somehow missed.

"Amanda, get down here!" Her hurried footsteps padded down the heavy stone, and she was at his side in seconds. "I was so busy checking out the gargoyles that I didn't notice it."

"Fray Marcos's symbol," she breathed. "Do you think…?"

"It's got to be." He said. "The entrance to this place was under the tenth step. The symbol here is…"

"Under the tenth step!" She squeezed his arm with delight. "I wonder why ten and not seven?"

"Who cares? Let's go."

The clover outline was carved in shallow relief, but the cross in the center was cut deep. A closer look revealed a thin circle two feet in diameter encompassing the symbol. Bones slipped his fingers into the grooves of the cross and twisted. Nothing. He tried again. Still nothing.

"Maybe counterclockwise?" Amanda suggested.

"What am I thinking?" he muttered. "Righty tighty; lefty loosey." He changed his grip and heaved with all his might. The stone moved an inch, then another, and slowly began to turn until it had rotated ninety degrees and then stopped. Bones kept pushing, but to no avail. He stepped away from the wall, about to try out some of Crazy Charlie's favorite Cherokee curse words, when a hissing sound filled the pit and the stone shot back into the wall with a pop like a champagne cork.

"They hermetically sealed it!" Amanda whispered. "You must have broken the seal and the suction pulled the stone through."

"Glad I wasn't still holding on," Bones said, imagining tumbling down a dark tunnel with his fingers stuck in the disc like a drunken bowler on ten cent beer night. He shone his light through the hole and saw another set of stairs leading down into more blackness. He went headfirst through the opening, with Amanda close behind. From somewhere down below, a sound came like a whisper but, as they drew closer, grew to a roaring crescendo. Water. As they continued their descent, a hazy, green glow emerged in the distance, first as a fuzzy pinpoint of light, growing to an arched doorway ten feet tall.

They stepped out onto a walkway running above an underground river cutting through an oval-shaped cavern. Shining bands of green twisted in irregular paths through the natural rock all around them, giving the entire chamber an ethereal glow.

"What's making it glow like that?" Bones asked. "It's nothing biological; it's in the rock." He knelt to get a closer look at one of the glowing streaks. "Radiation?"

"Radioactive material doesn't typically glow," Amanda said. "But sometimes radiation can cause other minerals to glow. I wrote an article on it once." She stood and took his hand as they paused, admiring the sight.

On the far end, water poured out of a clover-shaped

opening forty feet up the wall, and tumbled over a series of seven terraces before emptying into the channel that flowed beneath them. The walkway on which they stood ran directly down the middle of the channel, ending at the seven-terraced waterfall.

"Where is all this water coming from?" Amanda asked.

"We're pretty far below ground level," Bones said, consulting his Pathfinder. "I suppose some sort of underground stream runs through here."

"Well, this fits, at least. I think the next two clues go together," Amanda said, taking out her notes. "'On the third terrace in the cave on the eastern side inside the waterfall.' Looks like we're going to get wet."

"And to think I didn't even bring my umbrella," Bones said. "Who'd have thought we'd need one down here?"

From the stairwell behind them a cold voice spoke.

"I wouldn't worry about that. You won't be needing it."

Chapter 27

Issachar knew something was wrong the moment he entered the chamber. A foul stench filled the air, the faint sound of something… many somethings running, and then…"

A vicious snarl, and then a bloodcurdling scream. Confused shouts. Gunfire. Muzzle flashes. Confused interplays of light as the squad members searched for their attackers. And then he saw one.

A flash of gleaming white fangs, a slick, black snout, and burning eyes hurtled toward him from out of the darkness. He brought his Kalashnikov up and blew its head apart. So they could die. That was all he needed to know.

A flare blossomed in the darkness, setting the cavern aglow. Some of the creatures shied away from it, but others continued to attack. The surviving members of the squad fell in together, keeping up a steady fire and moving as one across the cavern.

Issachar picked off another leaping beast. In the glow of the flare he could see a little more of them. Their low-slung bodies were lithe, like greyhounds, and covered in dark hide. What were they?

"This way!" The Elder shouted. "Keep moving!"

Another squad member fell to one of the creatures. Issachar fired at it and missed. The beast began dragging the body away. He fired again and brought it down.

Reaching the far side of the cavern, Issachar and Benjamin laid down a steady rate of fire, trying to keep the creatures at bay as the men climbed into the passageway, but the creatures had fallen back into the darkness. Issachar caught a glimpse of booted feet as the beasts dragged the corpse of one of their men away into the darkness.

That's everyone, Elder," Benjamin said as Issachar scrambled into the tunnel. "The rest are dead. The creatures are…" he paused, his face twisted in disgust. "The creatures are dragging their bodies away. They're even dragging away the carcasses of their own dead." Sweat shone on his florid face, and he voice quavered.

"What are they?" Levi asked in scarcely more than a whisper.

"I don't know," Benjamin said. "Their heads are like wolves, but their teeth…" He shuddered and swallowed hard. "I wish I had could have gotten a better look at them. I've never seen anything like them."

The Elder had gotten a good enough look at them, however. In the first chamber they had found Jacob's remains buried under a rock fall, and had just seen the passageway above the pillar, when surprised shouts and agonized screams shattered the silence. As the rattle of gunfire filled the air, he turned back to a horrific sight. Like a macabre slide show, each muzzle flash revealed demonic creatures, somehow doglike, reptilian, and catlike at the same time. He mind could make no more sense of them in the strobe-like flashes of gunfire and wavering beams of their high-intensity flashlights. They stood little chance against these lightning-quick creatures that could apparently see in the dark. He had dropped a flare and guided his men to the escape, but already his elite twelve had been reduced to seven.

"It doesn't matter what they are or what they look like." Issachar's voice was a low rumble like a rockslide. "They can be killed. That's all that matters." He stood, his hulking form seeming to fill the tunnel in shadow.

The Elder nodded. He stood and shone his light down the passage ahead of them, seeing nothing threatening.

"We are seven now," he said. "A fitting number for uncovering the secret of the legend of the Seven Cities. God has seen fit to cull our flock. We will not be taken unawares again. Naphtali, you will be the rear guard. Keep an eye out behind us." The hulking blond man nodded. "Benjamin, watch for any passages or trapdoors on our right, Asher you mind the left. Levi will be on the lookout for anything coming from above. I will take the lead." His words seemed to renew his men's confidence, and they set forth at a slow jog.

The Elder set his jaw, channeling his frustration into a sense of righteous rage. It was his destiny to bring the Dominion to power. No longer would they be a clandestine organization, little more than a well-funded paramilitary group. The treasure would bring them greater wealth, no doubt, and the notoriety associated with the discovery would certainly cause many true believers to finally abandon the Mormon church and join the Dominion. But the true prize was something none other than him even suspected. Not even Ihara knew what the Elder believed lay beneath these stones. He suppressed a shiver of excitement as he thought of the moment he would finally lay hands upon it and the Dominion would truly live up to its name.

"Put your hands up very slowly." A man stepped out from the shadowy passageway, his pistol trained on Bones. He was just a shade over six feet tall, solid and muscular. His flat-topped hair was prematurely gray and looked like it had been cut with a laser level. He fixed his intense gaze on Bones. "Ihara, will you please relieve them of their weapons?"

Jade stepped out from behind the man. She did not meet Bones' eye as she relieved him of his Glock and Amanda of the .22. She didn't check his boot sheath, which struck Bones as odd. He was certain she knew about the knife he always carried.

"I remember you now," Bones said. "You're the idiot whose car I stole at Mesa Verde." Bones said. "Where's Maddock?"

Jade did not answer. She stepped back to stand beside the man with the gun and went about storing the confiscated pistols in her pack before drawing her own weapon, a snub-nose .38 revolver, and trained it on Amanda.

"Maddock is dead," the man said. "You can thank Ihara for that."

"Shut up, Jarren," Jade muttered.

"I'll kill you," Bones whispered. "Slowly and painfully." He wasn't sure which of them he was talking to. Right now he wanted them both dead. He might have taken his chances going after Jarren, but not at the risk of Jade killing Amanda. "You're both going to die."

"You'd better do it quickly," the man said. "As I'm about to kill you. I just wanted to give you some time to think about it before you died. You deserve to suffer a little. As a matter of fact," he lowered his gun from Bones' chest to his abdomen, "I think I'll make it slow and painful, as you suggested."

"You might want to think again." He was trying to think of anything to keep them talking. Anything to buy time in hopes that Jarren would make a mistake and give him an opening. "We've heard from Jimmy again. Seems he made some mistranslations in the final steps." It was almost true. "We saw what happened to your little friend in the first chamber, so you know what a bad idea it is to proceed without complete information."

"We'll take it off your dead body," Jarren said.

"I didn't write it down, you half-wit. It's in my noggin."

"We should keep them alive anyway," Jade said. "In case the treasure is booby-trapped. Let them lead the way and they can spring whatever traps are waiting for us."

"Not a bad idea," Jarren said. "But we don't need both of them to do that. And since Bonebrake here is the one with the knowledge, that makes his girlfriend expendable. Kill her."

It was like Bones had been dunked in freezing water.

His eyes locked with Jade's and he saw her look from him to Amanda and then at Jarren. Her face was a mask of uncertainty. She looked at Amanda and frowned, as if trying to communicate something. Her eyes fell, as did her hand in which she held her gun.

"Ihara?" Jarren turned his head to look at Jade. That was all Bones needed.

He leapt forward, striking Jarren's wrist with a vicious downward chop that numbed his fingers. He ripped the gun out of Jarren's grasp, but before he could get control of the weapon, Jarren knocked it out of his hands. Green light glinted off the barrel as it spun through the air and splashed into the water. At the mouth of the passage, Amanda had leapt onto Jade, and was grappling with her, trying to wrest the revolver from her. Bones landed a solid right to Jarren's jaw, sending him tumbling backward. He leaped past Jarren, stumbling as he dove for the weapon.

He, Jade, and Amanda landed in a heap at the mouth of the passageway. Bones grabbed the short barrel of the revolver and pointed it up toward the ceiling, aware that Jade's finger was still on the trigger.

"No!" Jade grunted. "You… don't … understand."

Bones twisted onto his side, and with his right hand, pushed the hammer back, and forced the webbing of his hand inside the hammer, preventing it from firing. With a snarl of pure rage, he ripped the pistol away from Jade. Before he could turn the weapon on Jarren, though, burning agony exploded inside him as Jarren landed a solid kick to Bones' groin. Dizzy with pain and grunting with the effort, he rolled onto his back, raising the revolver. Jarren kicked it out of his hands and leapt onto Bones, his hands clutched around Bones' throat.

Bones had plenty of experience in ground fighting, but the direct blow to the groin had weakened him. He struggled to get the clutching hands away from his throat. He worked Jarren's right hand loose, and struggled in vain to wrap it up. He pushed with both feet and twisted, trying to turn the man over, knowing he did not have the leverage or remaining strength to do so. His air almost completely cut out, his vision swam and Jarren's eyes glowed in triumph. Bones twisted again, trying to free himself. Amanda could not help him; she was still struggling with Jade. He knew the fight had lasted only a minute, if that, but the moments stretched into eternity as they struggled for their lives.

Jarren ripped his hand loose from Bones' weakening grasp and clenched his fist, ready to rain down blows, when something caught his eye. Bones' pants leg had slid up and Jarren had seen the knife. Before Bones could react, Jarren wrested it free and raised it above his head.

"Time to die."

Chapter 28

Dane burst into the glowing cavern, his eyes taking in the scene in a split-second. Jade and Amanda wrestling on the floor, rolling precariously closer to the edge of the walkway and the dark water that waited below. A man with an upraised knife. Bones clutching desperately at the man's arm.

His Walther useless, having expended his bullets fighting off the dark creatures that whose lair he had penetrated, he sprinted forward, leaping into the air and catching the man full in the chest with a flying side kick. The man fell onto his back, still clutching the knife. Dane tumbled to the walkway, catching most of the impact of his fall on his shoulder, rolled over, and sprang to his feet.

"Jarren! No!" Jade shouted. She and Amanda lay on the ground, their fight forgotten, both staring open-mouthed at Dane. Bones rolled over onto his stomach, choking and gasping for breath.

Jarren crept forward, his knife held low, a vicious look in his eyes, still panting from the fatigue of his fight with Bones. He chanced a glance behind him, apparently to gauge how long he had to dispatch Dane before Bones was able to join the fray. He sprang forward, slashing at Dane's inner thigh, trying to sever the femoral artery.

Dane slipped out of the way just in time, the blade slicing a shallow cut across the outside of his thigh. He sprang forward, driving his elbow into Jarren's throat. Jarren reeled backward, gasping, but immediately resumed the attack, stabbing at Dane's midsection. Dane pivoted and, with an open palm, knocked Jarren's knife hand to the side. As the blade thrust met empty space, Dane trapped Jarren's elbow with his right arm and struck him twice in the side of the neck with vicious palm heel strikes. Jarren's knees buckled and the knife clattered to the ground. Dane released his grip.

As Jarren staggered away, Bones stepped in front of him.

"I owe you this," he said, and drove a devastating right cross into the man's temple. Jarren's eyes went glassy. He took two steps to his right, and then went limp. He tumbled like a rag doll over the edge of the walkway and into the water below. They watched the current carry him out of sight.

Bones grasped Dane by the shoulders and held him at arm's length, looking at him like he had not seen him in ages.

"Bro, I thought I'd never see you again," he said. His eyes grew suddenly hard and he whirled about, picked his knife up off the ground where Jarren had dropped it, and stalked down the walkway toward the women, who were standing and looking at him in trepidation. "All right, Jade. What do you want me to cut off first: your fingers or your toes? I would cut your eyes out, but I want you to watch yourself bleed to death."

"Bones! What the hell are you talking about?" Dane shouted. He couldn't believe his friend was saying this.

"She's one of them," Bones snarled. "She's part of the Dominion. All along, it was her feeding information to them. As soon as Jimmy sent us the final translation, they sent men to kill us. They killed Saul and almost got us. She," he pointed at Jade, "was supposed to kill you. She told them she had."

Dane felt like a detached spirit floating in blessed unfeeling. He had not felt this numb since Melissa died. Everything fell into place. She had used him, used *them*, to help her find the clues she sought. When she didn't need them anymore, she drugged him and left him to die in the desert, and left the others to be taken unaware by the Dominion men."

"Don't kill her," he said in a voice like ice. He couldn't

bring himself to do that. "Find something to tie her up. We'll figure out what to do with her after we find the treasure."

"Dane, no!" Jade cried, her voice cracking. "You read my note, didn't you? I explained everything!" Tears welled in her eyes, and she took a tentative step toward him.

"What note?"

"They wanted me to kill you, but there was no way I would ever do that. I gave you something to put you to sleep and left you somewhere safe I knew of, somewhere close by, until I could come back for you. I explained it all in the note."

"You left me in the desert to die." He said.

"I left you in a sheltered place with six bottles of water, a bag of trail mix, and a note telling you to stay out of sight until I came back for you because the Dominion wanted you dead. Don't you remember when we stopped for coffee? The paper bag I carried out of the convenience store?" She was pleading now. "I tucked it between you and the wall of the overhang."

Dane vaguely remembered her taking a paper bag out of the back of the car. He certainly could have missed a brown paper bag stuck in a shadowy overhang of red rock. Could it be true? He wanted it to be, but he didn't know if he could trust her.

"Dane, if I wanted you dead, don't you think I could have killed you while you were asleep? Why do you think I left you so close to Zion instead of out in the middle of nowhere? How could you think I could do that to you after we… after…" Her voice faded away. Tears now flowed freely down her cheeks, but she did not look away from him. "Please," she whispered. "I really do care about you."

He couldn't take it. He had tried so hard not to let himself have feelings for anyone since Melissa had died. There had been Kaylin for a short while, and then after last night, he had thought… He turned his back on her and stared into the water tumbling from the center of Fray

Marcos' symbol and down onto the glowing terraces.

"Explain a few things to *me*, then." Bones said, taking up the slack in the conversation. "You admit, then, that you're in the Dominion."

"No," Jade replied. "Dane, please look at me. I'll tell you everything. I promise."

"Telling me everything from the start would have been a good idea," he said, turning around to face her. "Now I don't know if you're going to tell me the truth, or a carefully crafted story."

"I know. When I first met you, I didn't want to scare you away by telling you. I actually knew your name, and yours," she said to Bones, "from reading about what happened in Jordan. Then things got dangerous, and I was afraid you'd bail on me, and I was scared and I needed you. When I realized I was falling for you, it had been so long that I didn't see how I could tell you after waiting all that time."

"Fine, just tell me whatever truth it is you want to tell me." He folded his arms across his chest and stared at her.

"My passion has always been solving the mystery of the Seven Cities. Saul was one of my students, and one day he approached me with something I had only dreamed of ever finding: the missing final page from the journal of Fray Marcos de Niza."

"Great. Another journal," Bones muttered, fingering his knife.

"Fray Marcos uncovered evidence of a "great and terrible" secret. That secret was somehow associated with an order that acted under the sign of the cross-and-clover, the one we now know as Fray Marcos's sign. He journeyed through the New World and managed to confirm the truth of that secret. Seeing the depredations they committed upon the native people, and not wanting the Conquistadores to discover his secret, he concocted the story of the Seven Cities of Cibola, both to explain his wanderings and to throw the Spanish off. He did not, however, think it was his place to hide this secret from the world forever, so he and Estevanico concocted a plan. He remained in the southwest, planting clues in places he and Fray Marcos had chosen. Fray Marcos returned to Mexico, telling everyone that Estevanico had been killed, and spreading his tale of seven cities containing more gold than the Incas ever dreamed of.

"Unfortunately for Fray Marcos, Coronado couldn't wait to get his hands on the gold. He took Marcos as his guide and set out to conquer the Seven Cities. When the Spaniards never found the cities of gold, Fray Marcos was branded a liar, and eventually died in disgrace. According the journal page Saul gave me, he hid a single clue that would unlock the secret. He hid it in a well in a remote outpost in Argentina."

"The breastplate," Bones said, still holding his knife.

"Right," Jade said. "When Saul showed me this, I dove into the research, and learned of a recently discovered Spanish outpost in Argentina. I wanted to get down there and investigate right away, before someone beat me to it. Saul introduced me to his father, who offered to fund my expedition through the organization of which he was a member. I would get all the credit for the find. The catch was, when I found the final location, his organization wanted to cherry pick a few of the artifacts before I documented the find. I thought it was a simple matter of black market artifact trading, which I loathe, but I didn't see any other way I could fund the expedition on such short notice. By the time I learned I was being funded by the Dominion, it was too late to back out. In part, I was afraid of what they might do if I broke our deal, but I have to admit that I had the fever. I probably would have taken their money had I known from the start, as long as it meant realizing my life's ambition."

"I don't get why they needed you," Amanda said. "If they had the journal page, why not go after the clue themselves?"

"I can't be one hundred percent certain." Jade's eyes

took on a faraway glint. "The only things they had were the journal page, which makes no sense if you don't know the rest of the story, and some local legends about a hidden treasure. They needed my knowledge and expertise. If you have a choice, why send a team of grunts when you can send an archaeologist who's studied the Seven Cities for her entire life? Besides, even if they had managed to find the well and uncover the breastplate, which I doubt they could have done without the benefit of my research, they would have had needed an academic to help them get the clues deciphered. They also had Saul to keep tabs on me, and I was required to report in to Saul's father on a regular basis. I guess the answer to your question is, 'Why not me?'"

"Then why did they show up at Chaco Canyon, Mesa Verde, and Hovenweep?" Dane asked. "Why did they snatch the clue at Shiprock before we did?"

"Actually," Amanda said, "Saul found that clue. He didn't tell us because he knew Jade was working with the Dominion."

"He did?" Jade looked flabbergasted. "I didn't think he knew. He didn't seem to know his own father was in the Dominion." She shook her head. "He must have wanted to find the treasure before them. Why didn't he tell me?"

"You still haven't answered my question," Dane snapped. He wanted desperately to believe her, to feel about her the way he had before learning of her connection with the Dominion. Anything that did not make sense, anything that did not strengthen her story, eroded the trust he was trying to rebuild.

"That was Jarren's doing." She gestured toward the spot where Jarren had been swept away by the current. "He works for someone who is known only as The Elder. He's the head of the organization. Jarren wasn't sure I could be trusted, so he took it upon himself to try to find the first piece without us. When I reported in, as instructed, he backed off. That is, until Bones showed up."

"Why did that matter?" Bones had sheathed his knife,

and now squatted on the walkway, listening in keen interest.

"You were a new variable. You had already made trouble for them by taking the sun disc, and by rescuing Orley. At Mesa Verde, Jarren and another thug showed up at Square Tower House. They wouldn't answer my questions, but they wanted the clue and they wanted you dead, though I think they were acting on their own in that respect. I told them you had just reported back to me that Square Tower House was a dead end, and I convinced them that I was going to ditch you anyway because I didn't need you. One of them cut your rope, and knocked me out 'just to be safe.'"

"So you didn't set them on Saul and me at Sun Temple?" Bones asked. Amanda had sat down next to him. Both seemed to believe what Jade had told them so far.

"No. I had reported that we were looking at both locations. I kept giving them only the minimum information: what we found, and where we thought the next location might be, so they never knew about the solstice connections, or any of our speculation. We were a little off regarding the site at Hovenweep, so we unintentionally threw them a curve there. And you guys held back the information about Rainbow Bridge until we were already there."

"We thought Saul was the mole," Amanda said, "but we weren't sure."

Jade nodded.

"When Jimmy made the connection that led to Zion," Jade continued, "I reported in that all the pieces were in place. I believed Saul that the Dominion already had the Ship Rock piece. They, in turn, assumed that when I said 'all pieces' that I meant I had all of them. I thought I could ditch you guys at the hotel, complete the mission, and then when the Dominion picked whatever artifacts it was they wanted, I could let you in on everything. But they told me to kill Maddock."

"Why only me?" Dane asked. Now they were at the

heart of it.

"I think they suspected there was something between us." She was looking him right in the eye. "It was a test of my loyalties. What I did to you was the only thing I could think of on short notice. I almost told you the truth that night, but I didn't know what you'd do. I was half afraid you'd hate me and half afraid you'd insist on going with me and manage to get yourself killed. I never planned to hurt you, and I did not know they would send men after the rest of you." She now knelt and spoke to Bones. "When I came into this chamber and saw you and Amanda here, I was in shock. It was like my brain was frozen. Jarren had his gun on you, and I didn't know what to do that wouldn't get you killed. You had to have noticed that I didn't take your knife, not that it did you any good." She took a deep breath. "I've never killed anyone. Never even dreamed of it. But I swear to you, I had just made up my mind to shoot Jarren when you jumped him. I swear."

Bones did not say anything. Apparently he was having as much trouble making up his mind as Dane was.

"I really don't like you," Amanda said. Both women stood and faced one another, Amanda's eyes ablaze and Jade's dull with remorse or regret. "But I believe you." She held out her hand, and after a moment, Jade took it in hers.

"Okay," Bones said, rising to his feet. "I don't know if I forgive you, but I believe you."

"Thank you," Jade whispered. She let go of Amanda's hand and turned to face Dane, the questioning look in her eyes making words unnecessary.

Dane did not know what to say. Though every fiber of his being ached to believe her, to forgive her, to take her in her arms and make things be like they had been, he just could not. It just wasn't that easy.

"Let's find this treasure," he said, his voice hoarse with emotion. He could not help but see tears flood Jade's eyes as he turned his back on her.

Chapter 29

The icy water drenched Dane as he ducked through the waterfall, chilling him to his core. It brought him to his senses after feeling dazed by Jade's revelations. Behind the waterfall, a door in the face of the rock led to a spiral staircase. As Dane led the way up, Bones filled him in on the events that had brought him and Amanda to this point, including the attack at the motel, Jimmy's updated translation, and their trek through the chambers beneath Angel's Landing. Finally, the stairway ended at an ornate stone door. The door was carved with an elaborate scene of a storm at sea, complete with angry clouds, crashing waves, and a sea monster writhing in the depths. Where a knob would be found on an ordinary door, the cross and clover was carved, hovering just above the horizon. Hebrew words were carved above the doorway.

"I've seen these words before," Jade said. "When I was studying the first temple. 'Shaar HaMayin. The Water Gate. I wonder what's behind there."

"Only one way to find out," Dane muttered. His anger had lent him a sense of reckless disregard. He pressed the symbol and the door slid back, revealing another glowing cavern. Here, the glow was more intense, the light brighter, and the chamber was noticeably warmer, almost humid. A cross-shaped channel ran down the center of the room, the water disappearing into a hole at their feet. On the far end of the chamber near the point of the cross, and on either side, lay circular pools, their dark waters speaking of great depth. "The cross and clover," Dane said, noticing the layout of the pools. "This must be the source of Fray Marcos' symbol."

"Either that, or Estevanico spent a lot of time with a hammer and chisel," Bones said with a smile. "So, what's the next clue?"

"At the edge of the canal on its northern side, six cubits toward the immersed pool," Amanda recited. "Which way is north?"

"To the left," Bones said, consulting his Pathfinder.

They skirted the edge of the cross-shaped canal. Reasoning that the northernmost point of the cross would be the logical place to begin, Dane led the others to the far left point of the cross.

"A cubit is the distance between a man's fingertip and elbow." The hurt was still evident in her voice. "So, probably about eight feet toward the pool."

Dane paced off the distance, dropped to his knees, and shone his flashlight across the floor. He saw nothing but smooth stone.

Bones dropped to the floor next to him and ran his fingertips across the smooth stone. He frowned.

"Shine your light here, Maddock. I think I feel something." Dane turned his light on the spot Bones indicated, and saw the cross and clover traced into the rock in such fine lines it would have been almost impossible to see if they had not been searching so intently for it. "But what do we do?" Bones asked. "It's just a picture." He pressed it, but nothing happened.

"Boys, how about that big chain hanging up above you?" Amanda asked, her voice playful

Dane looked up. A massive chain hanging down from the ceiling, ending about eight feet above them.

"How long have you known that was there?" Bones asked.

"Since we walked in," she said. "There's another one on the opposite side." She pointed to the far side of the channel where Jade stood looking up at the twin of the chain under which they stood. "I imagine there's an unpleasant surprise waiting for the first person who doesn't know his north from his south."

As she said those last words, Jade reached up to take

hold of the chain.

"Jade! No!" Dane took off at a sprint, leaping across the center channel and dashing over to her. She looked into his eyes in complete astonishment as he clutched her tight against him.

"I wasn't going to pull on it, Maddock," she whispered. "What's gotten into you, anyway?"

"You have," he said, so soft that only she could hear him. For in that moment he thought she might die, he knew his true feelings for her. All uncertainties and hurt aside, he had cared only that she lived. He cared. "We have a lot to work out between us, but I do care about you."

She did not reply, but twined her arms around his neck and kissed him very seriously. After what seemed like an hour, Bones interrupted them by loudly clearing his throat.

"Excuse me, but don't we have a treasure to find here?"

"I found my treasure," Dane said, holding Jade tight to his side. "Let's get out of here."

"Are you serious, Maddock?" Bones' eyes were wide and his mouth agape.

"Hell no," Dane said after a suitable pause for effect. "I was yanking your chain. How about you yank that one and see what happens?"

"I suppose you think that's funny too," Bones said to Amanda, who was covering her face.

"Of course not," she said, her smile belying her words. "I would never make you the butt of a joke."

"Forget it," Bones said. He took hold of the chain and pulled. A sound like thunder filled the room and the floor shook.

"Bones! Are you sure this is the north side?" Dane shouted over the roar.

"Trust me!" Bones called back. "Look there!" He pointed to a spot in the ceiling directly above the pool, where a circle of stone about twelve feet in diameter had begun to turn. As the stone rotated, it gradually descended, revealing another spiraling stone staircase. It settled to the floor with a thud, fitting perfectly over the top of the pool. "Told you," Bones said. "Trust me."

Dane again took the lead. As they ascended, he finally told them how Justin had rescued him in the desert and showed him the pool that gave him access to a back entrance through a long, spiraling tunnel, much like the one at the top of the peak through which the others had entered. Finally, weary from the climb, he had emerged in the center of the gargoyle-lined pit. He had immediately been set upon by the dark creatures from Justin's drawings. He had retreated back into the tunnel, where he could pick them off one at a time. Finally, he made his way back out, praying he would not meet any more of the beasts, as he had exhausted his ammunition.

Upon learning that his friend was unarmed, Bones gave Dane the .22 Jade had returned to him. She had given Bones his Glock back as well, but her revolver was lost. When they reached the top of the stairs, they were again faced with a stone door. This one was engraved with a large circle at the top, with seven lines descending from it, each ending in a hand.

"That's the same symbol that was painted in Orley's cave," Bones said. "And on the sun disc." He took the disc out of his pack and held it up for comparison. They were identical. "Do you think whoever painted it was here?"

"Whoever the artist was," Amanda said, "he certainly knew the way to Angel's Landing. His paintings led the way. And that giant spiral slope Dane climbed sounds a great deal like the spiral staircase that was painted in the cave. I'll wager," she said, reaching out to touch the disc, "that even if the artist was never here, the disc was once here."

"It's also the symbol of Aten," Jade said. "I think this just about seals the connection, if there was any doubt."

"Can you translate what's inscribed above this door?" Dane asked.

"Shaar HaKorban. The Gate of the Offering."

"Sounds promising," Bones said, putting the gold disc back in his pack. "Maddock, do you want to do the honors?"

This door pivoted as the others had done, and as he stepped through Dane was greeted by a sight that took his breath. Like the chamber below, a cross-shaped channel flowed through the middle, but this was a massive, vaulted chamber with ornate columns, all shot through with the same intensely glowing streaks, that climbed to a ceiling far above them, supported by shining arches. Here, the light burned with such intensity that it had lost most of its greenish hue, and was almost white. A similarly vaulted chamber was carved into either side. It was like a giant cathedral! It was not, however, the magnificence of the room that amazed him, but the treasure.

The floor was carved into seven terraces rising up from the channels in the chamber's center. Every inch was packed with more wealth than Dane had ever imagined. Huge chests had dry rotted and burst, spilling their contents upon the floor. Coins and ingots of gold, gold, silver and bronze coins lay scattered on the floor. Bars of gold and silver were stacked like firewood. Casks that probably contained oils or perfumes stood on the upper levels, interspersed with sculptures and pottery. Much of it was obviously Egyptian, but not all of it. As they made their way through the room, they saw other treasures. Some barrels held precious jewels, while others held ivory, or moldering bolts of what must have once been the finest cloth.

"Man, something's messing up my phone," Bones said, holding up his cell phone. "I wanted to take a picture. Bummer." He looked down at a pile of Egyptian artifacts that had spilled down from somewhere up above and lay strewn haphazardly across the bottom level. "This must be how that ranger found his ankh, and Justin found his treasures. They washed down the channels and eventually made their way out."

"Let's see what's in the transepts," Jade whispered,

using the name of the side chambers that gave cathedrals their cruciform shape. She took Dane's hand and led him forward. The left transept was shallow, perhaps forty feet deep, and held no treasure, but at the far end, perched atop the seventh tier, stood a golden lampstand larger than any Dane had ever seen. Three golden arms curved up on either side of its central column, and its solid base was inlaid with rubies. Jade squeezed his hand in a crushing grip. "Dane! It's the menorah! The menorah!"

"I can't get my camera to work either," Amanda said as she and Bones walked up behind them. "It's almost as if…" She stopped in mid-sentence as her eyes fell on the menorah. "I can't believe it. I thought the Romans took it."

"That was the one that was made after the Babylonian Exile," Jade said, her voice soft with reverence. "This must be the original. Many believe that the shape of the menorah is influenced by the Aten symbol."

"So what's in the other transept?" Dane found that he could not bring himself to speak above a whisper in the face of such a holy sight. Moving as one, they all turned slowly about, and again were stunned by what they saw.

This transept, too, held no treasure save what stood at the end.

"I have to get a closer look at this," Dane whispered. He leapt across the center channel, the others following behind, all in rapt silence. The steps of this chamber were lined with white marble, and the walls were lined with cedar. On the bottom level of the left side of the transept, spaced at three-foot intervals, stood a line of twelve golden lions. On the right, facing their counterparts, were twelve golden eagles. Each step at the far end of the transept was also flanked by a golden creature: A lion facing an ox, a wolf and a sheep, a tiger and a camel, an eagle and a peacock, a cat and a cock, and a sparrow opposite a dove.

"Six steps lead up to…" Jade whispered.

On the seventh step stood a throne of such magnificence that it almost hurt to look upon it. The seat was made of ivory, its frame of gold. Atop the seat stood a golden candelabra topped by a golden basin. Twenty four golden vines entwined above the throne, and topping it all was a dove clutching a tiny hawk in its claws.

"…Solomon's throne."

Dane dropped to his knees, and the others did the same. He took Jade's hand in his left and Amanda's in his right, who in turn took Bones' hand. They remained there, in reverent silence, gazing upon what, until now, had only existed in memory and legend.

"I don't understand," he finally whispered.

"Understand what?" Jade asked, turning to stare at him.

"There are more clues," he said, unable to take his eyes off the throne of the greatest king in Hebrew history. "This isn't the end. But what else can there be?"

Bones stood and one-by-one hauled everyone to their feet. He looked at Dane with an unreadable expression.

"As to that question, my friend, there's only one way to find out."

Chapter 30

At the far end of the chamber, the steps led to a simple doorway, so out of place amongst the splendor of the treasure that surrounded it.

"In the sepulchre, in the third course of stones," Amanda read. "Is that a sepulchre?"

"In ancient Hebrew practice, a sepulchre was usually carved into the side of a hill," Jade said. "Perhaps that's what the simplicity is supposed to symbolize."

Golden statues of Anubis guarded the door, each holding a spear. Bones paused for a closer look."

"Hey! They come out!" he exclaimed, removing one of the spears and hefting it. "It's heavy!"

"Put it back," Amanda said, as if speaking to a child.

"You're no fun," Bones said, but he returned the spear to its proper place and followed her up the steps.

The chamber they entered was nothing more than a perfect square carved into the rock. Down the center of the room stood a line of seven piles of loose rock. Dane and Bones immediately set to moving the third pile of stones, and soon they uncovered a manhole-sized cross and clover disc. Together, they lifted it from its place and moved it to the side. Dane could hear the rush of water down below, and another sound he recognized immediately.

"Get out of here!" He shouted, pushing Jade toward the door and drawing the .22. A dark blur burst from the hole, snarling with unearthly rage. Dane pumped three rounds into the beast, but when it hit the ground, it turned toward him and tensed to spring. Before it could leap, Bones blew a hole in the back of its head with his Glock. They weren't out of the woods yet, as two more of the beasts clambered out of the hole. Dane emptied the .22 into the first, then drew his knife, and backed up to the door, ready to protect Amanda and Jade. Bones put four rounds into the second beast, then moved cautiously to the hole and peered down inside.

"Here, kitty, kitty," he called. No sound came from the hole save the steady flow of the underground stream. "Hopefully that's it," he said. "What are these things?"

In the light, Dane could clearly see the beasts for the first time. He squatted down next to the nearest of the fallen creatures. Amanda and Jade returned to the room, Jade clutching her knife and Amanda holding one of the Anubis's spears. Amanda shrank back from the dead creatures, but Jade dropped down on the balls of her feet next to Dane.

The creature's body was long and sleek, with a broad chest and a sturdy rib cage. It was hairless, its flesh a mottled, dark green and as tough as old leather, with a pronounced spinal ridge that jutted up like the plates of a stegosaurus. Its haunches were so thickly muscled that they reminded Dane of a kangaroo. The front legs were also short and powerful. Jade lifted one of the padded front paws and squeezed it, causing its wicked, black claws to extend, and retract when she let go. The head was vaguely catlike, save for the long snout, with oversized ears and large, black eyes. Its mouth was filled with razor sharp teeth, two of which extended below the lower jaw line like fangs.

"Chupacabra," Bones whispered. "It's got to be!"

"Choo choo. Justin was trying to warn me of the chupacabra. He must have seen one sometime, and it scared him enough to draw those pictures. Unbelievable."

"So, do we go on?" Bones asked. "There could be more, and I don't have many bullets left."

"There could be more behind us as well," Jade said. "I didn't come this far to stop now. I vote we go on."

It did not escape Dane's notice that Jade was no longer taking the lead, but treating everyone as an equal member of the group. This was no longer her expedition, but a shared experience.

"Me too," Amanda said. "Let's finish this."

Dane went feet-first through the hole, landing on a stepping stone inscribed with the symbol that had become so familiar. He was in the middle of a fast-moving underground river. Stepping stones like the one on which he stood were set at three-foot intervals in five rows running the length of the passage all the way to the end, where another arched doorway waited. He was about to hop onto the next stone when something caught his eye. He stopped himself at the last second, almost losing his balance and flailing his arms as he fought to keep himself from tumbling into the fast-flowing current.

"Are you doing some kind of bird imitation down there?" Bones called to him. "What's the holdup?"

"There are stepping stones down here," he called back. "But they're not all the same. Some of them have the symbol on them, but some only have the clover. Pass the spear down here." Bones handed him the spear, and he reached out and tapped the stone upon which he had almost leapt- one with only a clover. It sank beneath the surface, floating back to the top when he pulled the spear away. He tested his theory on another stone that had both the cross and clover on the surface. It held. But would it support his weight? *Here goes nothing!* Bracing himself for a swim, he hopped onto the stone. It held.

"All right!" He called up to the others. "Come down one at a time, and only jump on the stones that have the cross *and* the clover. Make very sure where you're stepping. Got me?" He led the others on a zigzagging path through the river, testing each stone with the spear before moving on. Soon, he hopped out of the river to stand at the doorway.

"Beit Adonai," Jade again read the inscription. "The house of God."

Dane stepped through the doorway, and the spear clattered to the ground from his limp fingers.

The chamber was carved into the shape of the interior

of a pyramid, and all its walls were gold plated, save the cap of the pyramid, which was natural stone. The light that shone down from that small section at the top, and up from the floor, was so intense that it set the entire space aglow with a flickering golden light as it reflected off the water and the shining walls. High above him, a golden chain hung from the capstone, supporting a platform, though he could not see what it held. Water poured down through the seams of the capstone as well, soaking the hanging platform and falling in a curtain that enshrouded an island in the very center of the pyramid floor. Through the haze of falling water, Dane could just make out a stone sarcophagus on either side of the island. The island seemed to beckon to him, and he continued, as if in a trance, along the walkway that led to the island.

Jade moved to the first sarcophagus, and ran her fingers across it. The lid was carved in the image of a woman of unsurpassed beauty. Her striking face and swanlike neck were reminiscent of the famed bust of Nefertiti. She was not rendered in the Egyptian style, with royal headdress and accoutrements, but as she might have truly looked, with long, flowing hair and simple garments.

"Nefertiti," Jade whispered.

"And the other one?" Dane asked.

"Let's see."

The man on the lid of the other sarcophagus had the long face, prominent nose, broad cheeks, and hooded eyes of Akhenaten. His shoulders were narrow and his hips wide for a man, but nothing like the exaggerated images portrayed in art. Like Nefertiti, he was not rendered in his kingly Egyptian garb, but as a regular man. His hair was long and flowing, as was his beard. His slender arms lay folded across his chest, and in his right hand he gripped a staff engraved with Hebrew writing.

"The staff of Moses was reputed to bear the names of the ten Plagues of Egypt," Jade said.

"So this is…" Bones said, his voice quavering.

"The mose," she said. "Moses."

"I have to see this for myself," Dane said. He didn't know why, but the compulsion was so strong that he could not help himself. He needed to see. "Bones, will you help me with this."

"Dane, maybe you shouldn't," Amanda began. "I mean, it's…"

"Babe," Bones said, "this is the only man on earth who's seen the dead body of Lucifer himself and lived to tell the tale. Amanda smirked, obviously assuming he spoke in jest, but Jade paled visibly.

They carefully drew back the lid. Dane peered into the stone coffin. There was no second, ornate sarcophagus, as was the Egyptian tradition. There were no mummified remains.

Moses lay in the bottom of the sarcophagus, his body somehow perfectly preserved despite the thousands of years.

"He looks like he could stand up and walk out of here," Jade said, peering over the side along with Dane and Bones.

"Wrong testament," Bones said.

Dane reached down and touched Moses' staff. Unlike many of the legends, it was not made of sapphire, but of solid wood, polished to a high sheen. The Hebrew words were there, worked in gold along the length of the staff. The ends were capped in bronze, with the symbol of Aten etched in the top.

Amanda screamed and the turned to see two dark-clad men burst into the room. They dashed across the walkway, the first clutching a military-style knife, the second holding the spear Dane had dropped. Bones brought down the first man, a powerfully-built blond man, with two well-placed shots. His final shot went wild as the man with the spear, a veritable brute of a man with dark-hair cut G.I. style and arms and legs like tree trunks, bore down on them.

Without thinking, Dane grabbed the closest weapon,

Moses' staff, and dashed out to meet him. The man thrust the spear at Dane's chest, but Dane parried the blow and cracked his opponent's elbow. It wasn't much of a blow; enough to sting, perhaps, but the man hissed as if he had been burned. Dane pressed his momentary advantage, driving the larger man back. Staff met spear with crisp, sharp clacks. His opponent was not tiring, he was obviously in peak condition, but his inability to penetrate Dane's defenses was clearly frustrating him, because he began taunting Dane, trying to distract him.

"You think you can win, little man?" He bared his teeth in a predatory grin. "Issachar has killed better men than you."

"Does Issachar always speak of himself in the third person?" Dane shot back. The surreal nature of this entire experience gave things a dreamlike quality, and with it, a subtle feeling of unreality, as if nothing could harm him, no matter how reckless he might be.

"Funny man!" Issachar growled. "You'll die whimpering like those pathetic beasts I killed in the tunnels. I ran out of bullets and had to strangle the last one with my bare hands." His blows rained down harder, but Dane turned them with ease. A quick side thrust to the chest and Issachar gasped in pain. Now, clearly frustrated, he barreled forward, seeking to knock Dane down by main force, but Dane was too quick. He dodged to his right, swept Issachar's feet from under him, and gave him a smart rap to the back of the head. The blow would have rendered a weaker man unconscious, but Issachar bellowed with rage and kicked out, catching Dane's heel and bringing him down hard on his backside.

They both sprang to their feet, but once again Dane was quicker. As Issachar tensed to make an impaling thrust, Dane whipped the staff around with all his might, cracking Issachar on the right temple. Issachar screamed in agony, covered his face with his hands, and staggered backward. Dane pursued him, the staff whirling like a windmill.

Issachar shrieked as each blow struck him. To Dane's great surprise, everywhere the staff struck his opponent, angry boils rose on his flesh and slowly began to spread. Issachar drew his hands away. The festering sores now covered all of his exposed flesh. He cried out again, this time in sheer horror, and dove into the water. His cries trailed away as he vanished from sight.

"Most impressive." Dane recognized the cool pressure of a gun barrel pressed against the base of his skull. "Very slowly, hand me the staff."

Dane's first reaction was to fight, but even the feeling of invincibility that still flowed through him was not sufficient to conquer common sense. The man, whoever he was, need only to pull the trigger to end Dane's life. Careful not to make any sudden moves, Dane handed the staff back to his captor.

"Very good. Now, get down on the ground and put your hands behind your head." Despite the circumstances, the man sounded completely at ease, as if he was accustomed to his orders being obeyed. Dane complied with the man's instructions, lying face-down on the cold stone. With Dane no longer standing between them, the others finally got a look at the intruder.

"Mr. Zollinger!" Jade gasped.

"As in Jude Zollinger the bank president?" Amanda blurted.

"He's also Saul's father," Jade said.

"I am all of those things," the man replied, as if making introductions at a formal party, "but you may call me Elder."

Chapter 31

"You're the Elder?" Jade's ashen face reflected her stunned disbelief. "But… you had your own son killed."

"Saul was no longer a true believer," the man said. His voice was cool and uncaring, as if he was discussing something stuck on the bottom of his shoe. "He was no longer of use to me. Besides, the Lord has shown us that it is noble to sacrifice your son. You, however, might have earned your reprieve. I was going to kill you all, and I still might, but I think perhaps I shall let you live."

"Why?" Bones eyes burned with fury as he stared at the Elder.

"As Ms. Ihara is well aware, there are a few items of particular interest to me. I cannot remove them alone. I shall carry the staff, keeping my gun hand free, while four of you carry the other."

"And what item is that?" Dane asked.

"Oh, forgive me, Mr. Maddock. I have left you lying on the cold floor for too long. Please stand, keeping your hands behind your head of course, and proceed out to the island. If the rest of you would please move to the side and kneel, also with your hands behind your head?" The congenial manner in which he made his requests was chilling. "Please understand that I have no qualms about shooting any of you, and I have the skill to do so."

Dane complied, moving cautiously toward the island. The others also cooperated with the Elder, moving off to the side and dropping to the ground. Dane joined them, and they knelt there looking up at the Elder who leaned casually against Moses' sarcophagus. This was Dane's first good look at the man. He had a distinguished-looking man with intense blue eyes, graying black hair, but his athletic build and confident bearing removed any doubt as to whether or not he could handle himself.

"All of you seem to have forgotten that we have not exhausted the remaining clues. There is one discovery yet to be made, and it hangs above us."

Their eyes went to the platform suspended from the top of the pyramid. The intense glow that emanated from the walls of the pyramid made the water seem to sparkle and dance as it cascaded down. For the first time, Dane noticed a haze of steam around the platform. He thought about what he had seen when he had first entered the pyramid.

"You know, I don't think I would mess with that platform," Dane said. "That water isn't supposed to be coming down from there. It's leaking through the seams of the capstone. You try to bring that platform down, you might just bring the whole place down with you."

"I'm disappointed," the Elder said. "I thought yours was a more adventurous spirit than that." He turned to Jade. "Miss Ihara, as you are the last remaining member of my organization who has any knowledge of this quest, I shall permit you to do the honors. If you will please?" He pointed his gun at her. "I am not really asking."

"I'm not part of your organization," Jade muttered as she slowly rose to her feet and looked uncertainly from the Elder to Moses' tomb, and back to the Elder again.

"Details. The next clues read, 'Under the tomb, in the chain platform.' I assume there must be a hidden mechanism to lower whatever that is up above us." She cast uncertain eyes to the platform hanging above them. She moved to Moses' tomb and circled it, inspecting the floor all around it.

Dane kept his gaze fixed on the Elder, who moved away so that he could keep an eye equally on Jade and the others who remained on the floor. Obviously, they could charge him, but at least one of them would die in the process. He couldn't risk it… yet.

"It's not here," Jade said, her voice uncertain. "It's

either inside, or it's somewhere there." She nodded to Nefertiti's resting place. She looked inside the sarcophagus where Moses lay, inspecting every inch. Her eyes narrowed. "Could that be it?" she whispered. "Bones, give me the Aten disc." Once again focused on solving the puzzle, her air of command had returned.

Bones removed his backpack and tossed it to Jade, who retrieved the disc and leaned down into the sarcophagus.

"There's a space just above his head," she explained, "that looks to be the mirror image of the Aten symbol side of the disc. It might be nothing, but I wonder…"

Jade's hands were not visible from where he sat, but Dane could see the look of concentration on her face. He watched her lean back down into the sarcophagus, biting her lip. There was an audible click, and then a roar like the grinding of great, invisible gears. He looked up to see the platform descending toward them. He, Bones, and Amanda sprang to their feet almost as one.

"Careful, now," the Elder cautioned, training his gun on Dane. "I won't have you crushed underneath the platform. Move slowly toward me."

Dane took a hesitant step toward the Elder, his heart pounding. He needed an opening and he needed it soon, because he had just understood the final clue, and now he knew what lay on the platform. All the pieces fell into place: the glowing veins in the stone, the increased intensity of light and heat as they moved closer to this place, the decaying capstone, even the deformed creatures. It was all connected.

"Elder, you have the wrong translation of the final clue." He held out little hope that the man would listen to reason, but he had to try. "It should read '…the *ten* is impure.' Not the *tenth*. The *ten*."

"Meaningless." The Elder gave him a dismissive glance. His eyes flitted back to the platform and a beatific smile spread across his face. "The wealth of the treasure is a mere pittance compared to the power the Dominion will now wield."

"You can't even touch it!" Dane shouted. "It kills anyone who puts his hands on it! Don't you remember the stories?"

"You've seen too many movies, Mr. Maddock. Besides, I shan't touch it. The four of you shall."

The platform was no more than thirty feet above them now. Dane was sure he could feel heat emanating from it. His eyes locked on Jade's and a look of horrified realization dawned on her face. She understood. Her expression became stern, and she tilted her head ever so slightly toward the Elder. Dane couldn't say for certain how he knew, but the message was clear— *Let's get him.*

"Bones," he whispered. His friend gave an imperceptible nod and tapped Amanda, who paled visibly and also nodded her assent.

A golden light fell upon the Elder's face and he looked up toward its source, letting his grip on his gun slacken.

In a flash, Jade snatched the sun disc out of the sarcophagus and sent it hurtling, frisbee-style, at the Elder. It cracked across the bridge of his nose in a spray of blood, and he cried out in surprise and pain. Dane and Bones were on him before he could recover. Bones ripped the gun out of his hands and Dane wrested the staff away.

"No!" The Elder grabbed futilely for the staff, his eyes filled with tears from the pain of his broken nose. Dane cracked him across the forehead with the staff. Instead of boils, a dark stream of flies erupted from the Elder's forehead, and engulfed him in a dark, buzzing cloak. The Elder shouted and staggered back, flailing his arms at the swarm that now completely enshrouded him.

"Come on!" Dane cried, taking Jade by the hand and sprinting down the pathway toward the exit. He heard an anguished scream behind him, and he stole a glance over his shoulder. The platform had completed its descent, settling neatly between the tombs of Moses and Nefertiti, and the Elder had not made it out from underneath. His head, arms, and shoulders jutted out from beneath the massive stone block. The swarm of flies was gone. Dane heard Bones gasp, and he realized they had all stopped in the doorway, staring back at what the platform held.

The Ark of the Covenant.

Jade took two steps back toward the island, entranced by the sight. Dane took her by the arm and yanked her back, not bothering to be gentle.

"You can't," he said. "Don't you feel it?" His body tingled as if he was badly sunburned. "We have got to get out of here!" As if to punctuate his statement, the water that had been pouring from the leaking capstone chose that very moment to become a deluge. The movement of whatever mechanism it was that operated the chain had put undue stress on the surrounding rock. Cracks appeared at the pyramid's peak, creeping down the walls like the claws of a hungry predator. "The ceiling's going to come down! Let's go!"

Chapter 32

Dane led the way back across the stepping stones. The water level was rising, and by the time he reached the final stepping stone, it was underwater. He clambered out of the hole and helped the others out. They dashed through the cathedral-like treasure vault, where the canals there were also roiling with the increased flow of water. He spared a glance at Solomon's throne as they sprinted by, a pang of regret pinching the back of his throat as he realized it might be the last time human eyes gazed upon its beauty.

"Maddock!" Bones shouted. "Behind us!"

Dane looked over his shoulder to see a pack of the chupacabra creatures pour out of the doorway from which they had just fled, and hurtle toward them with relentless rage, gaining ground with every leap. *Where were these things coming from?* "Keep running!" he shouted to Jade and Amanda, and turned to face the beasts.

Bones dropped to one knee and opened fire with the Elder's gun. He brought down the one in the lead, but the others leapt over it and kept coming. When he brought down two more, the rest slowed down. Apparently they had some degree of intelligence, because they spread out, encircling Bones and Dane.

"Any ideas?" Bones muttered, letting the Elder's gun fall uselessly to the floor and drawing his knife.

Dane's mind raced. Could they survive an attack from seven of these beasts? Then he realized he was still holding the staff. In his desperation to think of a way to get everyone safely away, he had not spared it a thought. It obviously had power. The creatures slunk closer.

"Maddock?" Bones' voice was strained.

What could the staff do? Assuming what happened with Issachar and the Elder held true, he could kill one of the creatures by striking it, but one at a time was not going to be good enough against these lightning-fast predators.

"Get back!" he shouted, striking the end of the staff to the floor. He immediately felt foolish. Were these beasts truly going to obey him like a well-trained pet? But then…

"What the hell?" Bones stepped back as a hole appeared in the floor where the staff had struck it, and out poured… frogs!

Hundreds of the small amphibians poured forth, hopping in all directions. The chupacabras began to turn in all directions, sniffing the air and snarling.

"They're confused! They must rely on their sense of smell!" How long would it be, though before they singled out the scent of humans? He and Bones took off toward the exit, leaving the confused beasts behind, but not for long. They had not gone forty yards when the monsters again took up the pursuit. "Leave me. Find the girls and get them out of here."

"No way. We stay together."

They turned to face the charge of the remaining beasts.

Figuring he had nothing to lose, Dane struck the floor again, and this time a writhing, contorting ball of bronze grew out of the floor. The ball split into seven pieces that each twisted into a bronze serpent that slithered out to meet the chupacabras. The beasts never smelled the snakes, which must have been actually made of bronze. The snakes went for the creature's throats, and with each bite came instant death. Dane and Bones slowly backed away from the scene as, one by one, the bronze serpents swallowed the beasts. Then, as the final creature was devoured, the serpents flowed together, melted into a ball, and dissolved into the floor.

"Time to go," Dane whispered.

They sped out of the cathedral and down into the water gate chamber. Here, the canals had overflowed, and the water was an inch deep. The spiral staircase that descended to the room of waterfalls was now a waterfall itself, and they took care to keep from falling. Jade and Amanda waited at the bottom.

"Thank God!" Jade cried as she wrapped her arms around Dane.

"You don't know how true that statement is," Dane replied. "Let's go."

"There's a problem. Amanda and I already tried going through the waterfall. The bottom level is completely submerged. You can't even see the tunnel we came down. We could try to swim for it, but the current..." She shrugged and stared at the curtain of water that blocked their view of the next room.

"Should be no problem," Bones said. "You've got Moses' staff. Did he ever let a little water get in his way? You know, '...and Moses stretched out his hand over the sea...'"

"'The waters were divided,'" Amanda whispered.

"You two left out a little bit in the middle," Dane said, "but I get your point." Dane's first thought was that Bones was crazy. There was no way he could do what his friend suggested.

"You already made boils, flies, and frogs, Mister Plague-Bearer. Then you made serpents that devoured the chupacabras. Does somebody need to whack you over the head to make you see the obvious? Now hurry up! This water is cold."

Bones was right. Even more water poured out of the stairway behind them, and the level had risen almost to his calves. His feet were going numb from the cold. He extended the staff.

Nothing happened.

And then, as if a strong breeze were blowing into it, the waterfall in front of them wavered, and then the curtain of water parted. Down below, a channel opened along the pathway that led to the way out.

They walked between walls of roiling water. It surged and pulsed, and with every step he took, Dane was more and more certain that it was all going to collapse in on them at any moment.

"It's like Sea World!" Bones said. "But without all the cool fish."

They reached the other side safely and ascended the exit tunnel that was now a vortical tube of water.

"Anybody else feel like a hamster?" Dane asked, watching as the water raged around the circular passage. The path opened for them as they made the climb, and closed behind them when they passed. The glowing cavern was soon left behind, and they had to rely on their flashlights to light their way.

They emerged in the gargoyle pit, which was now an angry vortex. Water gushed from the gargoyle's mouths, swirling about the circular pit and spiraling into a violent maelstrom that was swallowed up by the tunnel through which Dane had originally entered the pit. He had hoped that would be the avenue of their escape, but now they would have to retrace the path by which Bones and Amanda had come.

Dane extended the staff again, and a pathway opened that led them to the stairs that wrapped around the pit wall. He took the steps two at a time, the narrow beam of his flashlight bobbing as he climbed.

When he reached the top, a flash of movement caught his eye, and before he could react, something struck him hard above his right ear. He crashed to the ground, landing hard on his back, the staff slipping from his grasp. He reached out in desperation, but only succeeded in brushing it with his fingertips before it rolled out of his reach and disappeared over the edge of the pit.

He didn't have time to even think about what had happened, because something was hurtling directly at him. Bones and the others had not reached the top, but the faint light cast by their flashlights shone on Issachar, his face now little more than a mass of bleeding boils. With a bellow of inhuman rage he hurled himself at Dane. Dane drew his knees to his chest and caught Issachar stomach on the balls of his feet, and grabbed his shoulders. Using his attacker's momentum to his advantage, he kicked up, somersaulting Issachar into the pit.

He rolled over, snatched up his flashlight, and shone it down into the depths of the pit below. He saw nothing but dark, angry water.

"It's gone," he said in disbelief as the others arrived at his side. "I just lost the staff of Moses."

"Brother, at the rate we're going, there won't be any biblical treasures left in a few years." Bones clapped Dane on the shoulder. "Next week let's blow up Noah's Ark."

Faint lines of pink brushed the velvet sky on the edge of the horizon when the weary party found their way back to the top of Angel's Landing. They replaced the cover stone and heaped mounds of loose rock over it. No one before them had found it, and likely no one would again, at least not for a long time. There had been no more sign of the Dominion or the chupacabras though they did find a Kalashnikov lying in a sticky pool in one of the chambers and had taken it with them just to be safe.

Now they stood together letting the first rays of the morning sun wash away the memories of their hellish night underground. Jade leaned against Dane's shoulder and he slipped his arm around her waist.

"None of it seems real now," she whispered. "My life's ambition realized and lost again in one night. And what do I have to show for it?"

"You're alive," Dane said. "And hey, you've got me."

"So it's kind of a wash," Bones said. "Life with Maddock can be an absolute pain."

"So the Ark of the Covenant was radioactive?" Amanda asked after a long silence. They had all been too focused on getting out alive to discuss what had happened.

"I think the plates on which the Ten Commandments were carved were highly radioactive. Unbelievably so considering the half-life it must have for it to still be radioactive today."

"How did you guess?" Now that they were back in the real world, Amanda was regaining some of her reporter's instincts.

"I kept wondering what could be a greater treasure than what we saw in the cathedral chamber. What is associated with Moses besides the staff? Then I remembered what Bones said about Jimmy's corrected translation: The ten is impure. The Ten Commandments! I thought of the Ark of the Covenant, and how the Bible said that if someone touched it, they died. And then it all fell into place: the glowing veins of minerals in the stone, the fact that every cavern seemed to get warmer and brighter as we moved closer to the final chamber, the chupacabras, which are probably descendants of population of native animal, maybe a mountain lion that has mutated for generation after generation. Their lair smelled of wild cat. Justin's grandmother told me that her family has lived in that spot for generations. They've probably been drinking contaminated groundwater."

"Why wouldn't it affect the park?" Jade asked.

"I don't know. It would probably take years of drinking it to have any effect. Besides, think about how far we traveled down there. The chambers are miles from here."

"I get it!" Bones said. "The Ark of the Covenant is gold-plated, which acted as an imperfect shield. You could get close, but not too close."

"How could Moses have carried the Ten Commandments down from Sinai if they were so highly radioactive?" Jade asked.

"The same way he parted the sea, caused the plagues, all that good stuff," Bones said. "No matter how much science you throw into the mix, you can never quite factor God out of the equation, can you Maddock?"

"I guess not," Dane said. He and God had not been on good terms since Melissa's death. The experiences of the past year, though, had made the universe a much bigger and more complicated place than he had ever imagined. It was certainly beyond his small capacity to comprehend. He looked at Jade, thinking of how he had every reason not to trust her, yet he trusted her. More than that, despite the hurt she had caused him, he wanted to give it a go with her. Maybe that was a small taste of what faith was like.

"Does it bother any of you," Amanda remained in reporter mode, "knowing that Moses was, in actuality Akhenaten?"

"I don't know." Bones looked out across the beauty of the landscape. "Does it bother you to know that Akhenaten was really Moses? It doesn't change what Moses did, or why he was so important. Heck, I think it's cool. Things like that sort of bring us all a little closer together. Shared history and all that. I don't know. It's not as bad as if we found out Elvis was really Tiny Tim."

"You can ask Elvis next time we see him," Dane said. He noticed that Amanda had turned away from the rest of the group and was staring up into the sky. "Are you all right?"

"I was just thinking that I just helped uncover the story to end all stories, and I can't tell anyone. It's got Pulitzer written all over it, but even if there is anything left down there, would it be a good idea for the world to know? Look at what the staff could do. What other powers might some of those treasures have? Imagine them in the hands of the crazies of this world."

"The Elder indicated that no one is left in the Dominion who knows anything about any of this," Dane said. "That leaves Jimmy and the four of us. Personally, I think Fray Marcos was right. It's too terrible a secret to share with the world. Someday, if it's meant to be, the right person at the right time will find it."

"So we weren't meant to find it?" Amanda asked, returning to Bones' side.

"I'm not a philosopher," Dane said. "But I think

maybe we were meant to stop the Elder from finding it. I know that's not much, but at least you know you were part of something important."

"Man! I thought *I* was being cheesy," Bones said. "But I think you're right."

"It's all right," Amanda said. "I think that with just a little digging I can come up with a major story on a respected bank president and community leader who was secretly the head of an underground paramilitary organization. I might even be able to blow the lid off of Central Utah University as well." She looked at Jade, concern in her eyes. "But what are you going to do? I mean, you can't go back, can you? Not with the university's connections to the Dominion. And finding out the truth of the Seven Cities was your life's ambition, and now you can't even take any credit. Oh Jade, I'm sorry."

"Thank you," Jade said. "But I did find out the truth, and that's what matters. I guess I need a new life's ambition. As for where I'll be working," she turned to look into Dane's eyes, "I'm a pretty fair diver. Know anyone who's hiring?"

"I just might at that," Dane said. "Bones and I have been talking about expanding our operation."

Now Bones turned to Amanda. "That leaves you," he said. "What are your plans?"

"My plan is for you to buy me a meal and give me the back rub of my life. Long term? When my story comes out, I'll be a girl in demand. Maybe I'll find my way down to Florida and blow the lid off some scandal or other. Think you'll be free?"

"You never know," Bones said. "I'm already a man in demand."

"I think it's light enough to safely make our way down now," Dane said, taking Jade's hand. "Are we ready?"

"We need to take it slow," Amanda said. "By the time we get to the bottom we should probably have a good explanation for the shootings at the hotel. Some of our names are bound to be on the hotel registry, after all."

"No they aren't," Jade said. "Saul always registered us in his father's name and paid with one of his father's credit cards. I never thought anything about it. Now, all signs point back to the Elder."

"The snake bites its own tail," Bones said. "Maddock, you ever notice how things just seem to go our way?"

"You know," Dane said as they stepped around a large outcropping and into the light of a new day, "I'm starting to think you just might be right."

Epilogue

Justin sat at edge of the pond, rocking back and forth, letting his bare feet soak in the cool water. The sun sparkled on its surface, lending a sense of joy to the early morning. He held up his hand, letting the dancing reflections of sunlight play across his palm. It was a favorite game of his, and could occupy him for hours at a time. But not today. Today he was worried about his new friend.

Justin had waited by the pond until almost dark, hoping his friend would come back, but he did not. What if the choo choo's had gotten him? He hoped not. His friend was nice. He liked Justin's pictures, and he didn't seem scared by Justin's funny eye. He talked to Justin like a regular person.

There still was no sign of him. No footprints around the pond. Nothing. The pond was bigger this morning, which was strange. The water went all the way past his favorite sitting rock and around the pine tree where he liked to get his shade. Probably his friend had found a different way out. He wouldn't have wanted to walk across the desert again. Yes, that was it.

Feeling much better, he decided it would be okay to leave now. As he stood, something in the water caught his eye. Down at the bottom of the pond, the sun glinted off of something shiny and gold. He had found shiny treasures in the pond before! His friend had liked those too. He waded into the water as far as he could, took a deep breath, and dove. He was a good swimmer—he could swim better than he could walk, anyway.

He reached the bottom and his hand closed around the shiny thing. It was much bigger than he had thought. It wasn't too heavy though. He swam back to shore, excited at his new find.

Back on dry ground, he held his treasure up so he could see it better. It was long, dark, and shiny, with golden letters that glowed in the sun. There were shiny things on either end, too. He liked it!

"Stick!" he said. There was a note of pride in his voice. This was the nicest stick he had ever found. He wouldn't show grandma. She always let him keep his sticks for a while, but in the winter she burned them in the wood stove. This stick would be his secret.

Happier than he had felt in a long time, and no longer worried about his new friend, he decided this would be a perfect morning for a long walk-- just him and his new treasure.

Under the tenth step entering to the east

Under the black stone at the Western entrance

Above the pillar of the northern opening of the cave that
has two entrances

Under the stairs in the pit

On the third terrace in the cave,
on the eastern side inside the waterfall

At the edge of the canal on its northern side

Six cubits toward the immersed pool

In the sepulchre, in the third course of stones

Under the tomb
In the chain platform

This is all of the votive offerings of the seventh treasure, the
ten is impure

From the Author

People sometimes ask, "How much of your story is true to life?" Much of this story is real. This tale was initially inspired by two discoveries: Fremont Indian ruins that had been kept a secret for years by the land's owners, and that of a previously-unknown Spanish outpost in Argentina. You may also visit any of the national parks and historic sites our characters visit.

Obviously, in a work of fiction such as this, I have taken liberties. The clues from the copper scroll are very close to actual translations, though I changed the wording in a few instances. A few of the sites, Rainbow Bridge and Angel's Landing in particular, are not situated precisely as they seem in the story, but I think you'll find the discrepancies are, for the most part, minor.

As to the biblical back-story, some of the powers attributed to Moses' staff in this book actually come from Aaron's rod in scripture, though many biblical scholars believe the two staffs are actually one and the same. As to the Moses and Akhenaten connection—probably not. The most reliable sources place them too far apart in history to have been the same person, but it is not beyond the realm of possibilities to think that Moses might have been familiar with Akhenaten's monotheistic beliefs.

Finally, if you've never visited the Four Corners area of the United States, I urge you to do so. Places like Mesa Verde, Chaco Canyon, and Hovenweep are among the most magnificent places I have ever seen. (Just don't break into ruins looking for hidden clues—It's just a story, folks!)

As always, thank you for reading! Drop by my website at www.davidwoodweb.com and let me know how you liked the book. Until next time!

David Wood

Other Titles From Gryphonwood Press

Street...Empathy by Ryan A. Span

"In the future, telepathy is no longer a fantasy; it's a job. Gina- just Gina- is a woman with no future, trying to make her living along the Street of Eyes, where people go to hire the desperate and the suicidal for their unique services. She is one of the sellers, the new underclass, who use "third eye" or "Spice"- a powerful drug that gives them the ability to read minds- as their way of making ends meet. The drug has only one downside- it drives the user insane. Gina no longer cares about the risks and is content to go on the way she has for years, not knowing fate has something very different in store for her when she accepts a mysterious job from an unusual buyer. Before she knows it, Gina finds herself embroiled in a dangerous mystery, hunted by gangs and madmen, consorting with hackers and assassins, and all the while trying to keep her mind from coming apart at the seams"

Don't miss Ryan A. Span's debut sci-fi/cyberpunk thriller. *Street* was a top-10 bestseller in both Technothrillers and High Tech Sci-Fi on the Amazon Kindle charts.

The Silver Serpent by David Debord

The frost creeps again... Taught the sword from childhood, Shanis Malan's only dream is to be a soldier, but a woman cannot join the Galdoran army. She thinks her dream has come true when Prince Lerryn hosts a tournament in her town, but circumstances snatch her from her home and carry her into the midst of a quest for a legendary artifact that can save the world from the minions of Tichris the Ice King. Join Shanis and her friends on a perilous quest for the Silver Serpent."

David Debord's epic fantasy was a top-100 bestseller on the Epic Fantasy chart, and a top-10 bestseller among Fantasy Series and Epic Fantasy on the Amazon Kindle charts.

Dourado by David Wood

"A sunken treasure. An ancient Biblical artifact. A mystery as old as humankind. On January 25, 1829, the Portuguese brig Dourado sank off the coast of Indonesia, losing its cargo of priceless treasures from the Holy Land. One of these lost relics holds the key to an ancient mystery. But someone does not want this treasure to come to light. When her father is mysteriously murdered while searching for the Dourado, Kaylin Maxwell hires treasure hunter and former Navy Seal Dane Maddock and his partner Uriah "Bones" Bonebrake, to locate the Dourado, and recover a lost Biblical artifact, the truth behind which could shake the foundations of the church, and call into question the fundamentally held truths of human existence. Join Dane and Bones on a perilous adventure that carries them from the depths of the Pacific to ancient cities of stone as they unravel the mystery of the Dourado.."

David Wood's adventure-thriller was a top-10 bestseller in four different categories on the Amazon Kindle charts, and reached number one among Smashwords e-books.

Seabird by Sherry Thompson

When Cara Marshall is transported to Narenta, she is proclaimed champion of its people against the sorcerous daemagos. Amid the grateful welcomes, Cara protests that she has been "world-napped," and wants neither her title nor her mission. "They've got the wrong person and they're going to get me killed because they won't admit it." With no knowledge of weapons or magic, can she save the Narentans and find her way home?

4893642

Made in the USA
Lexington, KY
12 March 2010